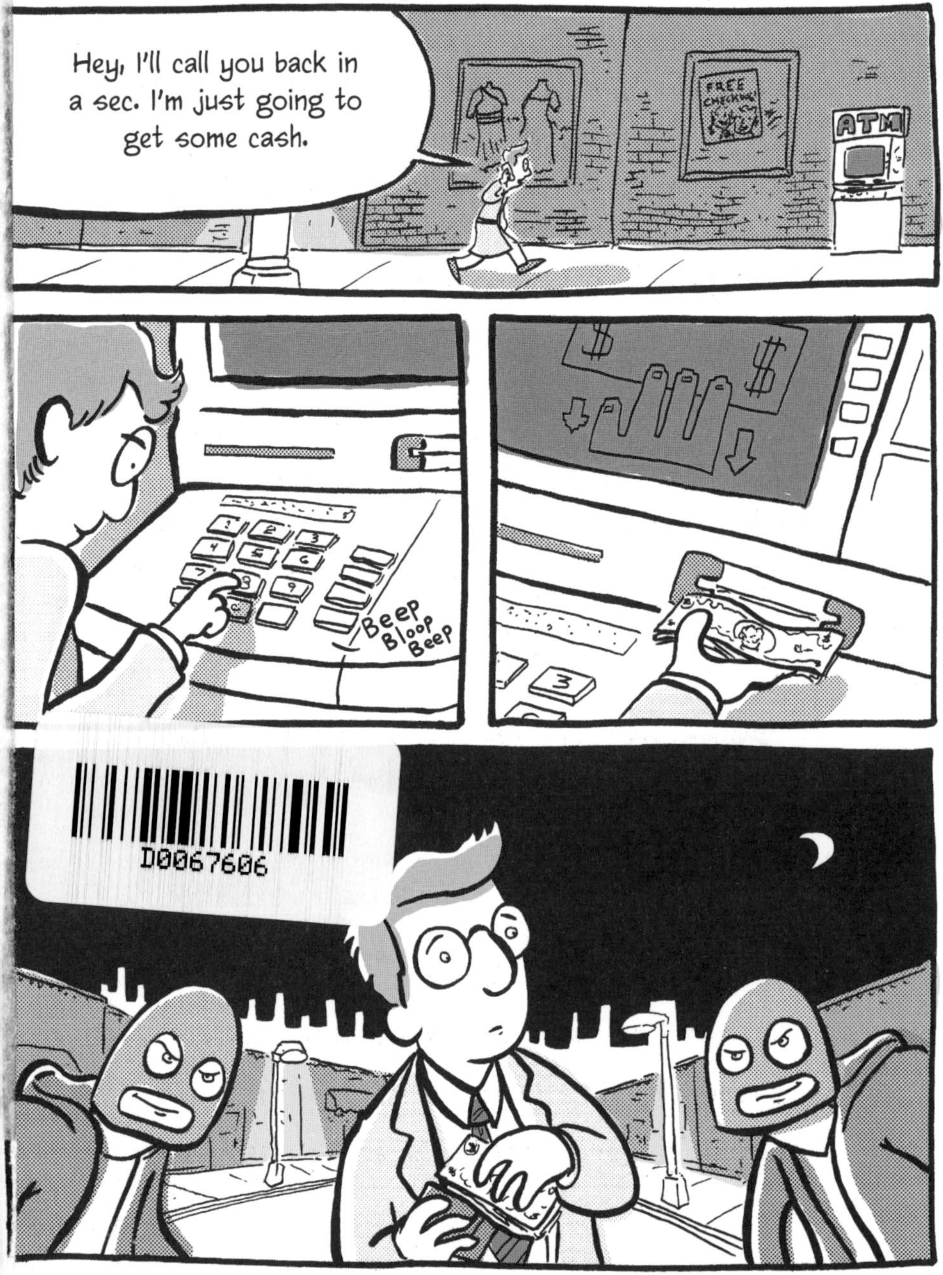
Hey, I'll call you back in a sec. I'm just going to get some cash.
FREE
ATM
Beep
Bloop
Beep

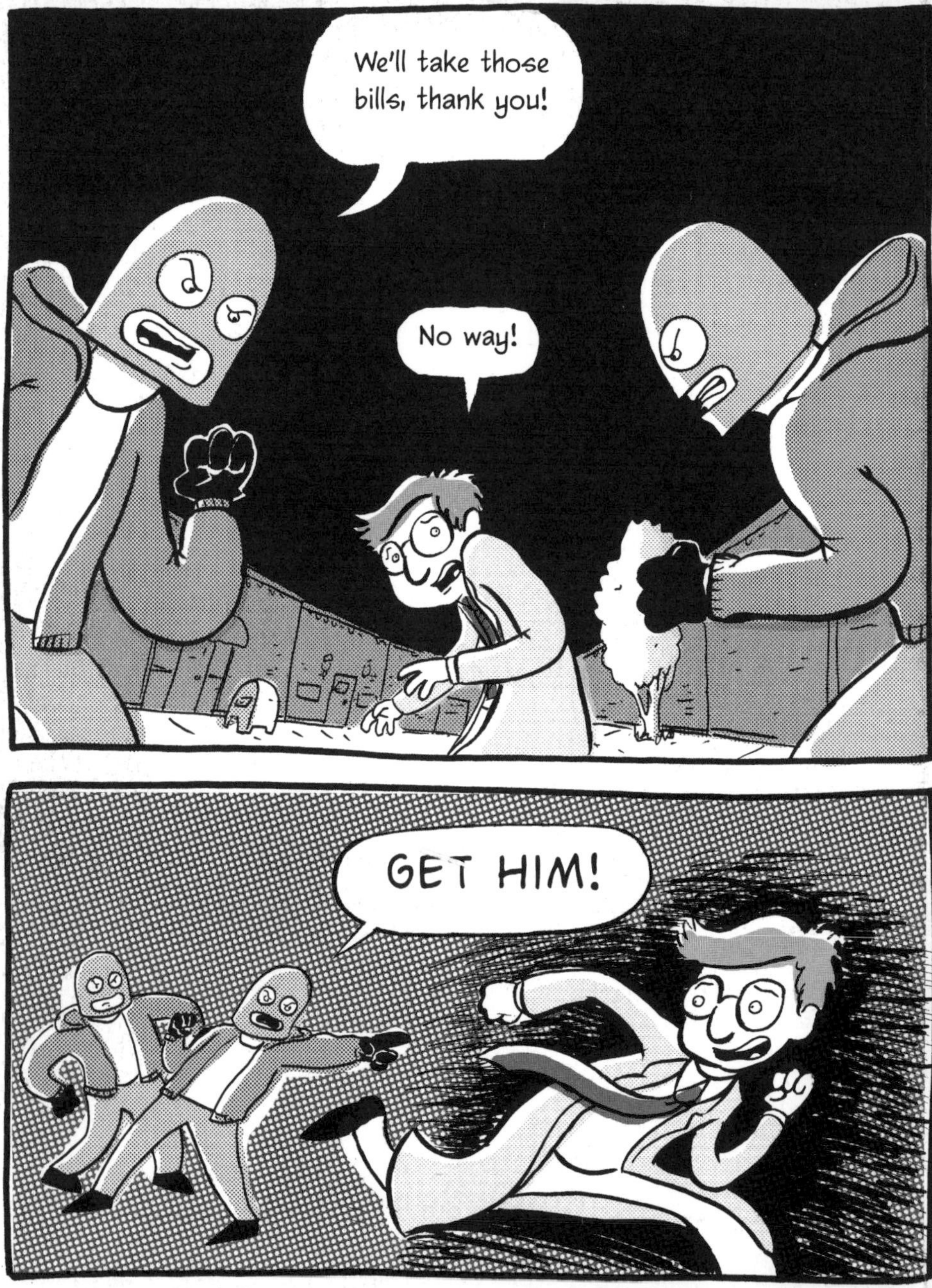
We'll take those bills, thank you!
No way!
GET HIM!

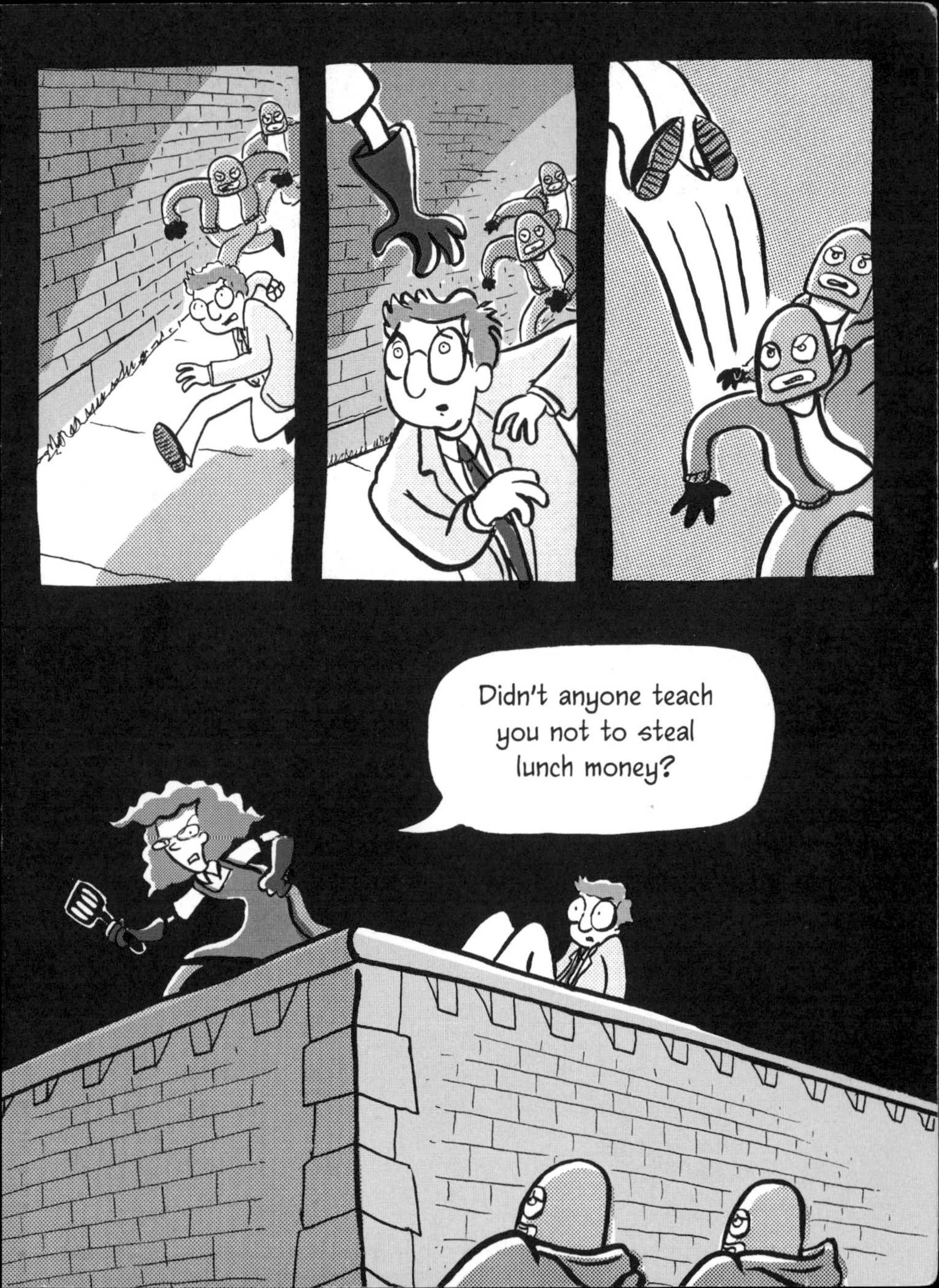
Didn't anyone teach you not to steal lunch money?

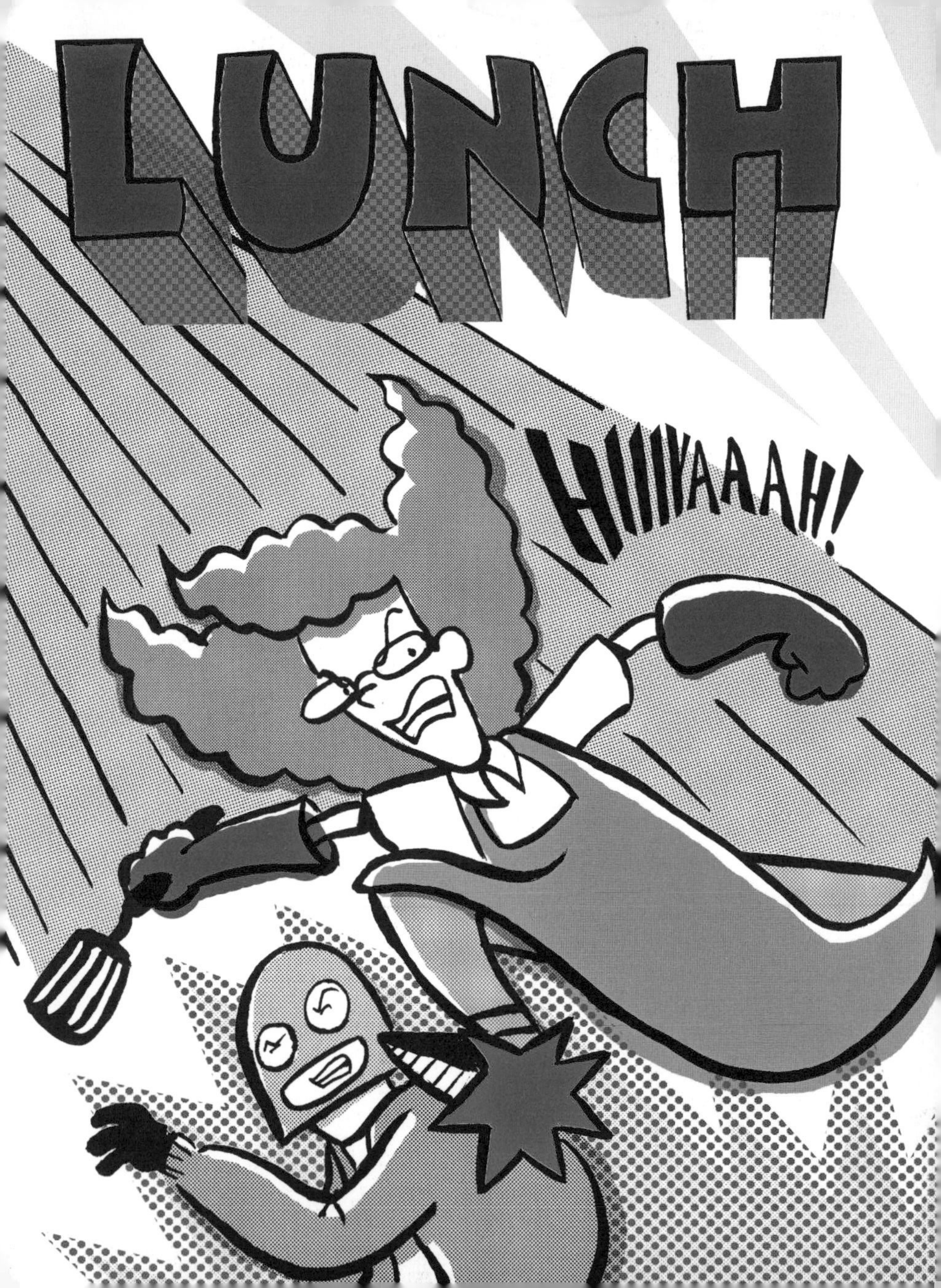
LUNCH
HIIIIYAAAH!

LADY

and the Picture Day Peril

Jarrett J. Krosoczka

Alfred A. Knopf New York

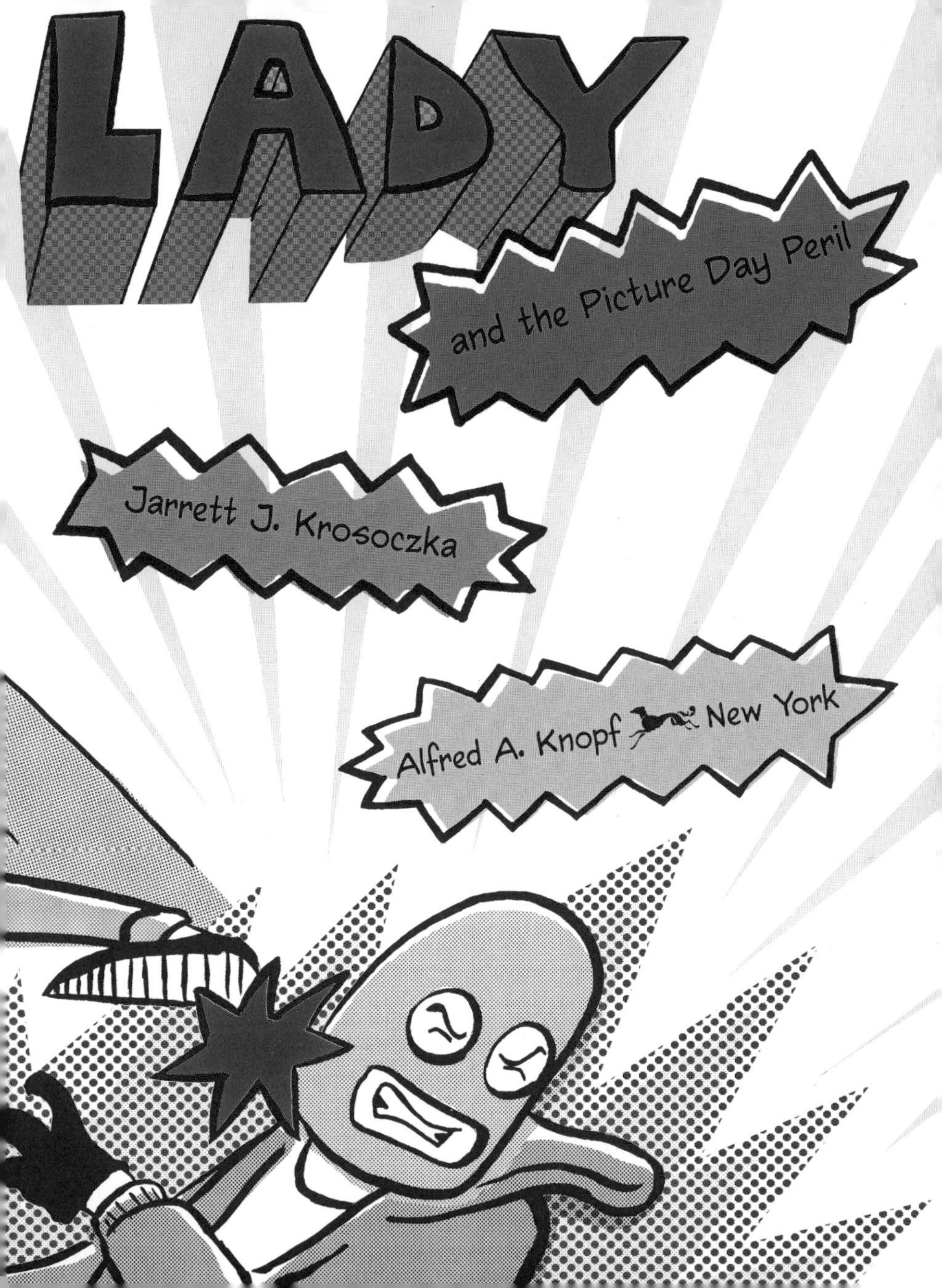

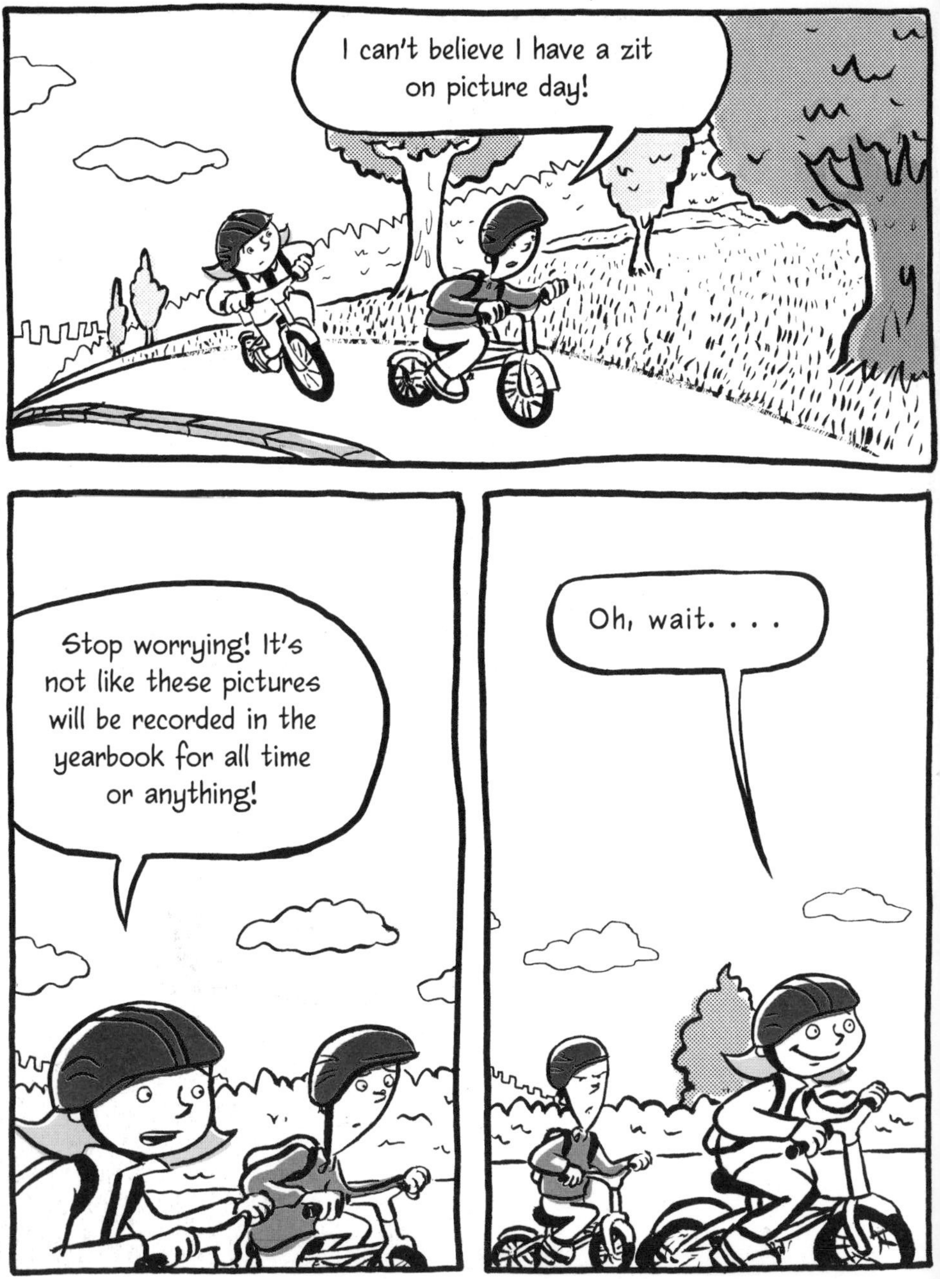
I can't believe I have a zit on picture day!
Stop worrying! It's not like these pictures will be recorded in the yearbook for all time or anything!
Oh, wait. . . .

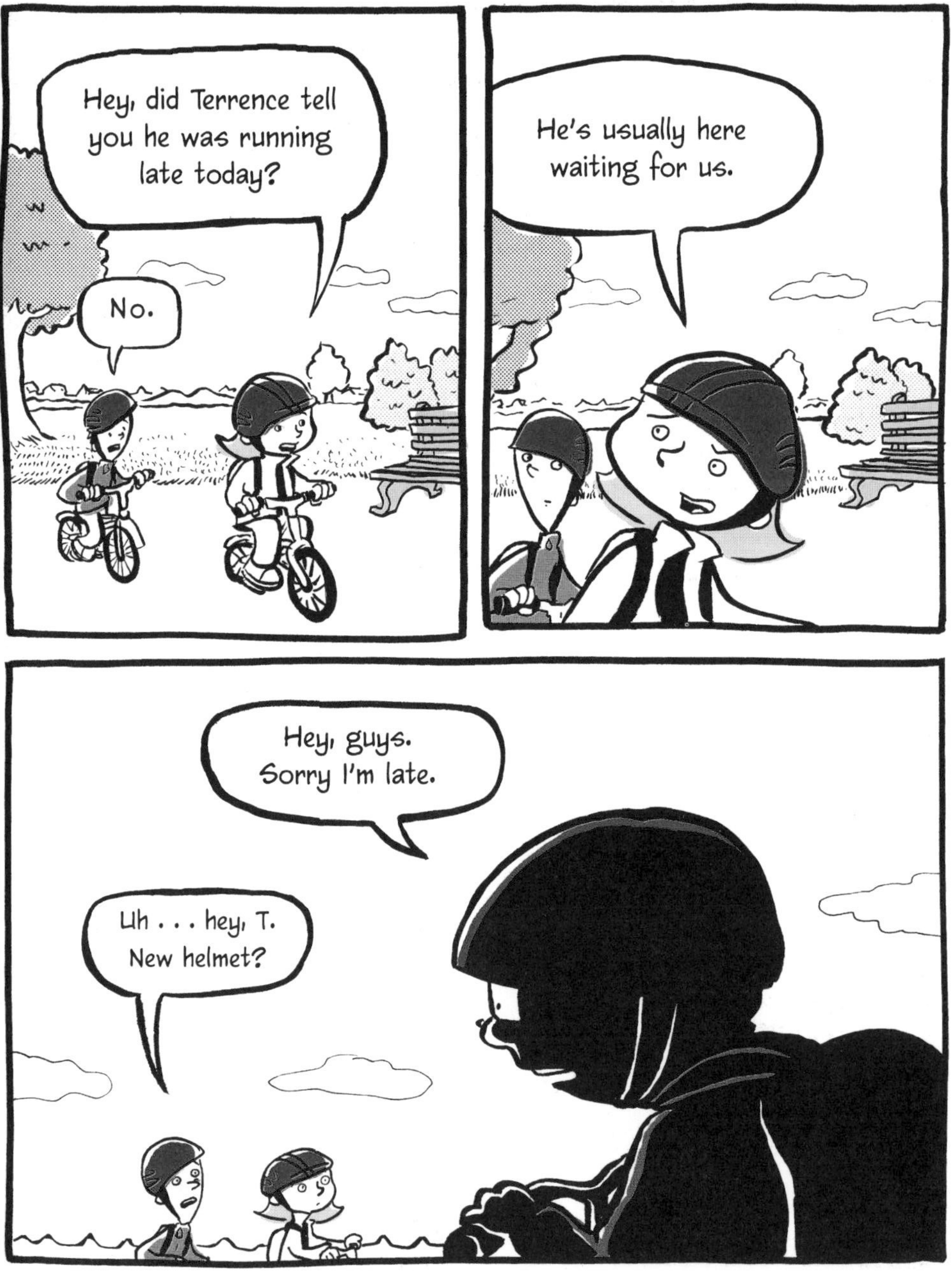
Hey, did Terrence tell you he was running late today?
No.
He's usually here waiting for us.
Hey, guys. Sorry I'm late.
Uh . . . hey, T. New helmet?

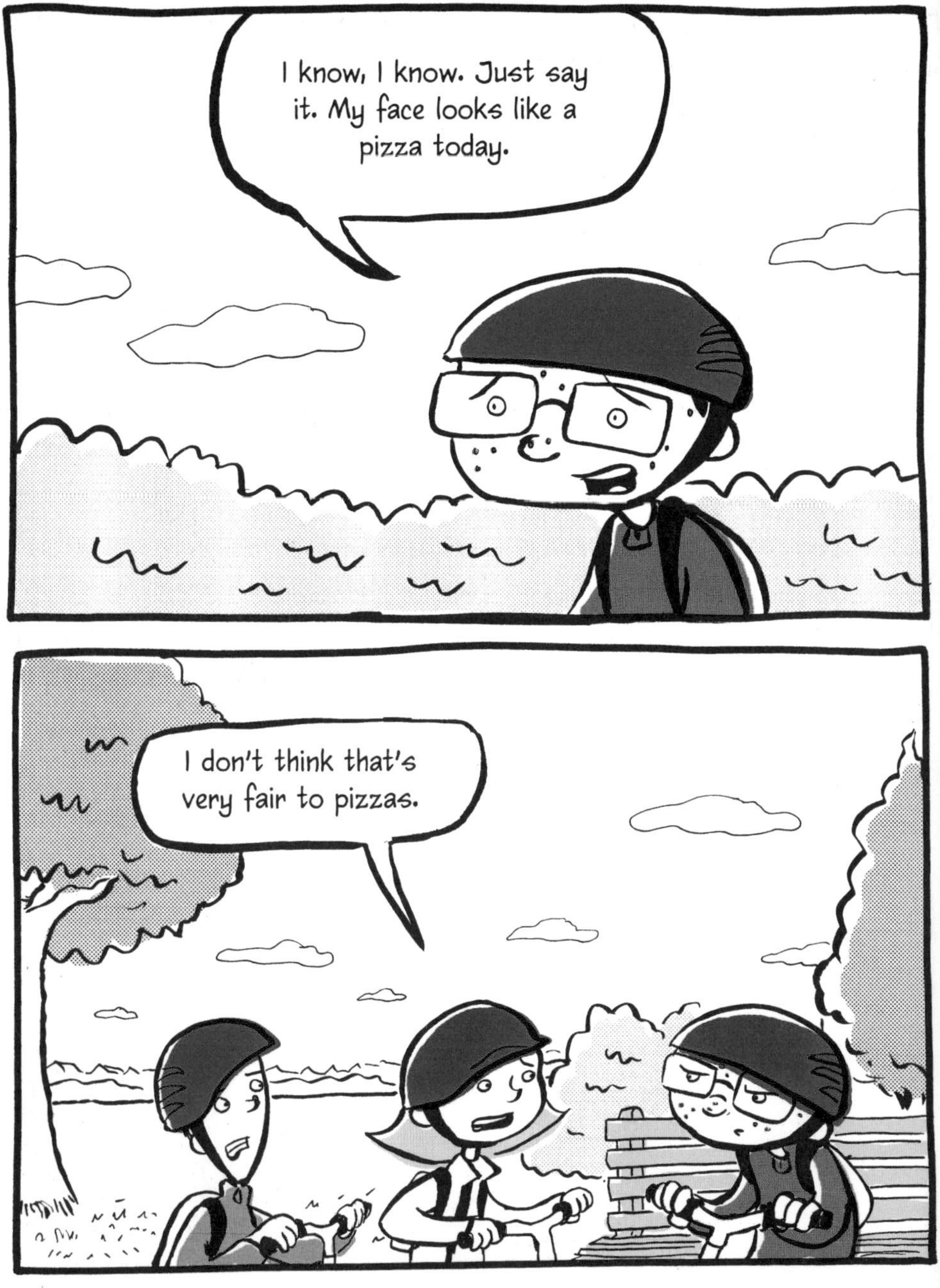
I know, I know. Just say it. My face looks like a pizza today.
I don't think that's very fair to pizzas.

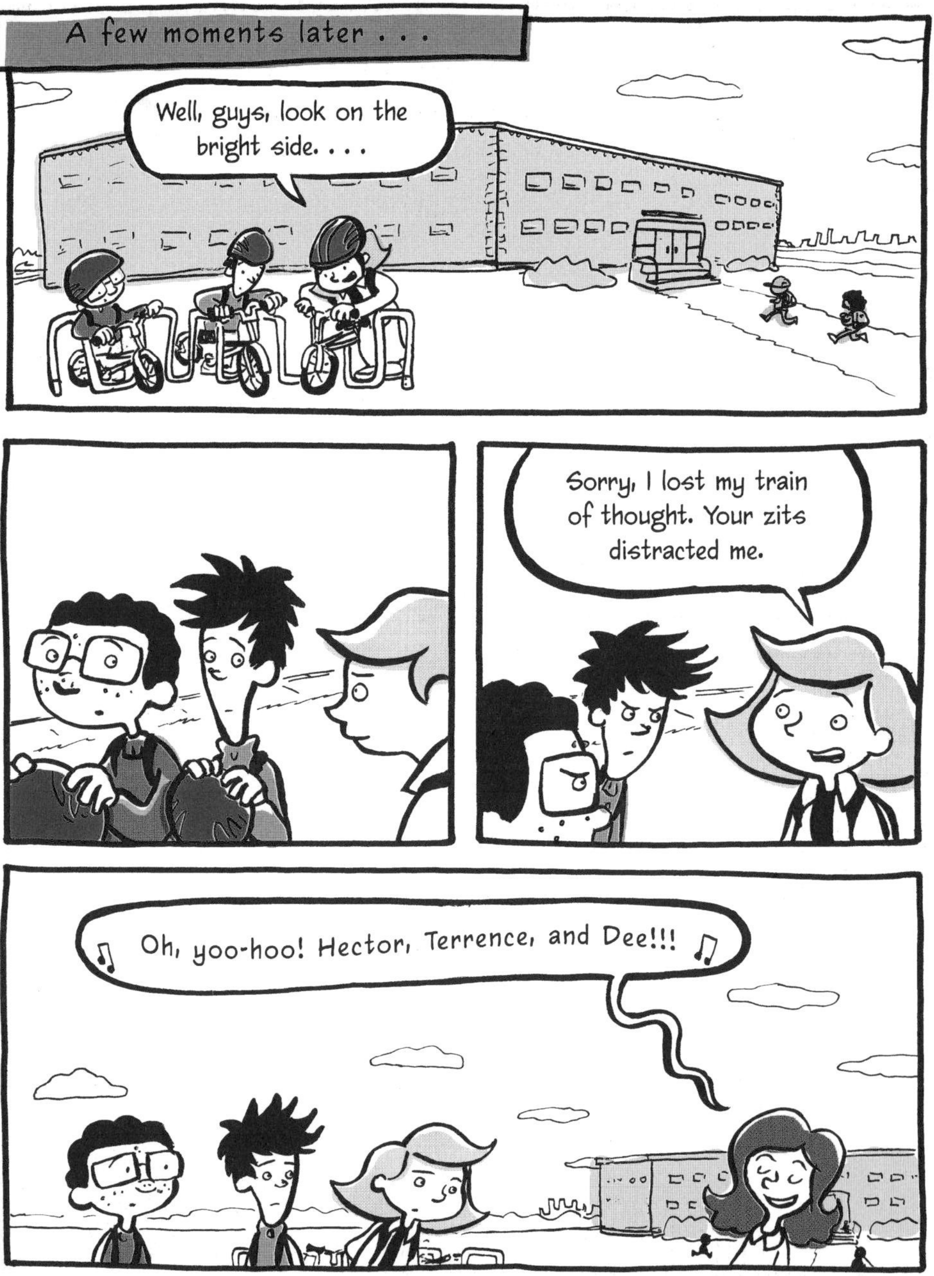
A few moments later . . .
Well, guys, look on the bright side. . . .
Sorry, I lost my train of thought. Your zits distracted me.
♫ Oh, yoo-hoo! Hector, Terrence, and Dee!!! ♫

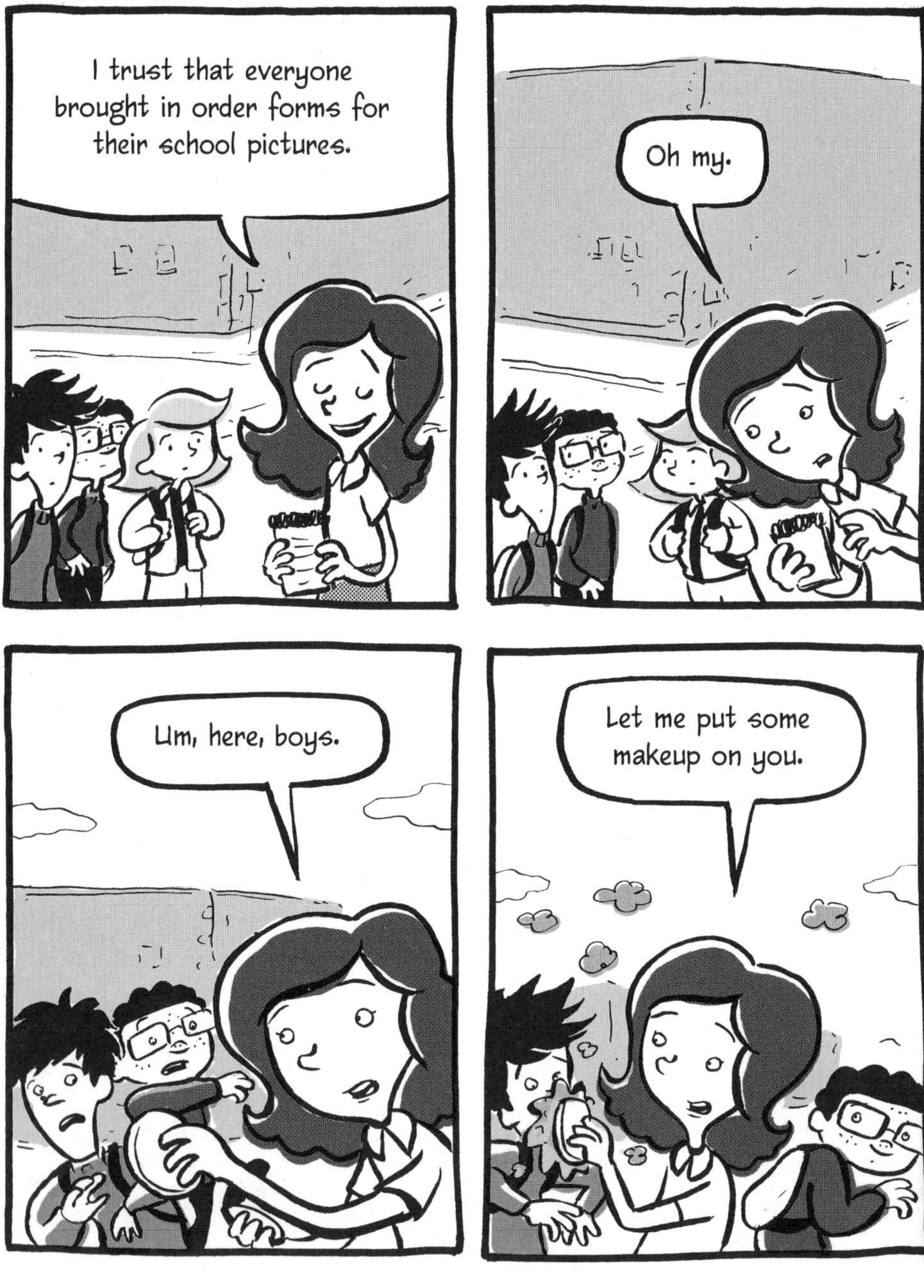
I trust that everyone brought in order forms for their school pictures.
Oh my.
Um, here, boys.
Let me put some makeup on you.

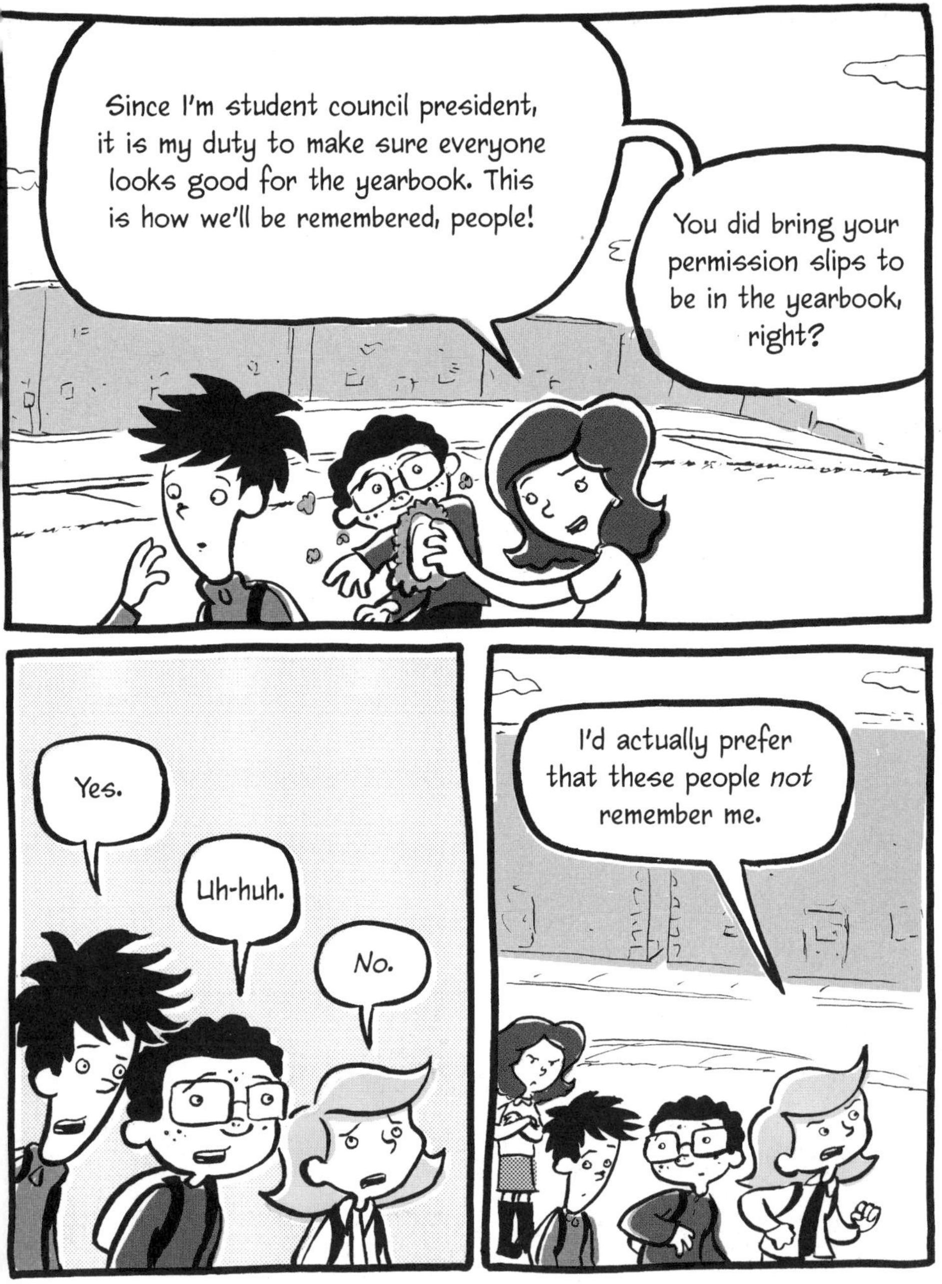
Since I'm student council president, it is my duty to make sure everyone looks good for the yearbook. This is how we'll be remembered, people!
You did bring your permission slips to be in the yearbook, right?
Yes.
Uh-huh.
No.
I'd actually prefer that these people *not* remember me.

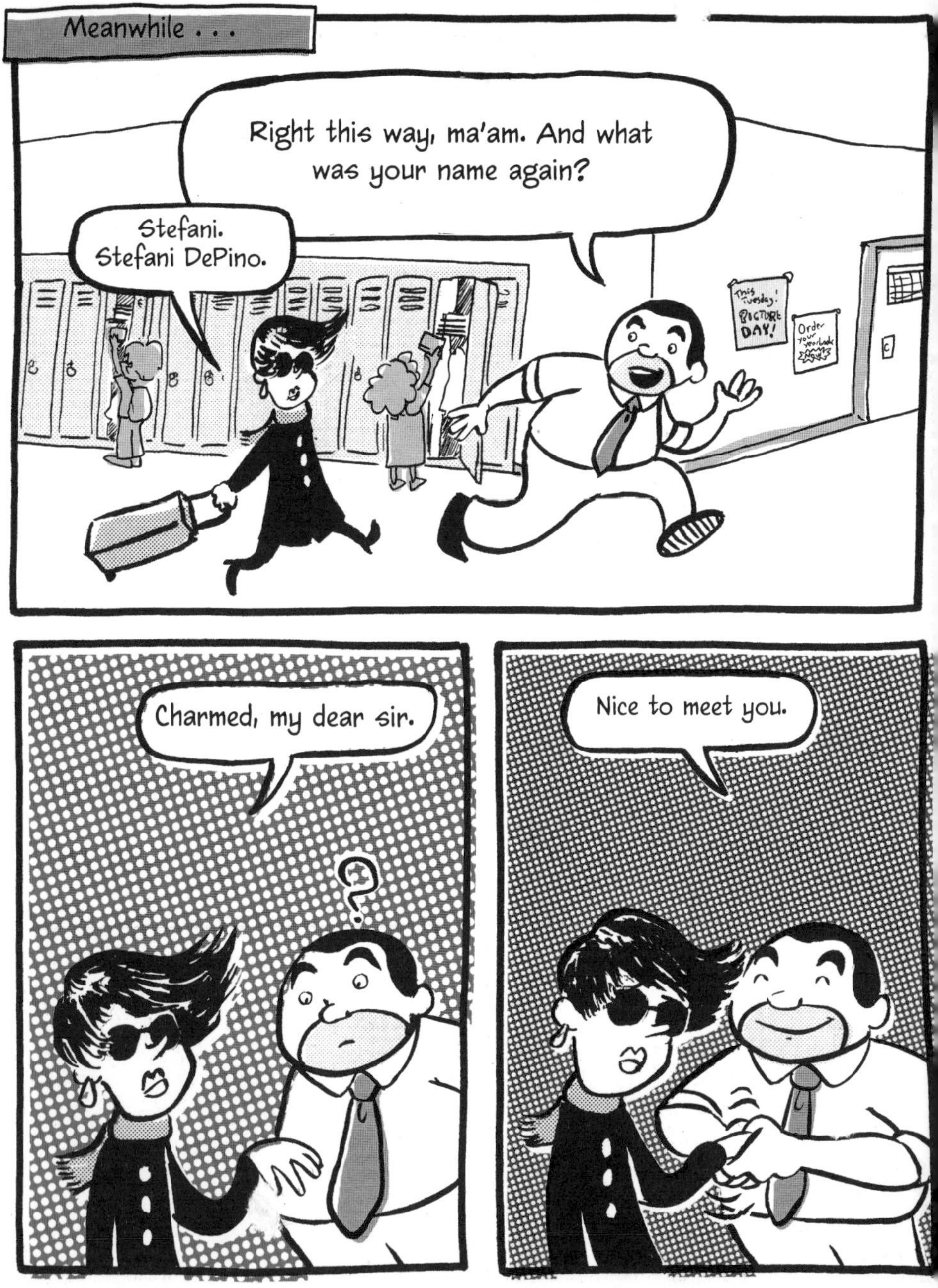
Meanwhile . . .
Right this way, ma'am. And what was your name again?
Stefani. Stefani DePino.
This Tuesday! PICTURE DAY!
Order your yearbook
Charmed, my dear sir.
Nice to meet you.

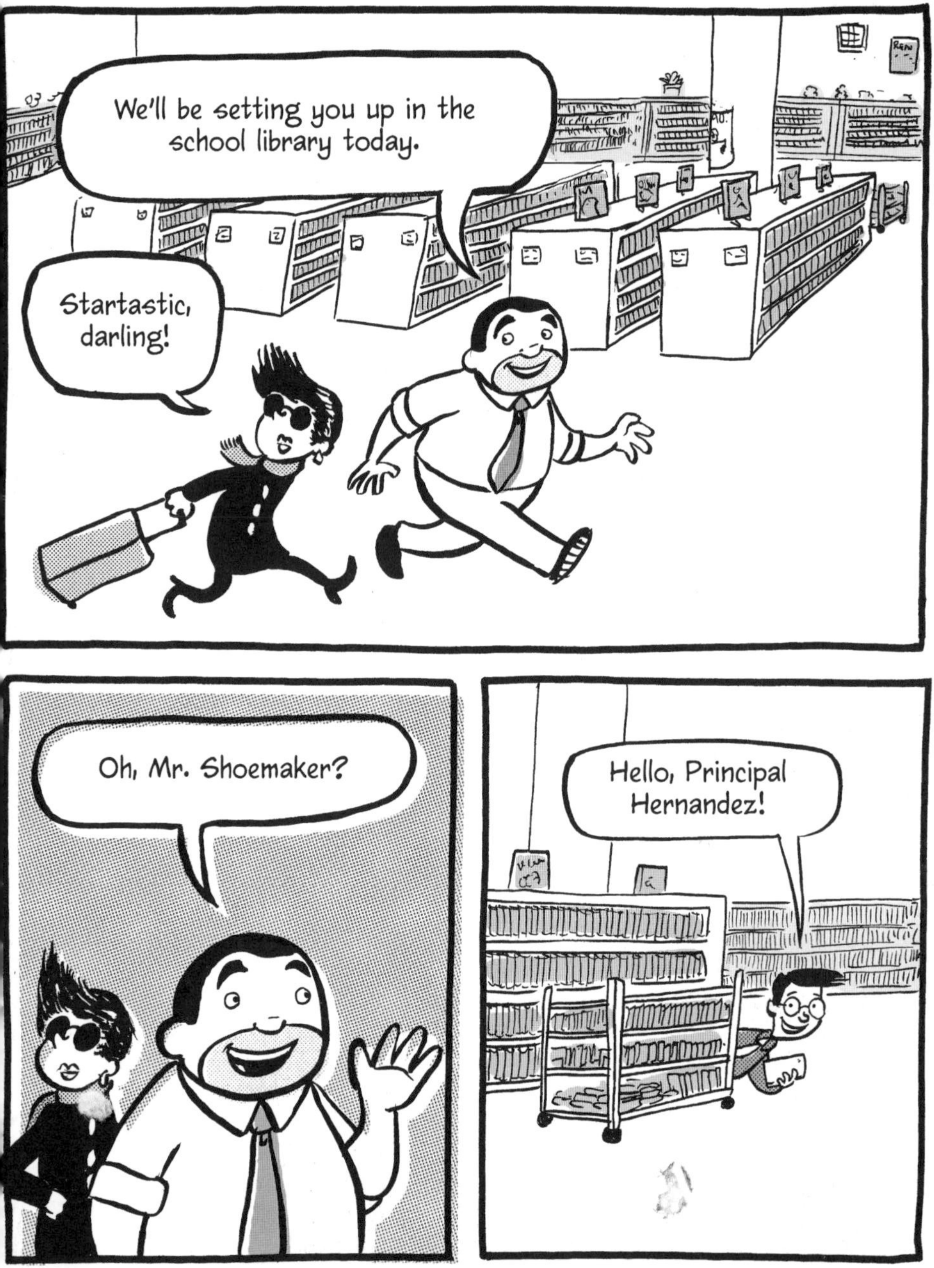
We'll be setting you up in the school library today.
Startastic, darling!
Oh, Mr. Shoemaker?
Hello, Principal Hernandez!

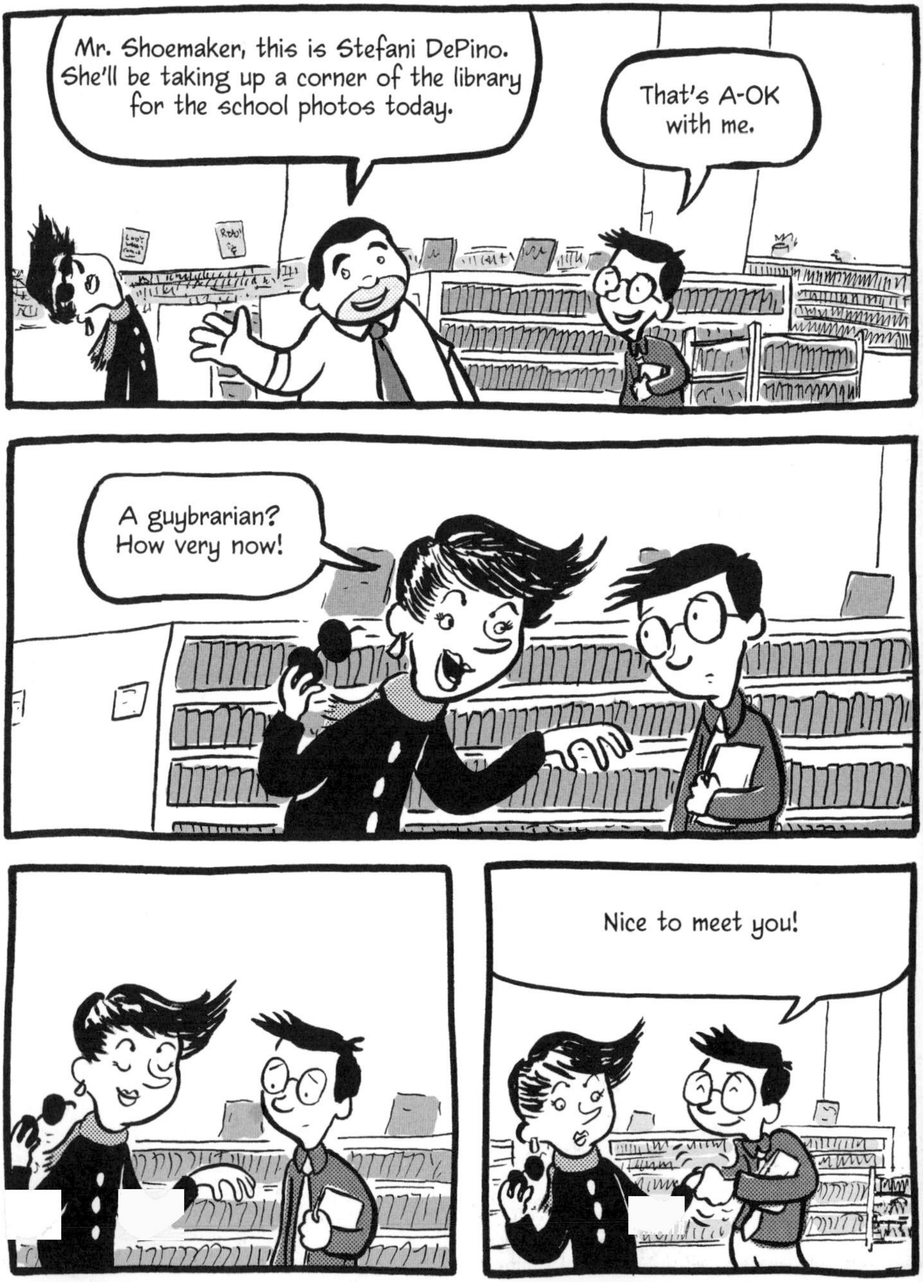
Mr. Shoemaker, this is Stefani DePino. She'll be taking up a corner of the library for the school photos today.
That's A-OK with me.
A guybrarian? How very now!
Nice to meet you!

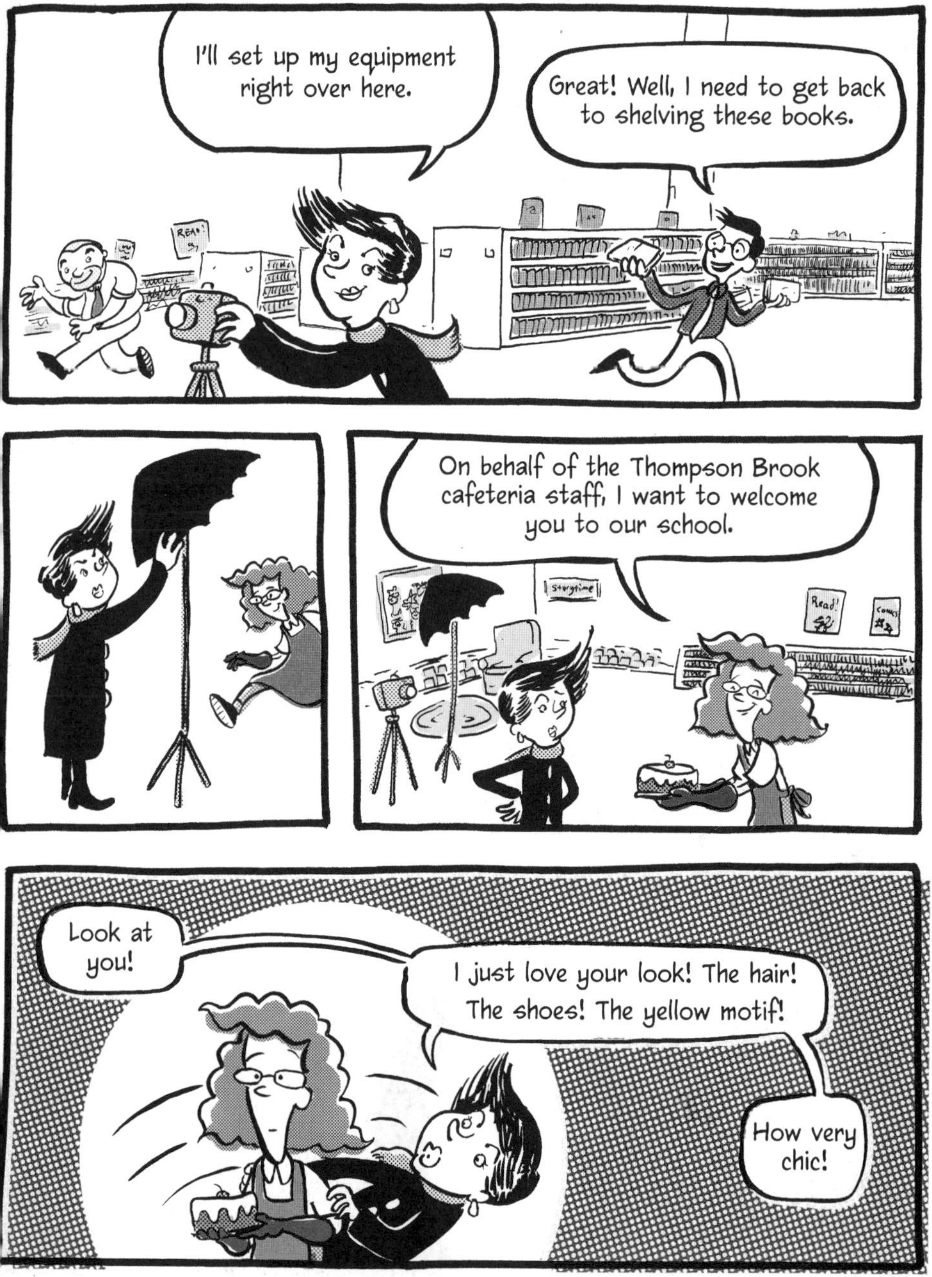

I'll set up my equipment right over here.
Great! Well, I need to get back to shelving these books.
On behalf of the Thompson Brook cafeteria staff, I want to welcome you to our school.
Storytime
Read!
Comics
Look at you!
I just love your look! The hair! The shoes! The yellow motif!
How very chic!

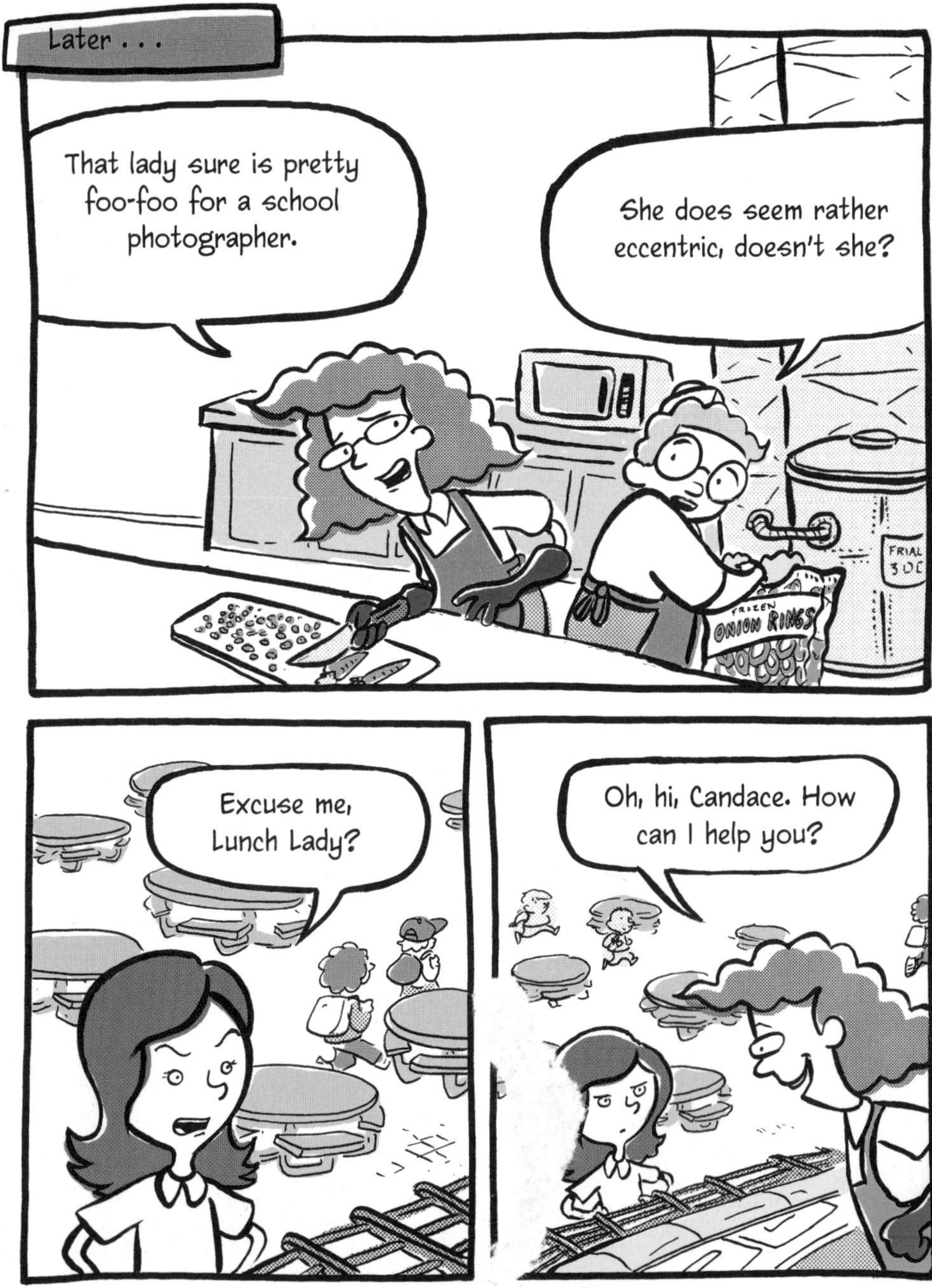
Later . . .
That lady sure is pretty foo-foo for a school photographer.
She does seem rather eccentric, doesn't she?
FROZEN ONION RINGS
Excuse me, Lunch Lady?
Oh, hi, Candace. How can I help you?

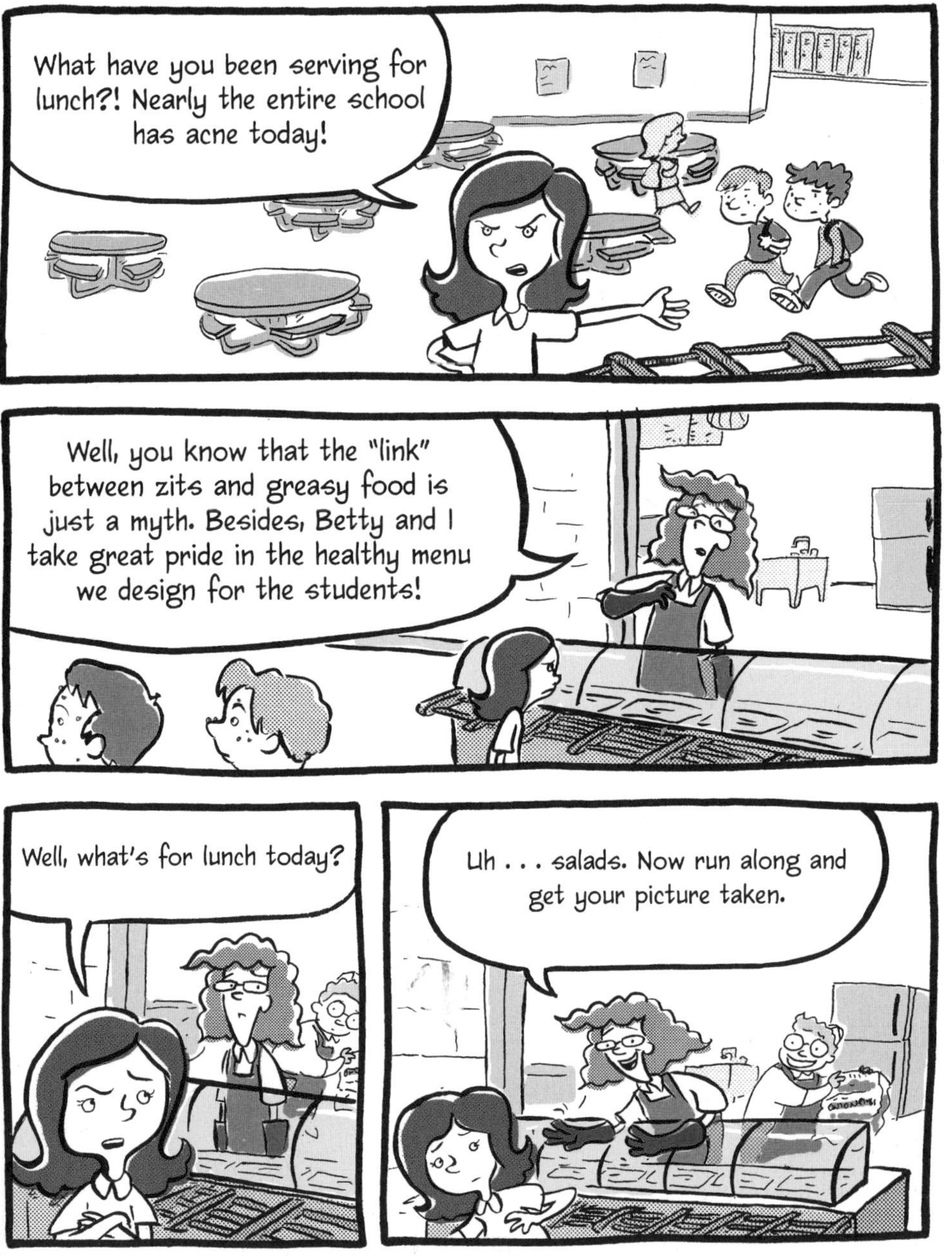
What have you been serving for lunch?! Nearly the entire school has acne today!
Well, you know that the "link" between zits and greasy food is just a myth. Besides, Betty and I take great pride in the healthy menu we design for the students!
Well, what's for lunch today?
Uh . . . salads. Now run along and get your picture taken.

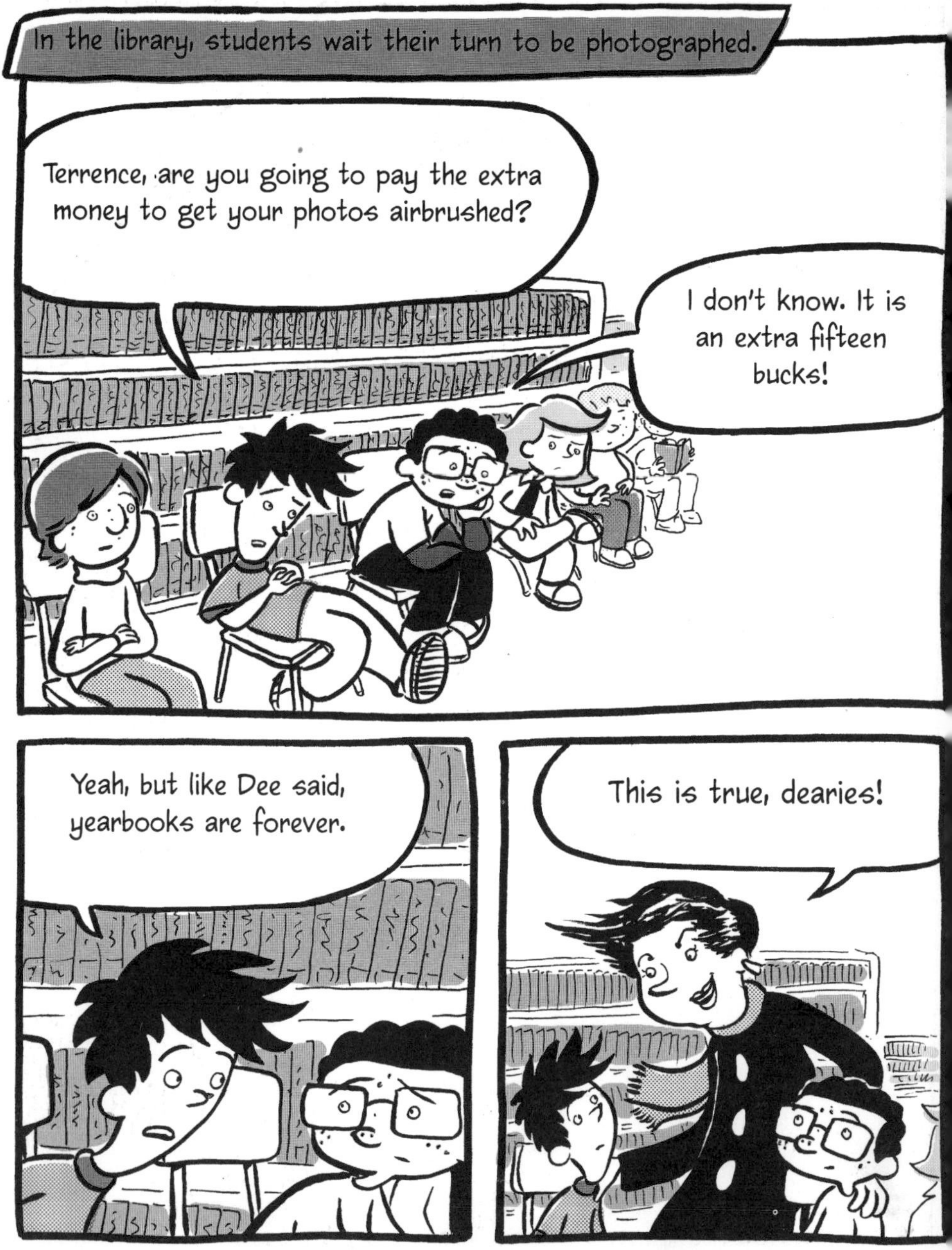
In the library, students wait their turn to be photographed.
Terrence, are you going to pay the extra money to get your photos airbrushed?
I don't know. It is an extra fifteen bucks!
Yeah, but like Dee said, yearbooks are forever.
This is true, dearies!

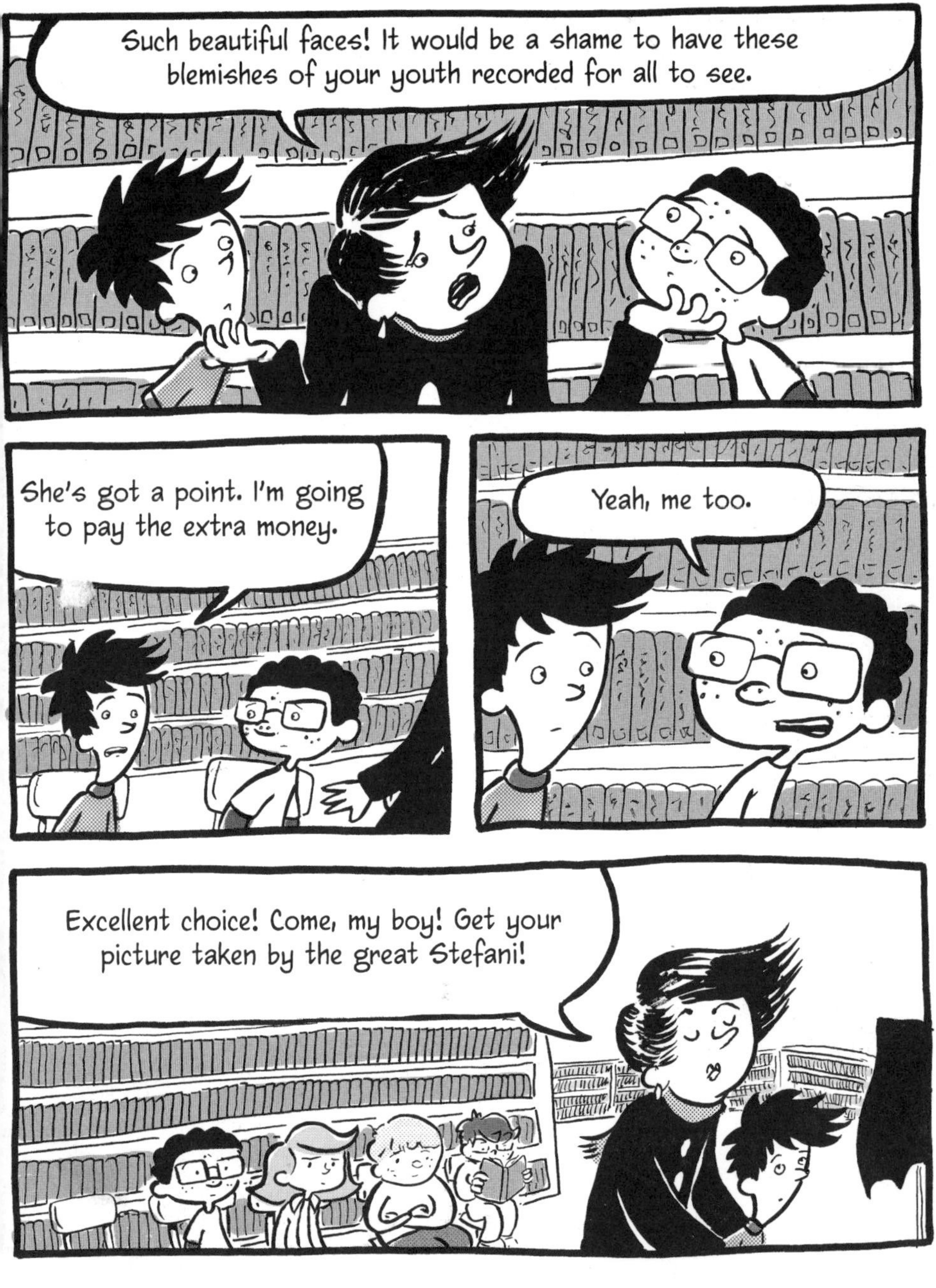
Such beautiful faces! It would be a shame to have these blemishes of your youth recorded for all to see.
She's got a point. I'm going to pay the extra money.
Yeah, me too.
Excellent choice! Come, my boy! Get your picture taken by the great Stefani!

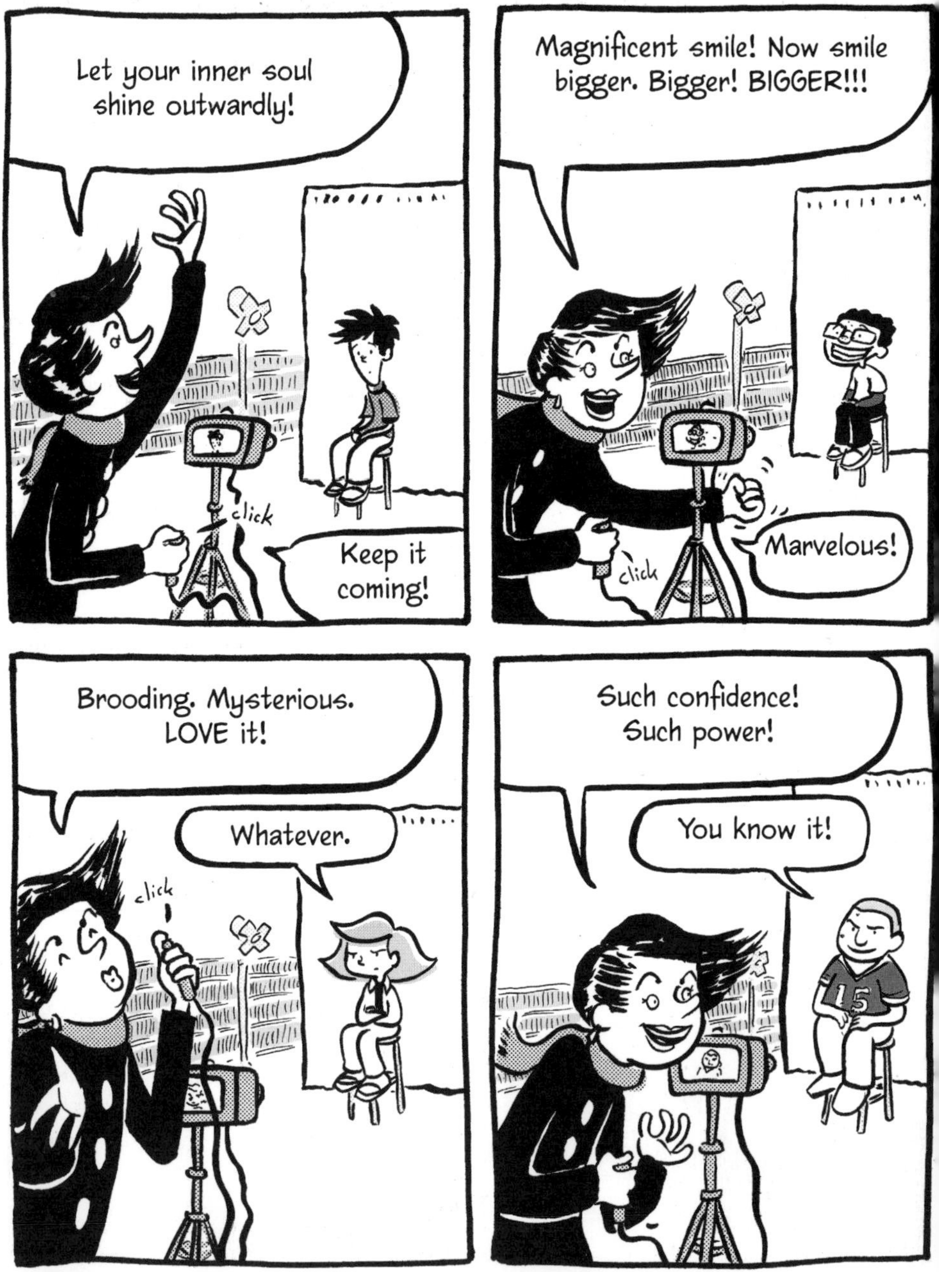
Let your inner soul shine outwardly!
click
Keep it coming!
Magnificent smile! Now smile bigger. Bigger! BIGGER!!!
click
Marvelous!
Brooding. Mysterious. LOVE it!
Whatever.
click
Such confidence! Such power!
You know it!
15

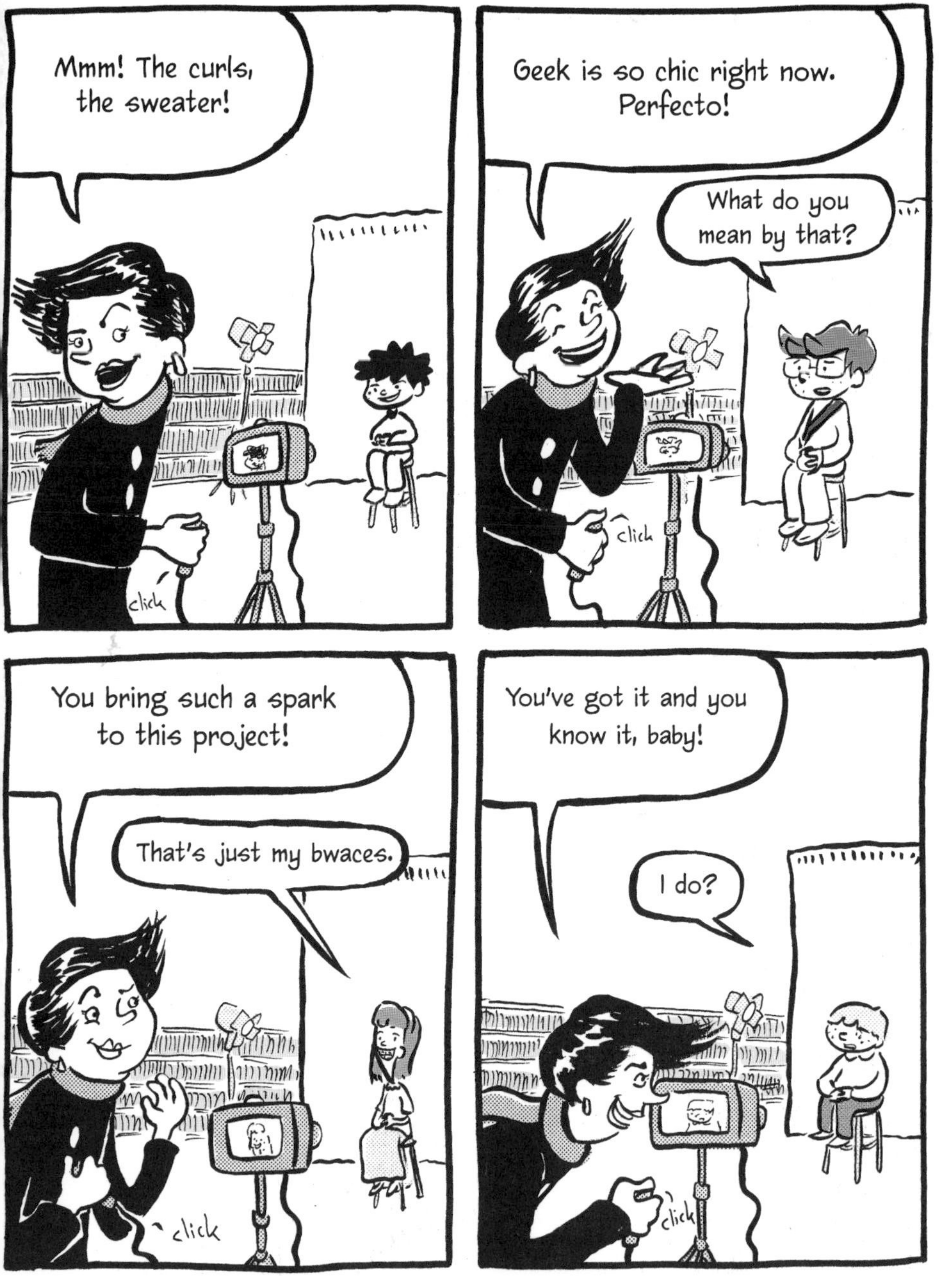
Mmm! The curls, the sweater!
click
Geek is so chic right now. Perfecto!
What do you mean by that?
click
You bring such a spark to this project!
That's just my bwaces.
click
You've got it and you know it, baby!
I do?
click

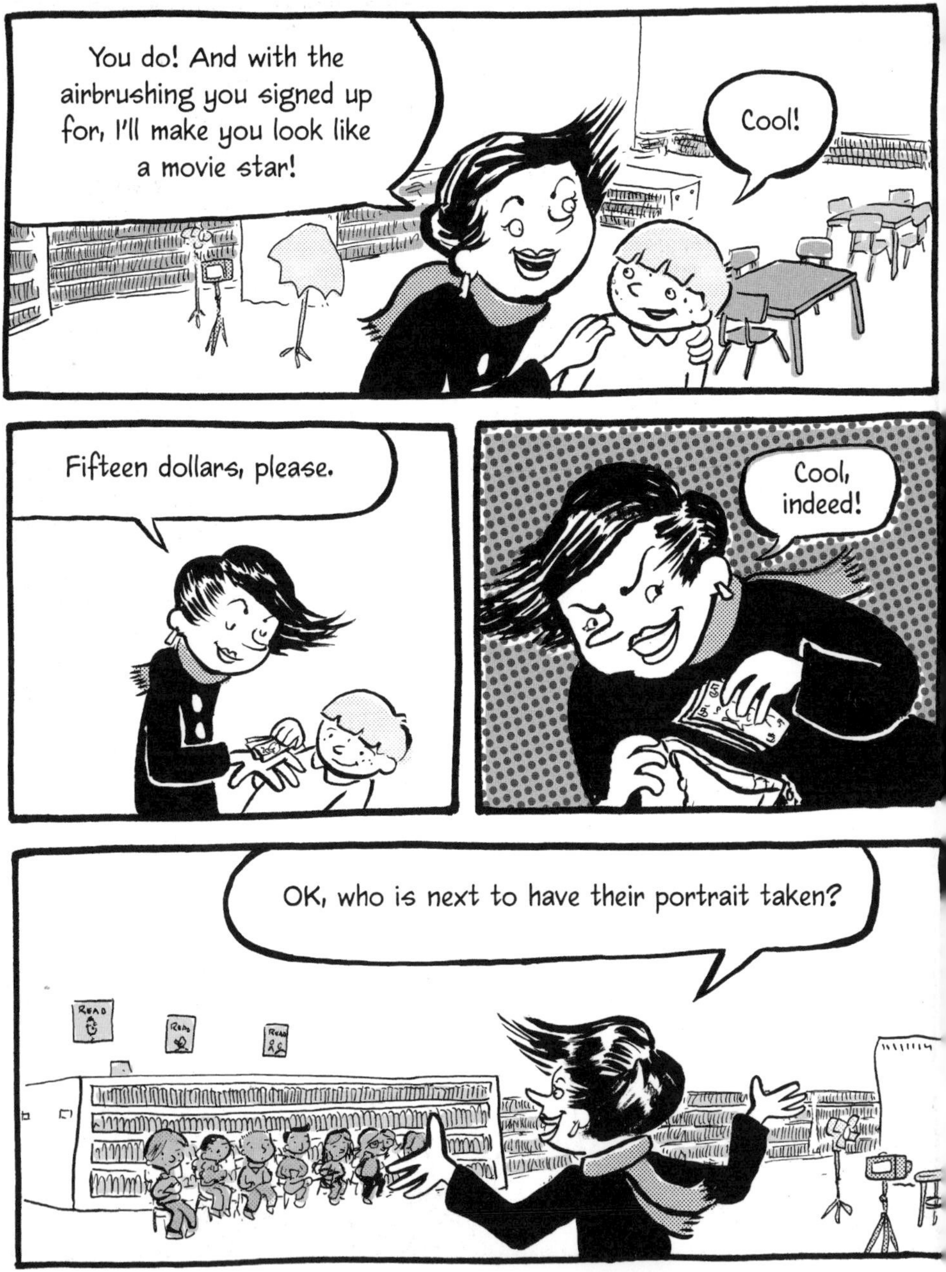
You do! And with the airbrushing you signed up for, I'll make you look like a movie star!
Cool!
Fifteen dollars, please.
Cool, indeed!
OK, who is next to have their portrait taken?
READ
READ
READ

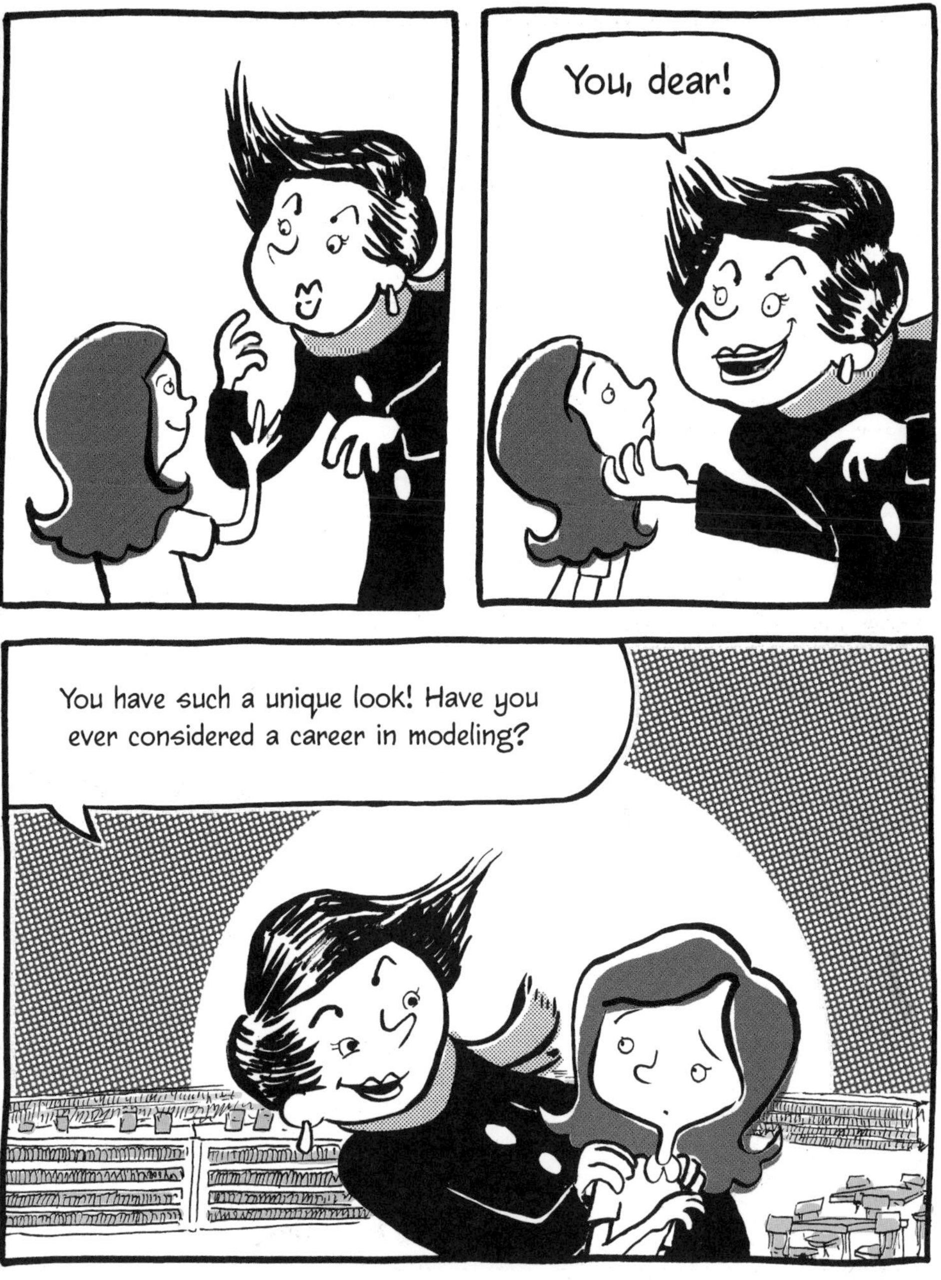
You, dear!
You have such a unique look! Have you ever considered a career in modeling?

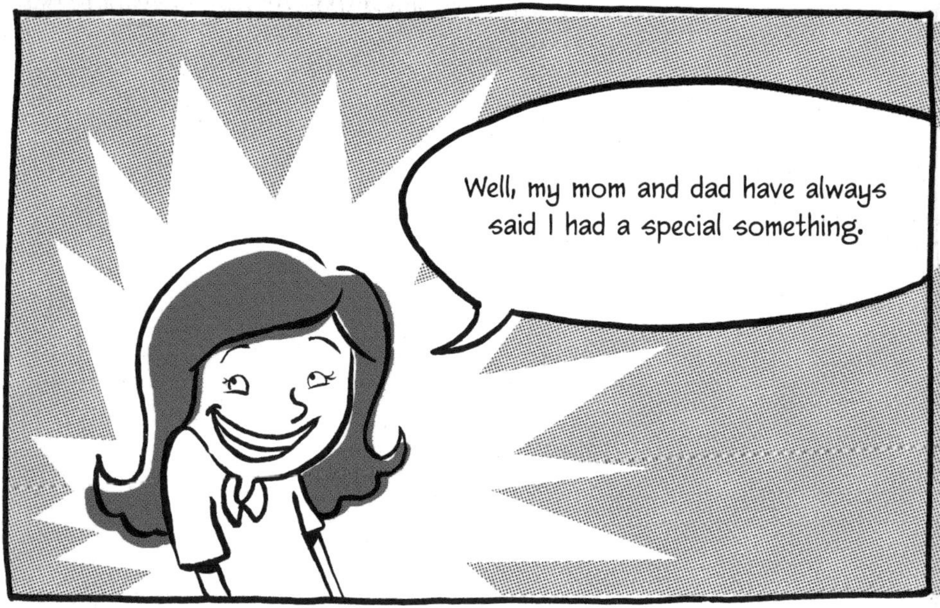
Well, my mom and dad have always said I had a special something.

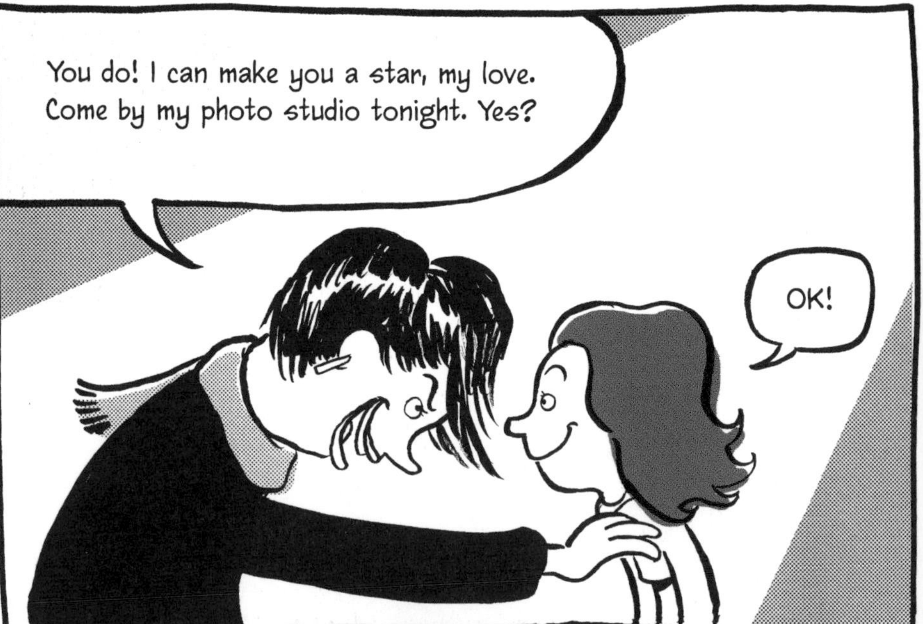
You do! I can make you a star, my love. Come by my photo studio tonight. Yes?
OK!

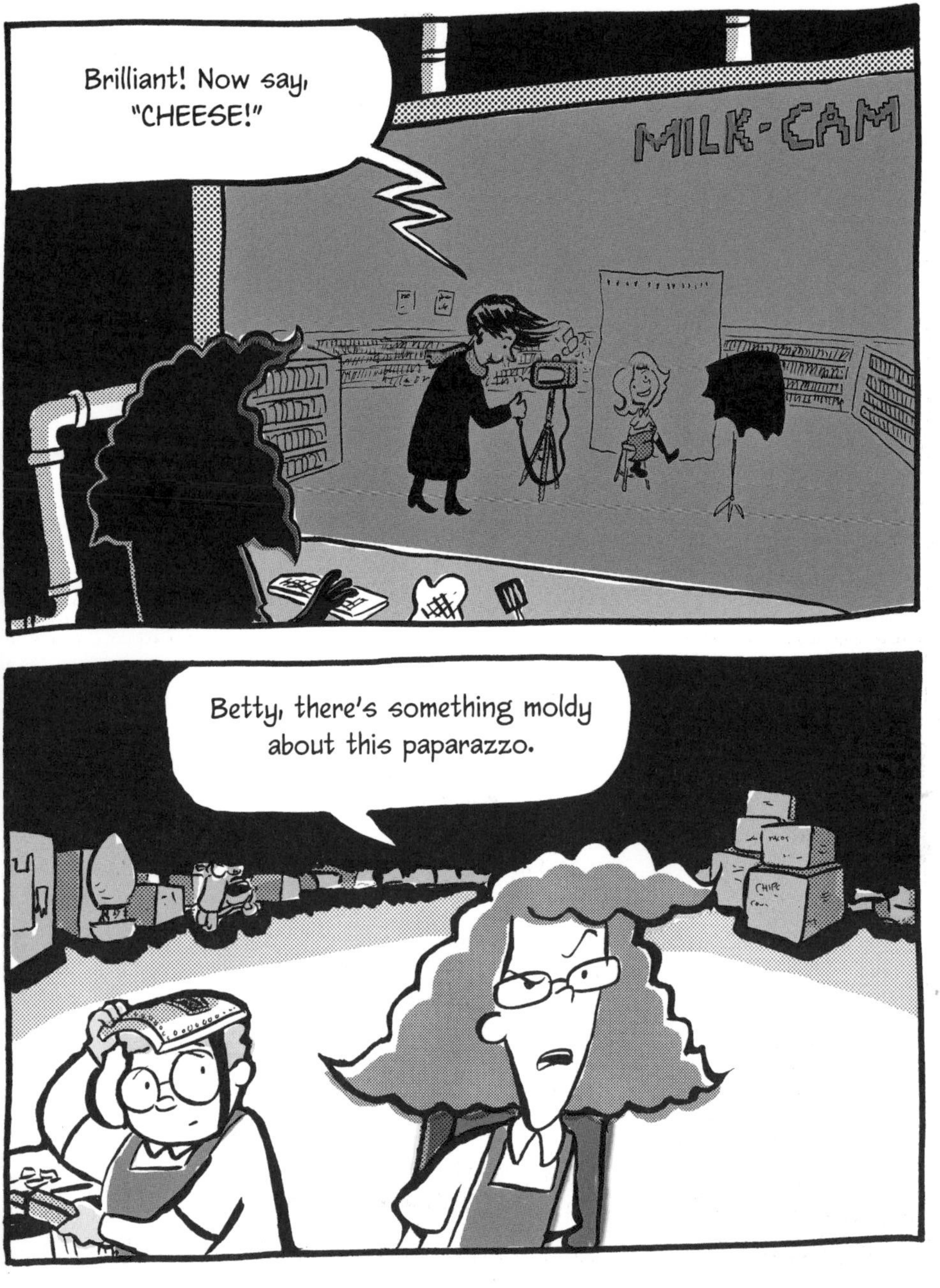
Brilliant! Now say, "CHEESE!"
MILK-CAM
Betty, there's something moldy about this paparazzo.

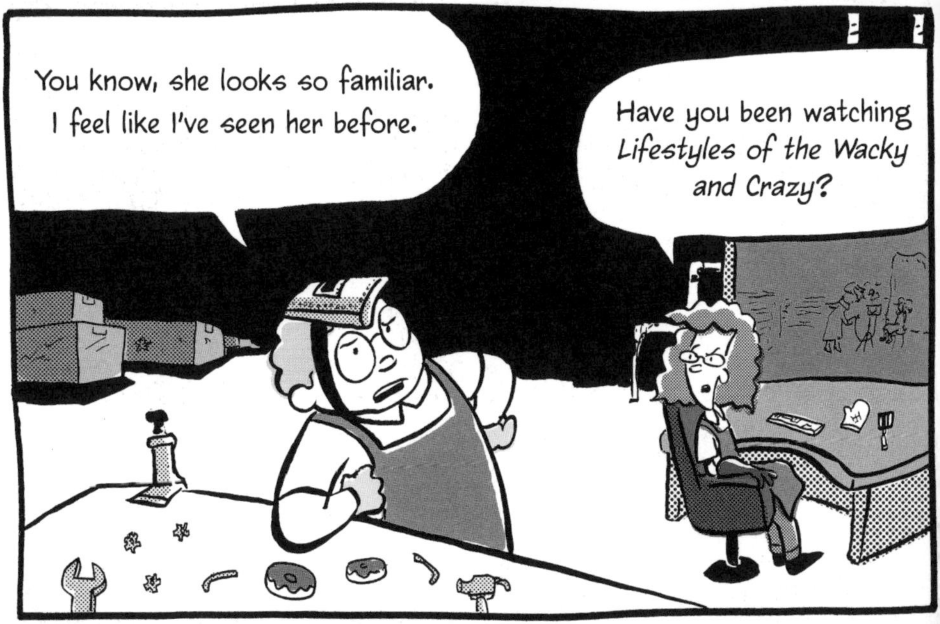
You know, she looks so familiar. I feel like I've seen her before.
Have you been watching *Lifestyles of the Wacky and Crazy?*

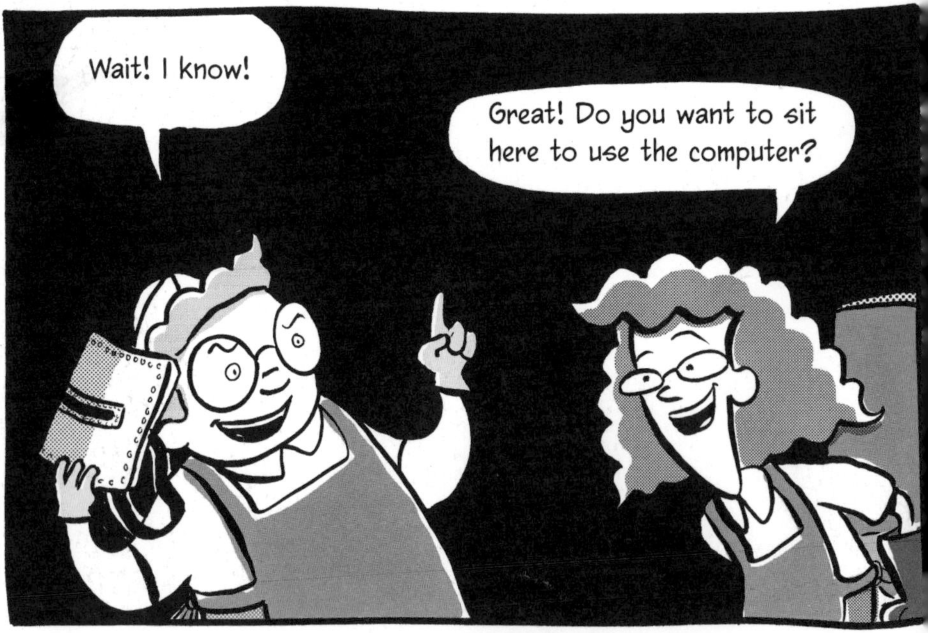
Wait! I know!
Great! Do you want to sit here to use the computer?

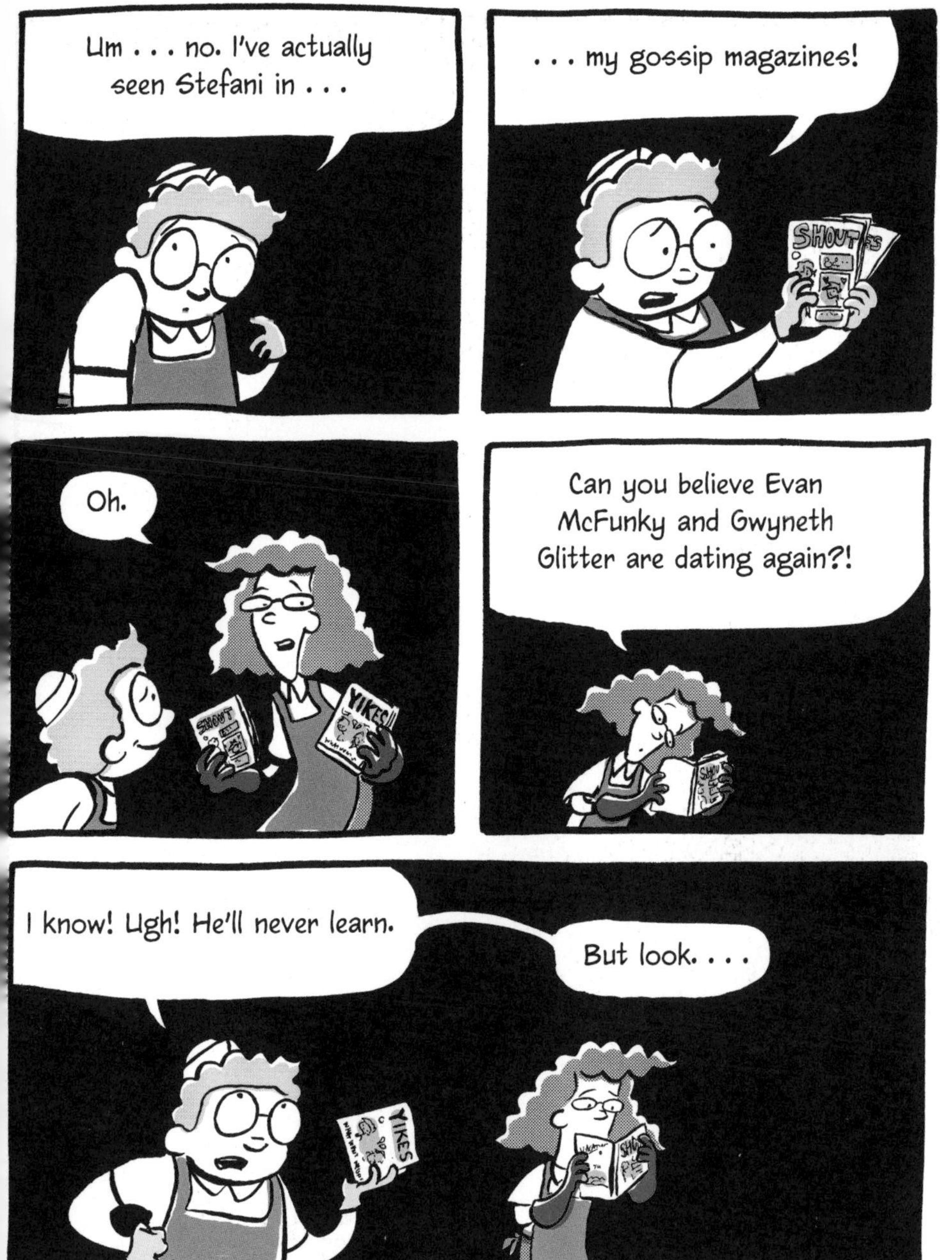
Um . . . no. I've actually seen Stefani in . . .
. . . my gossip magazines!
SHOUT
Oh.
SHOUT
YIKES!!
Can you believe Evan McFunky and Gwyneth Glitter are dating again?!
I know! Ugh! He'll never learn.
But look. . . .
YIKES

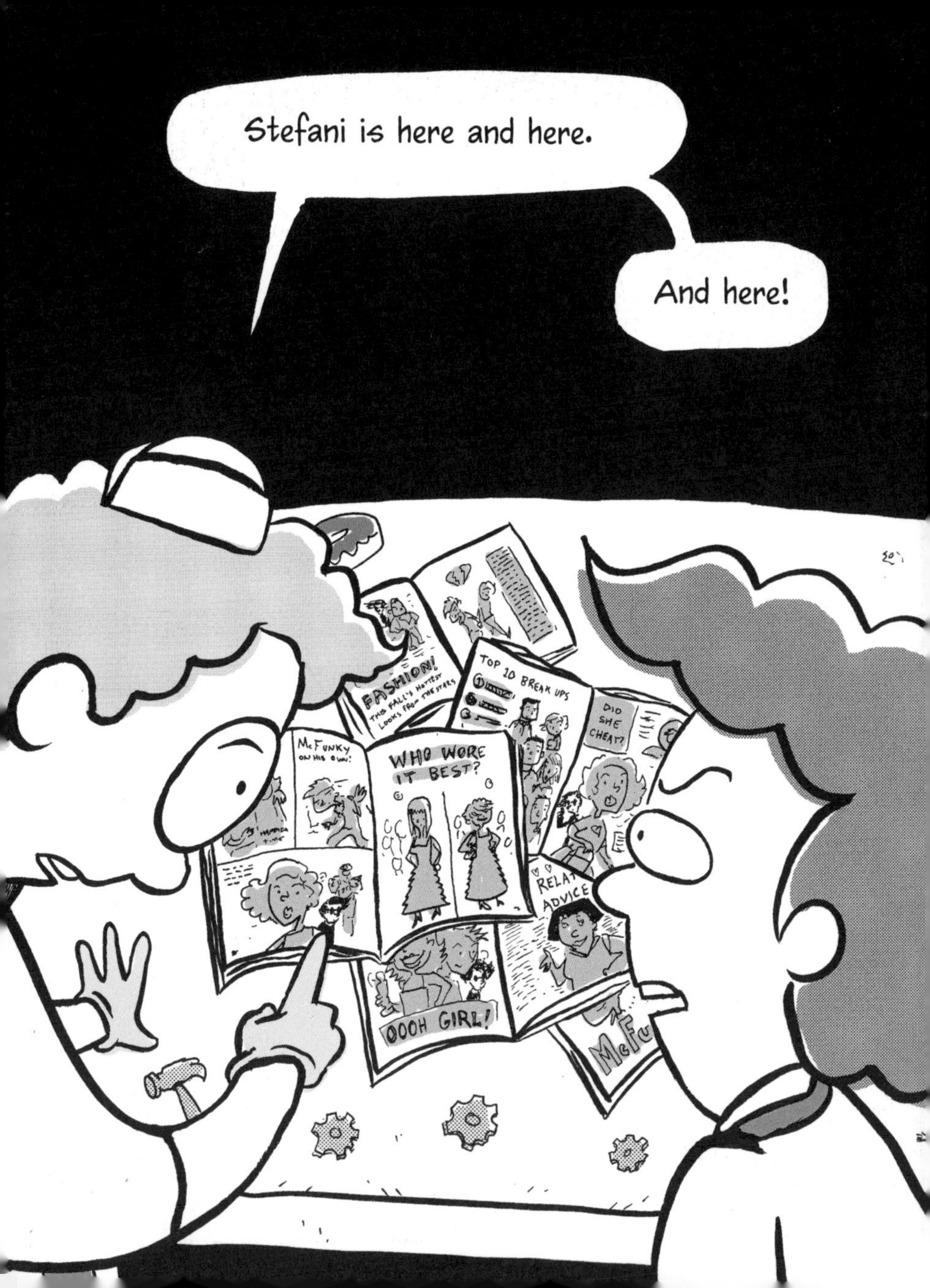
Stefani is here and here.
And here!
FASHION!
THIS FALL'S HOTTEST LOOKS FROM THE STARS
TOP 10 BREAK UPS
DID SHE CHEAT?
McFUNKY ON HIS OWN!
WHO WORE IT BEST?
RELAT
ADVICE
OOOH GIRL!
McFu

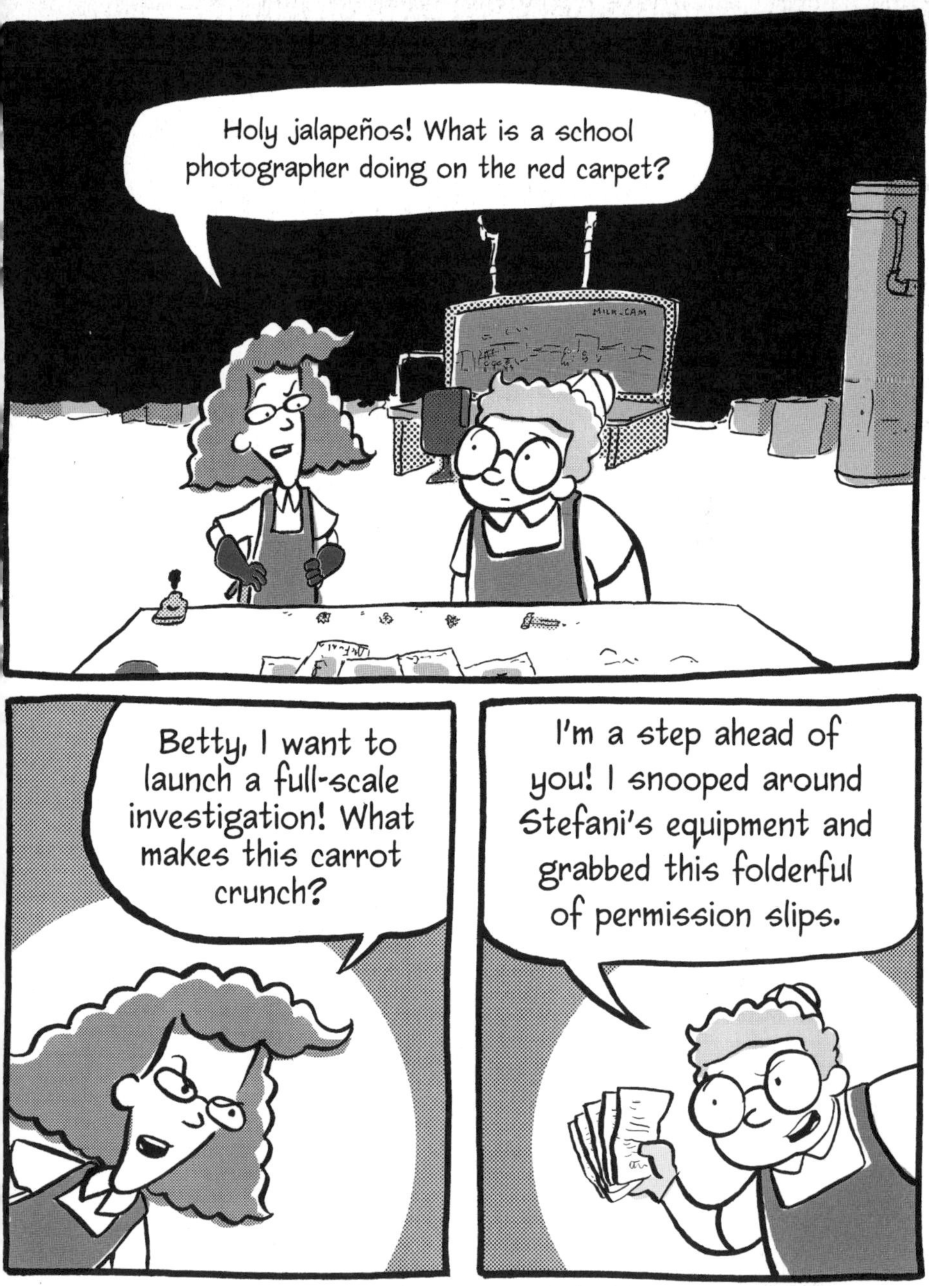
Holy jalapeños! What is a school photographer doing on the red carpet?
MILK-CAM
Betty, I want to launch a full-scale investigation! What makes this carrot crunch?
I'm a step ahead of you! I snooped around Stefani's equipment and grabbed this folderful of permission slips.

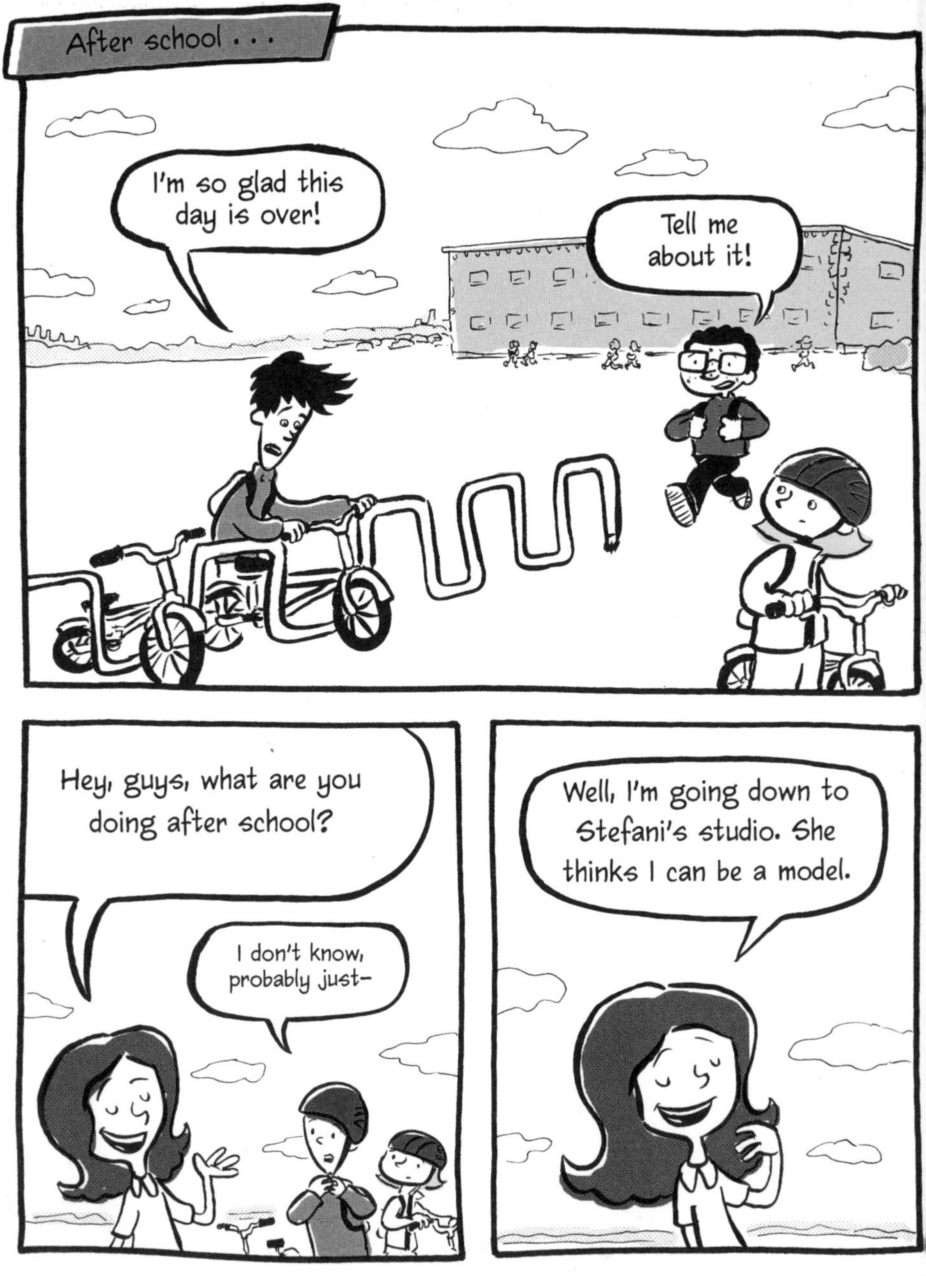
After school . . .
I'm so glad this day is over!
Tell me about it!
Hey, guys, what are you doing after school?
I don't know, probably just-
Well, I'm going down to Stefani's studio. She thinks I can be a model.

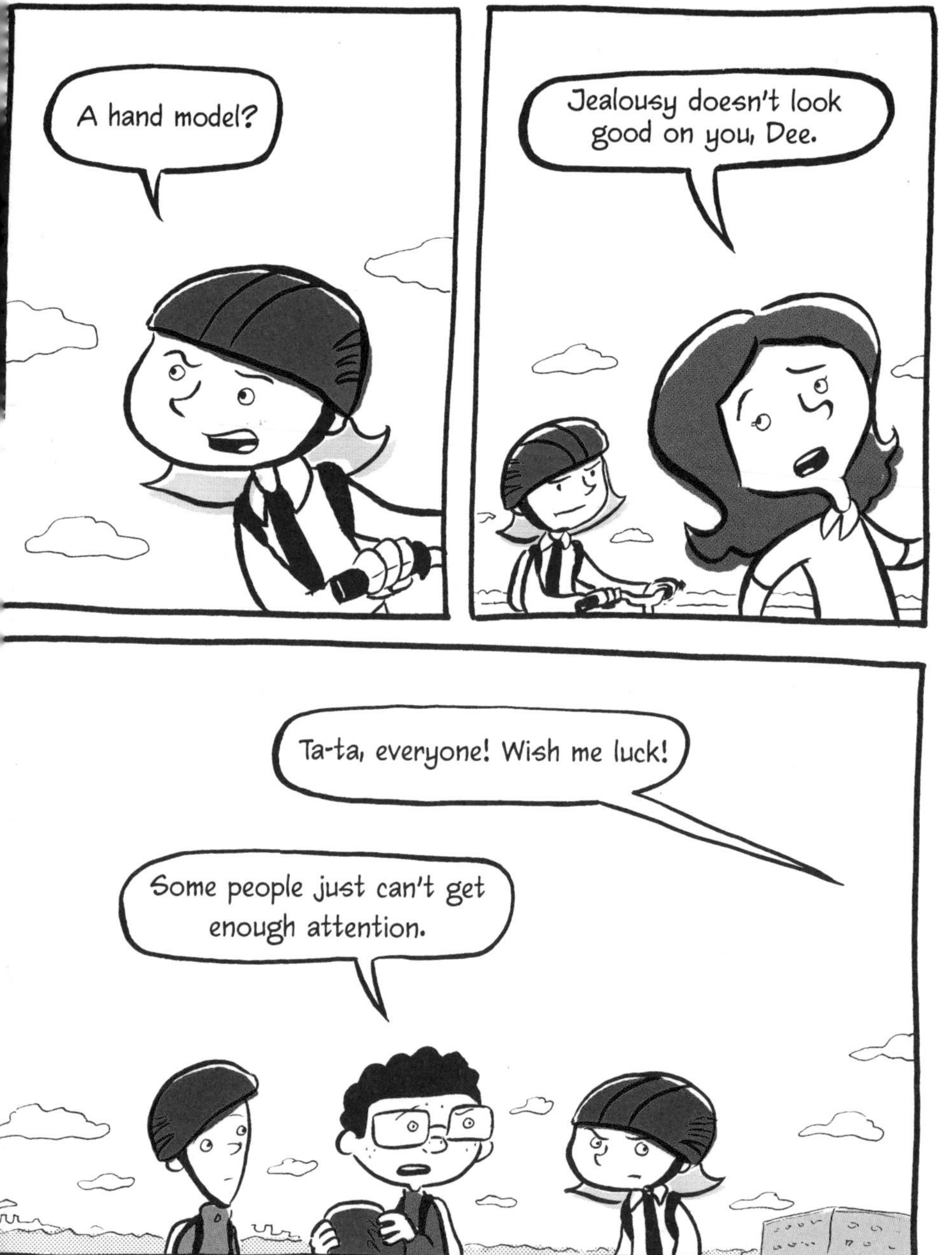
A hand model?
Jealousy doesn't look good on you, Dee.
Ta-ta, everyone! Wish me luck!
Some people just can't get enough attention.

A few days later, when Lunch Lady arrives at school . . .
She'll be comin' round the mountain when she comes . . .
LL
sniff
Sob
Sob
sniff
sniff

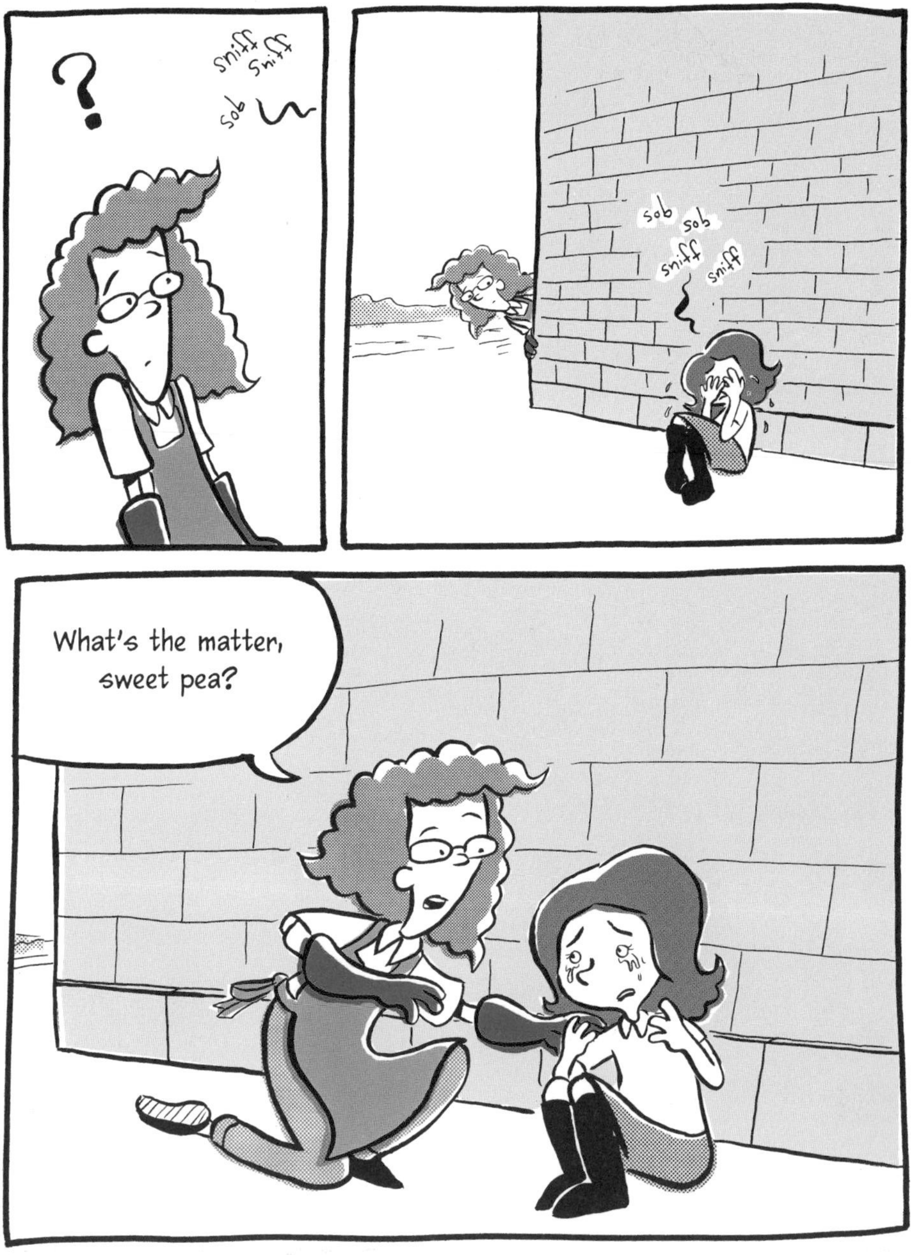
?
sniff sniff
sob
sob sob
sniff sniff
What's the matter, sweet pea?

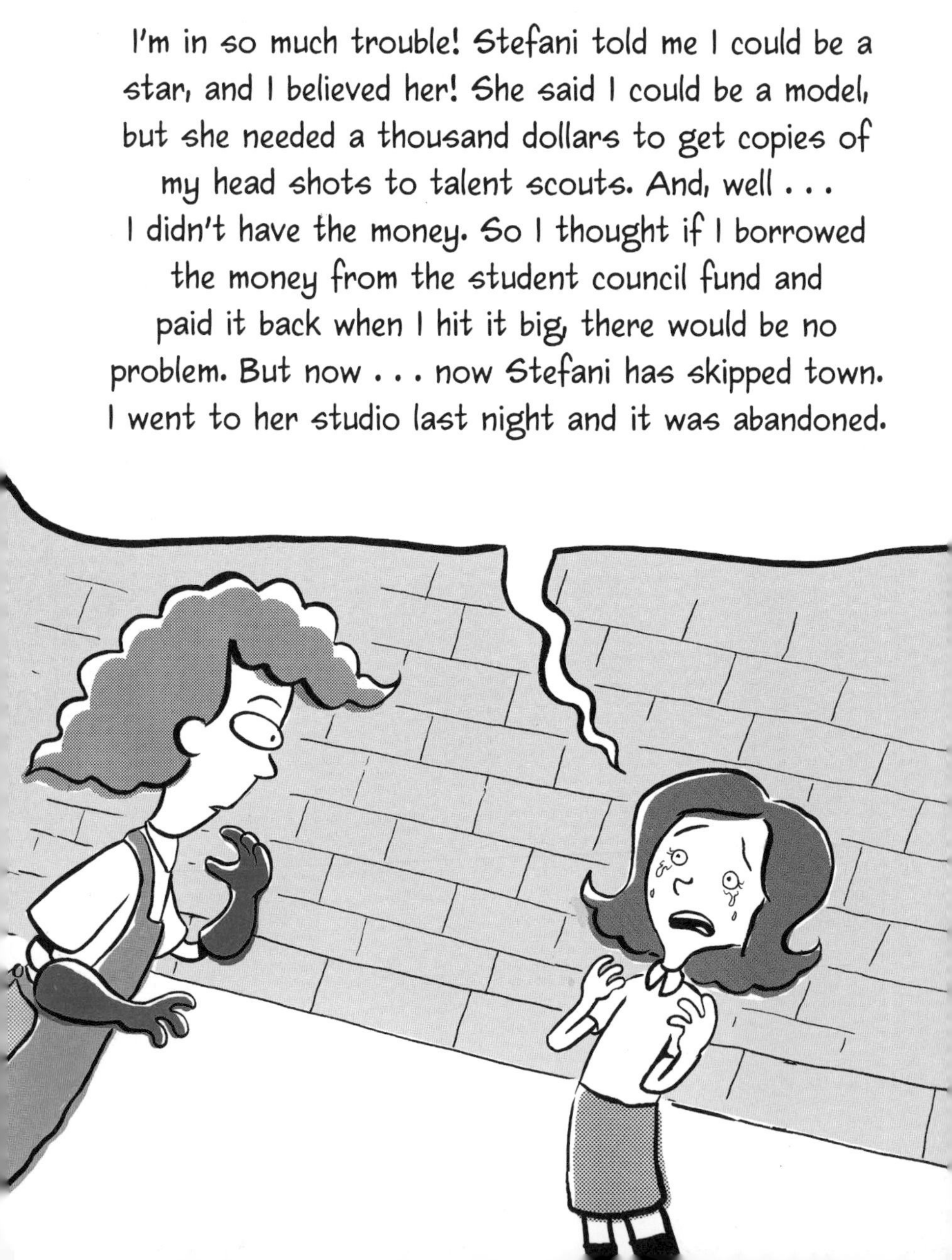
I'm in so much trouble! Stefani told me I could be a star, and I believed her! She said I could be a model, but she needed a thousand dollars to get copies of my head shots to talent scouts. And, well . . . I didn't have the money. So I thought if I borrowed the money from the student council fund and paid it back when I hit it big, there would be no problem. But now . . . now Stefani has skipped town. I went to her studio last night and it was abandoned.

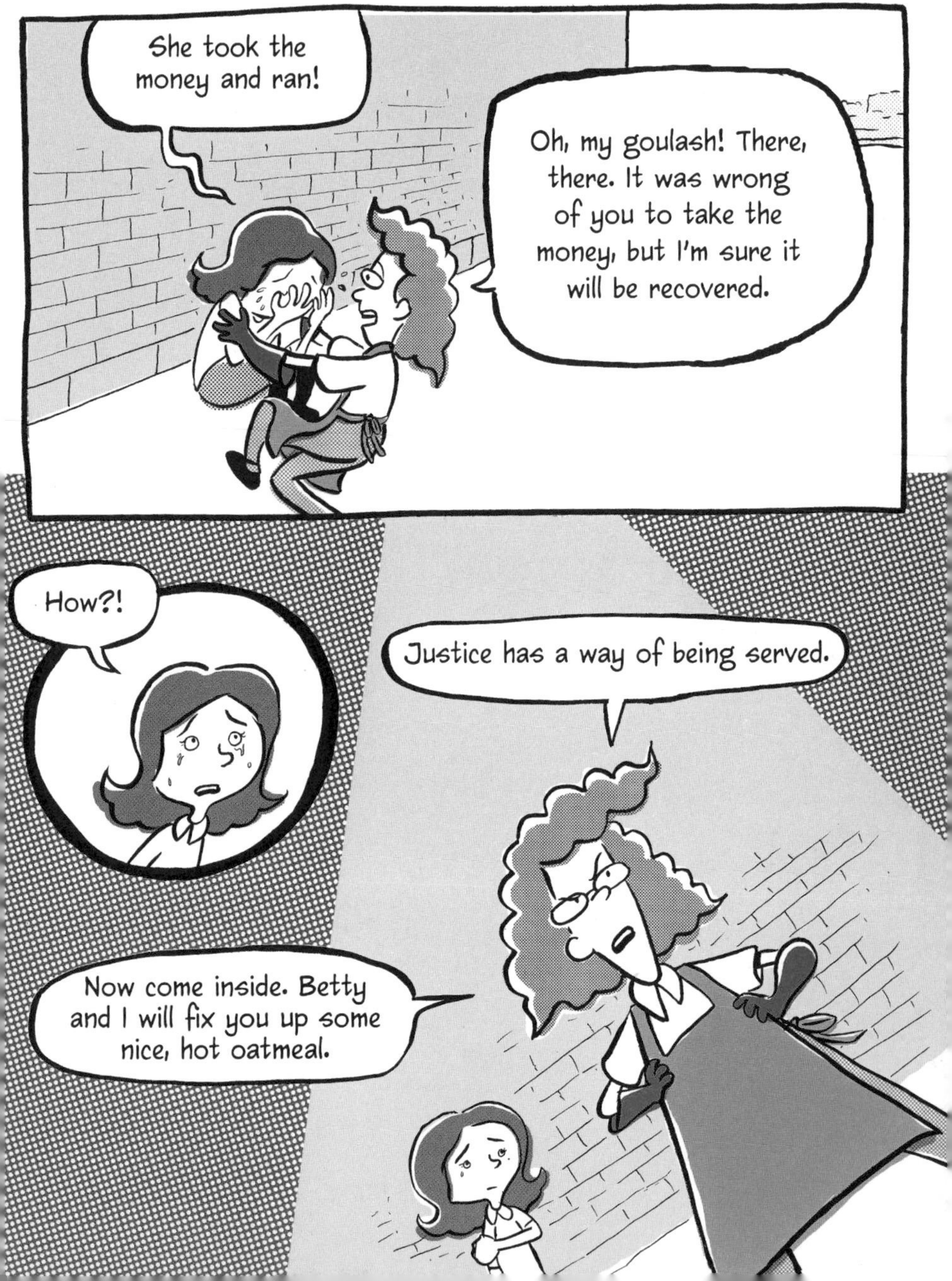
She took the money and ran!
Oh, my goulash! There, there. It was wrong of you to take the money, but I'm sure it will be recovered.
How?!
Justice has a way of being served.
Now come inside. Betty and I will fix you up some nice, hot oatmeal.

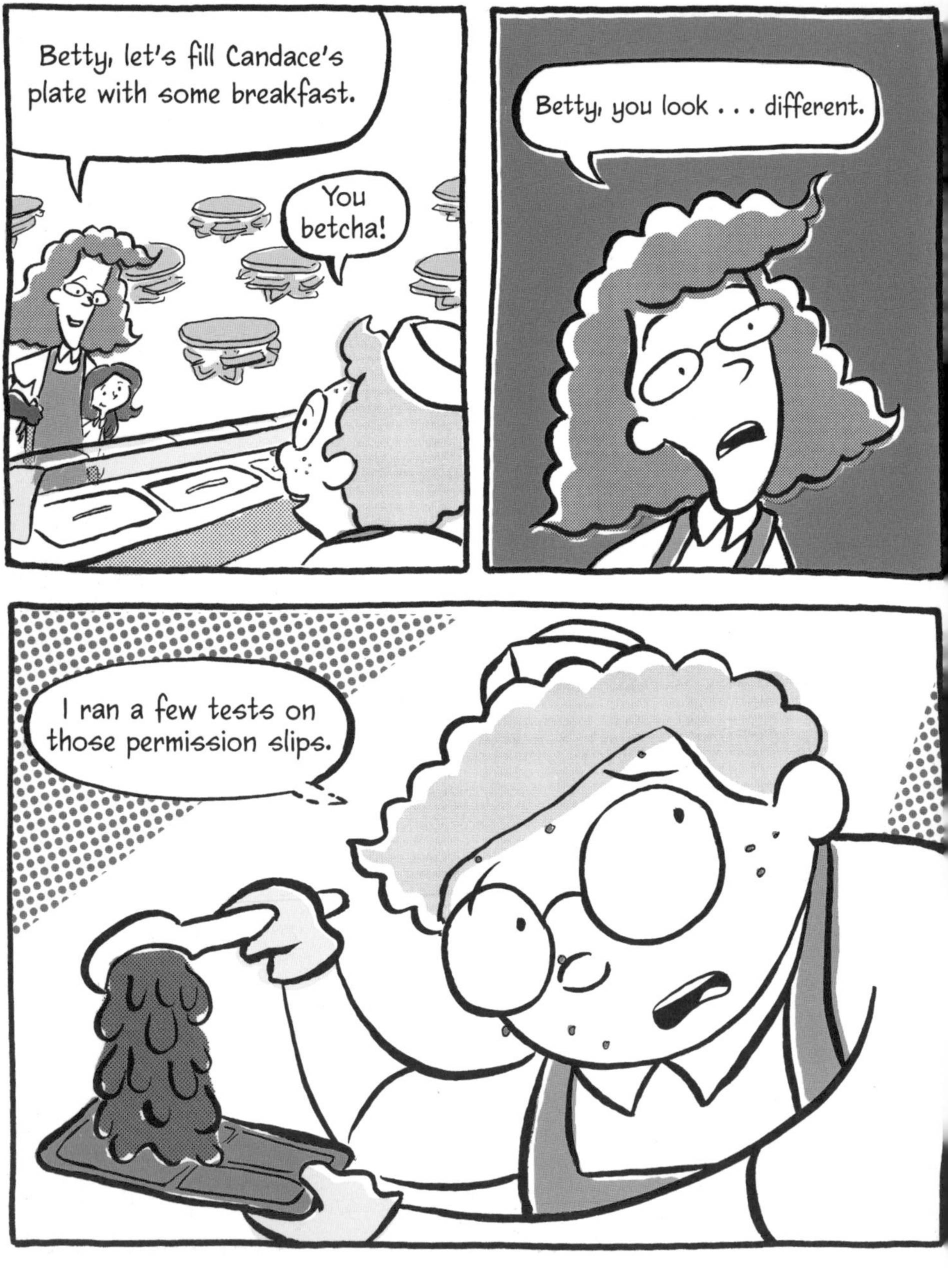
Betty, let's fill Candace's plate with some breakfast.
You betcha!
Betty, you look . . . different.
I ran a few tests on those permission slips.

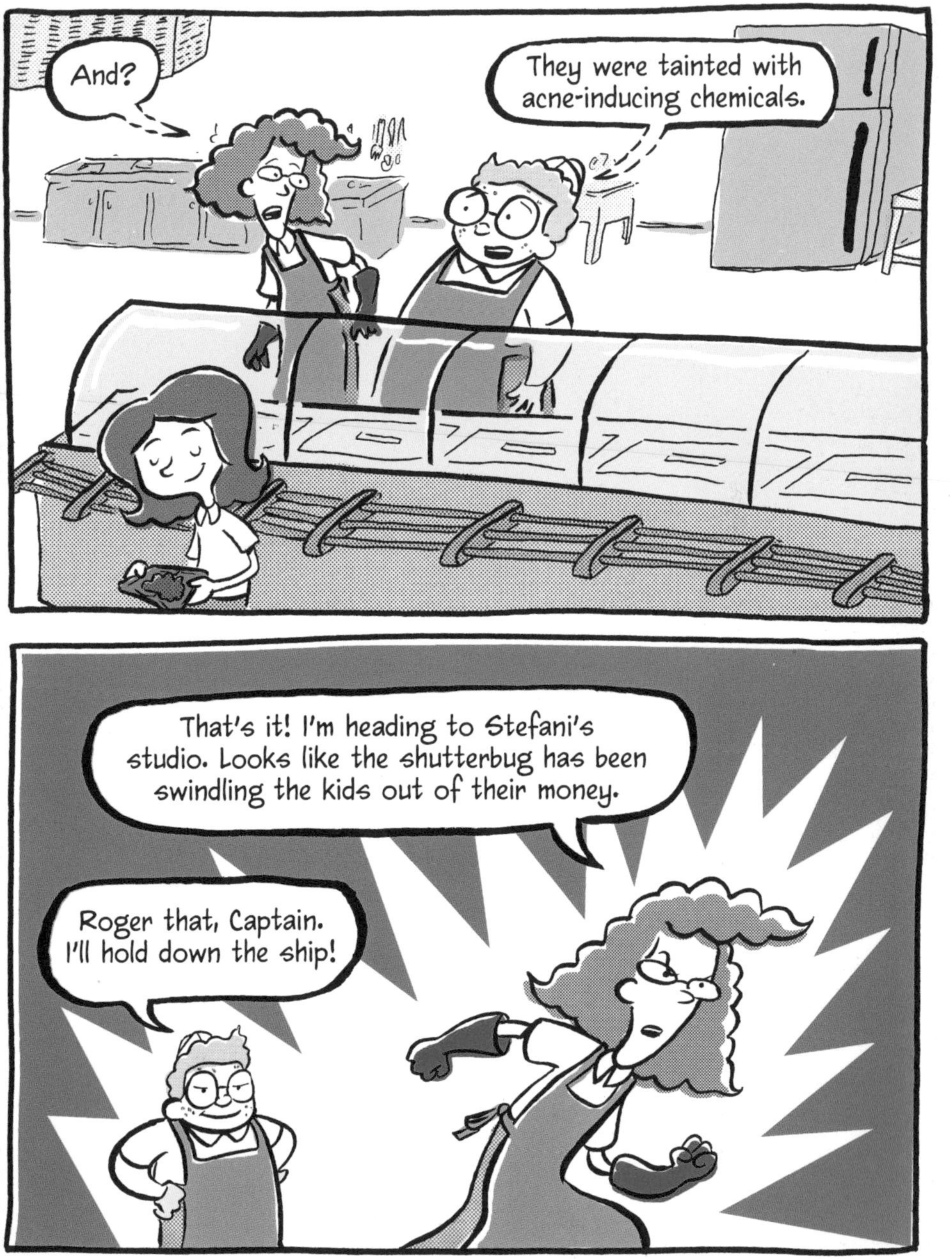
And?
They were tainted with acne-inducing chemicals.
That's it! I'm heading to Stefani's studio. Looks like the shutterbug has been swindling the kids out of their money.
Roger that, Captain. I'll hold down the ship!

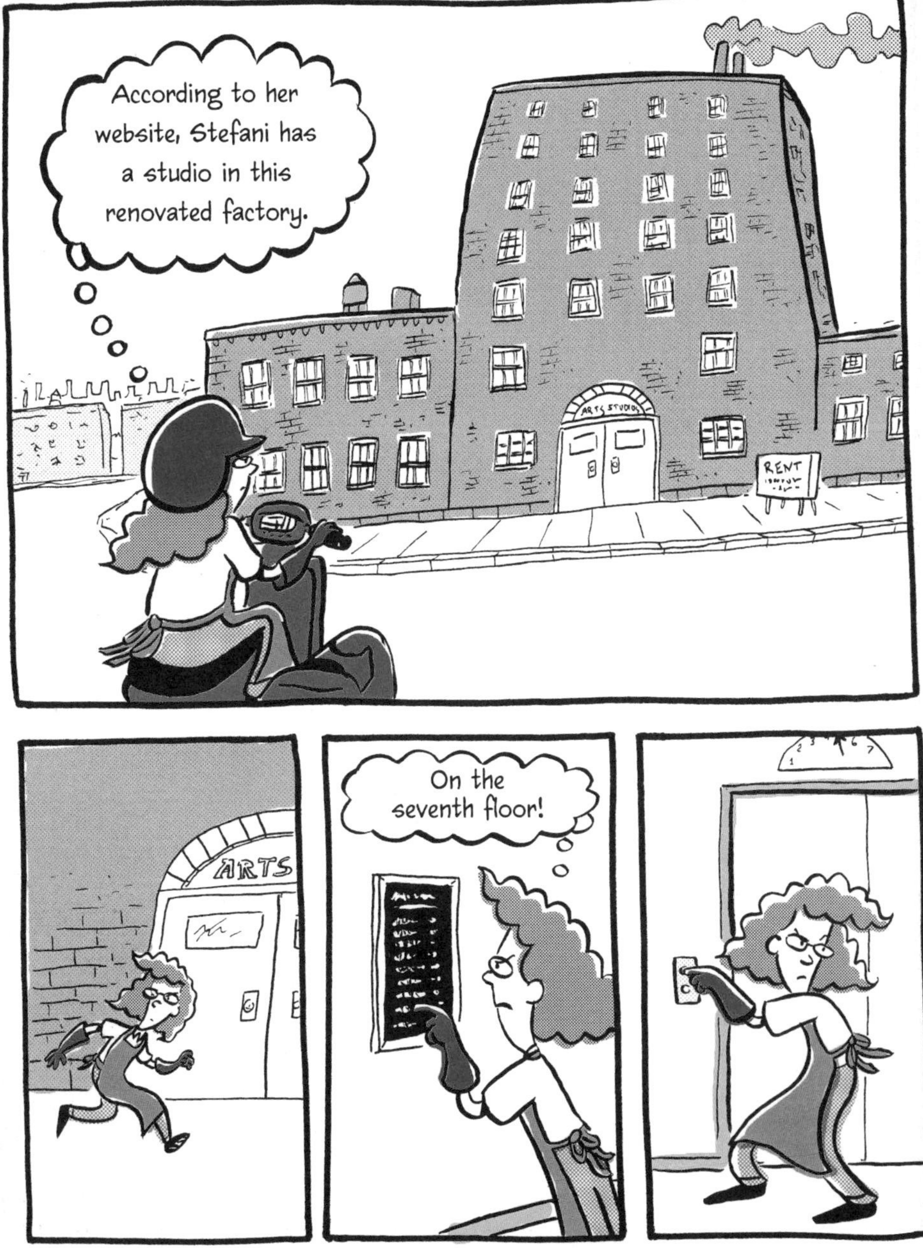
According to her website, Stefani has a studio in this renovated factory.
ARTS STUDIOS
RENT
ARTS
On the seventh floor!

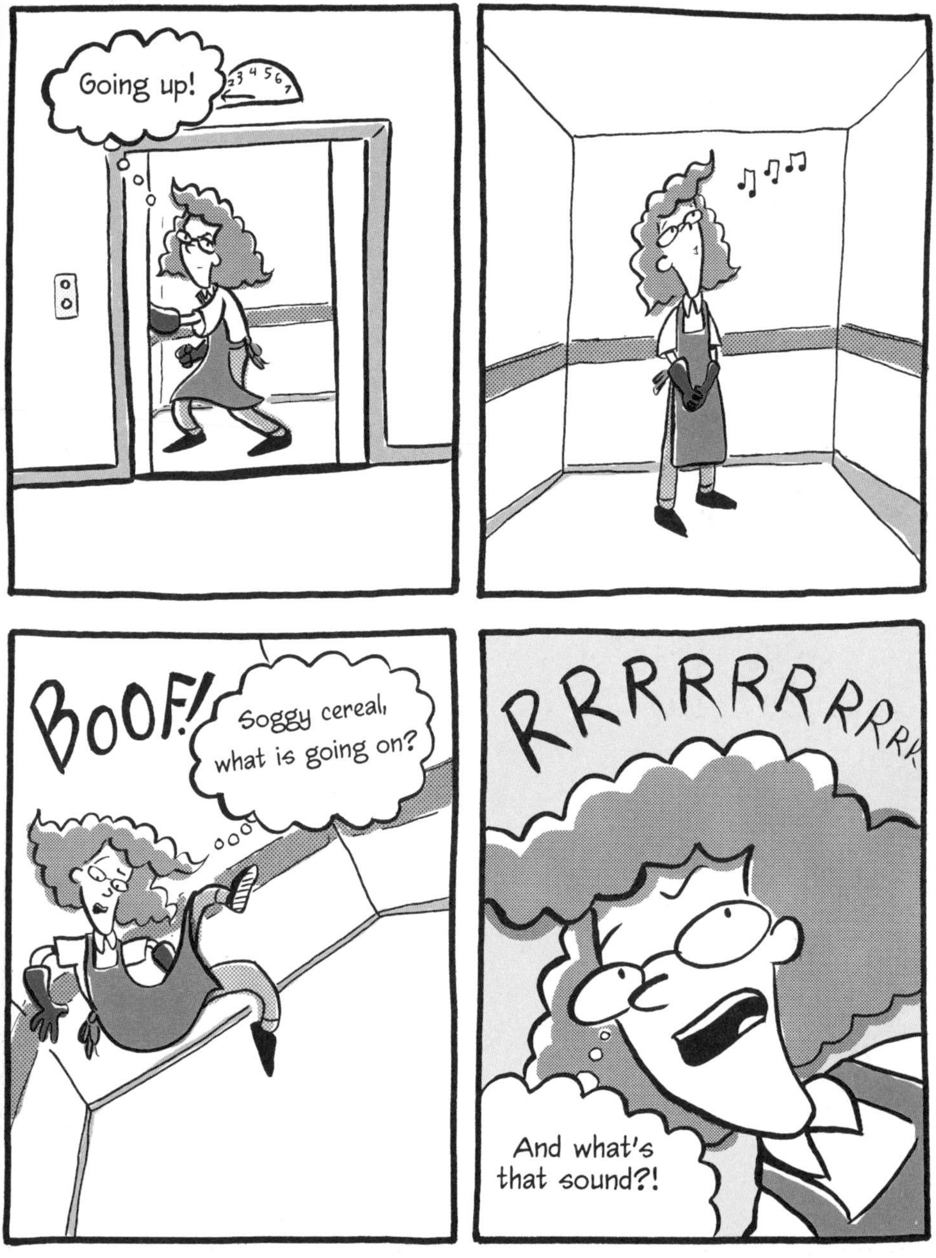
Going up!
2 3 4 5 6 7
BOOF!
Soggy cereal, what is going on?
RRRRRRRRRRR
And what's that sound?!

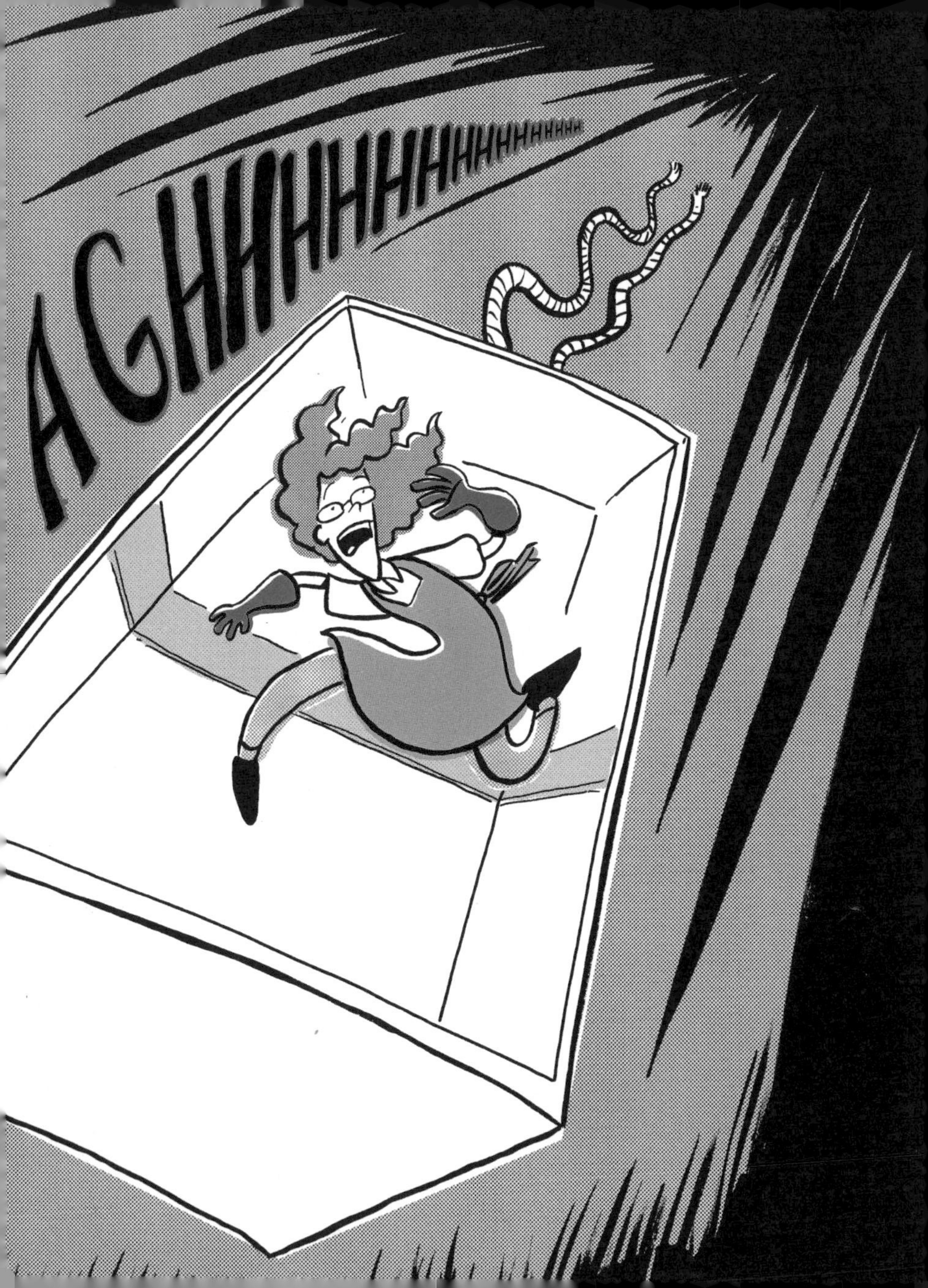
AGHHHHHHHHHhhhhhhhhh

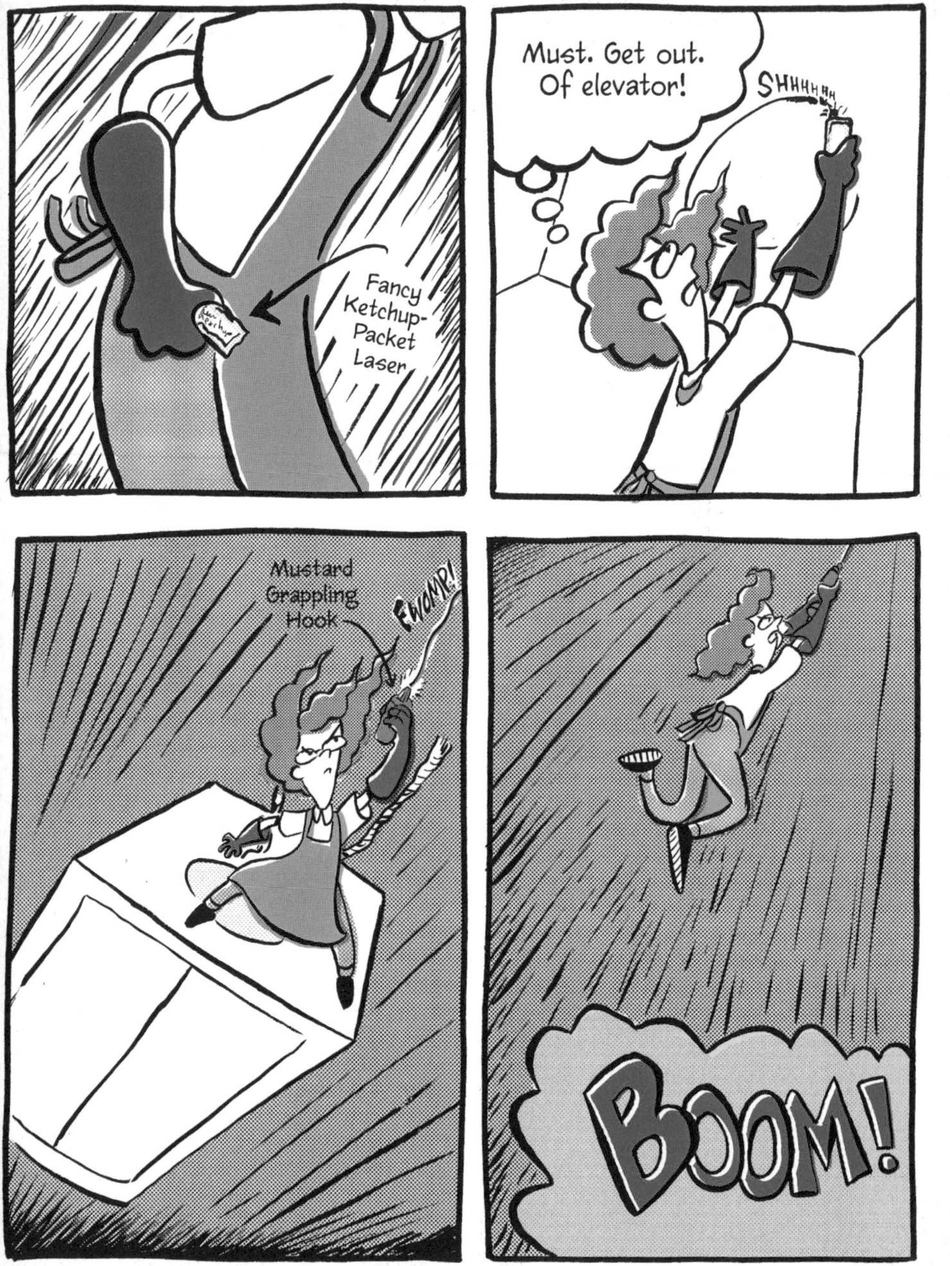
Fancy Ketchup-Packet Laser
Must. Get out. Of elevator!
SHHHHHH
Mustard Grappling Hook
FWOMP!
BOOM!

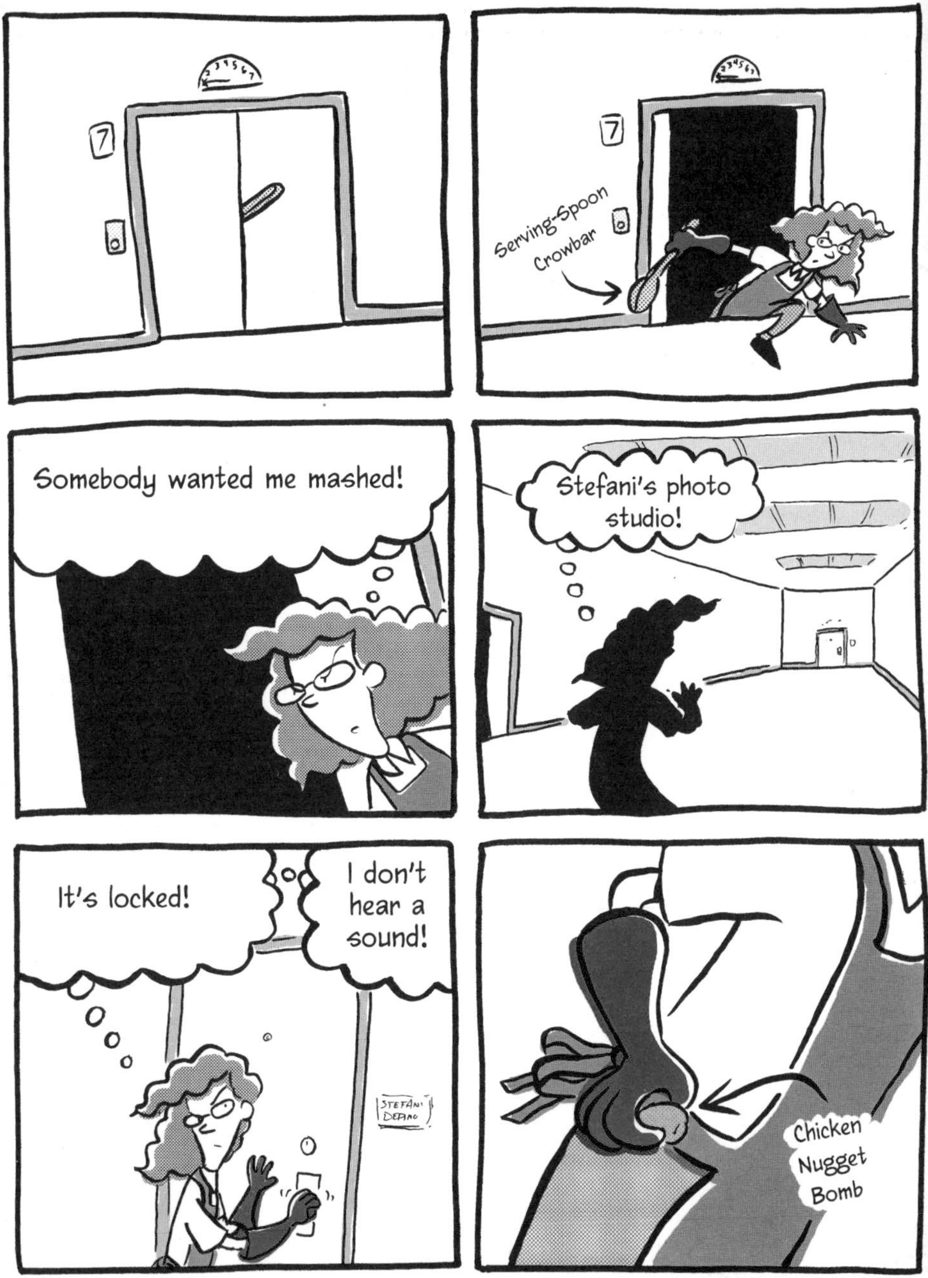
7
7
Serving-Spoon Crowbar
Somebody wanted me mashed!
Stefani's photo studio!
It's locked!
I don't hear a sound!
STEFANI DEPINO
Chicken Nugget Bomb

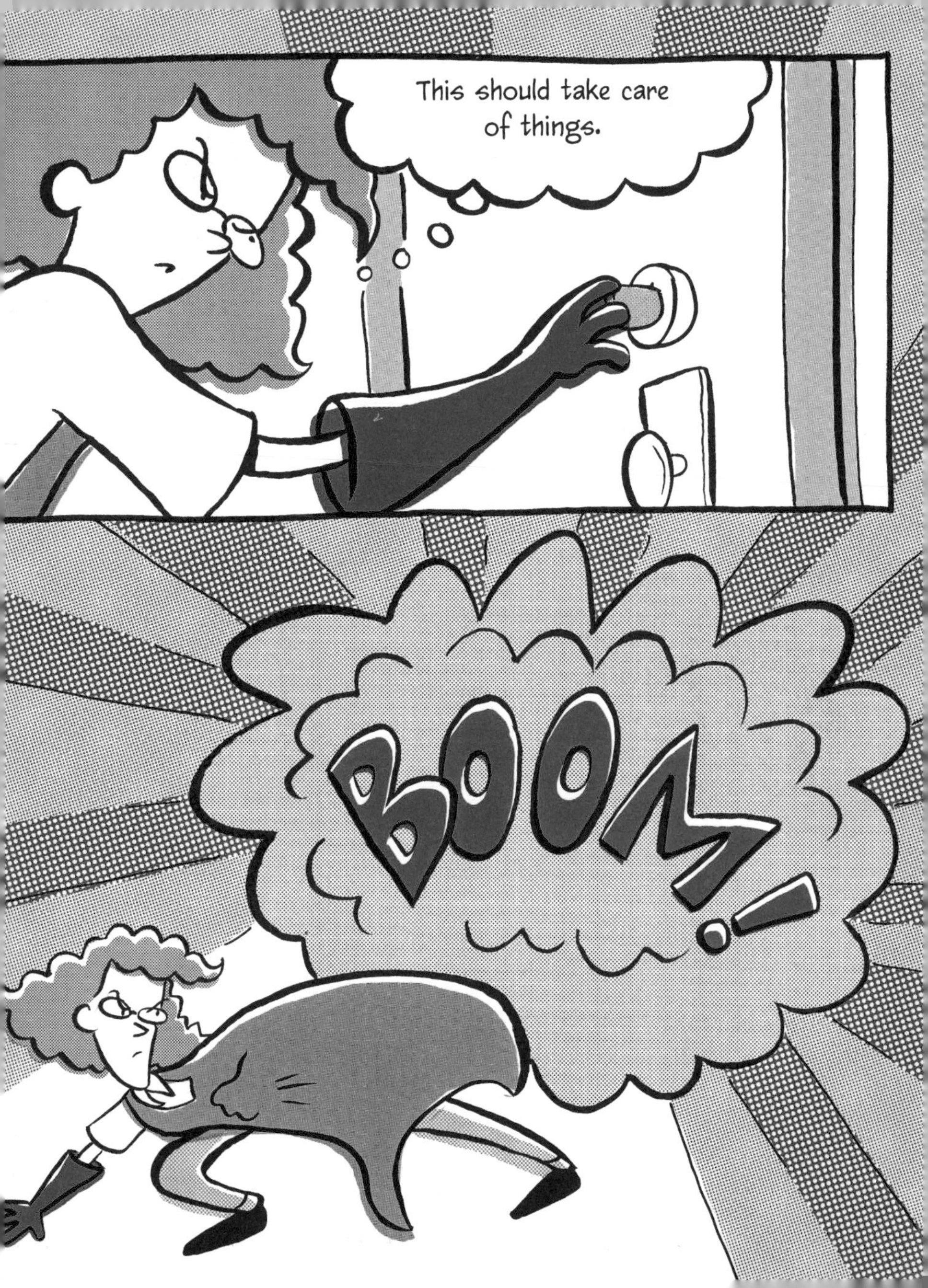
This should take care of things.
BOOM!

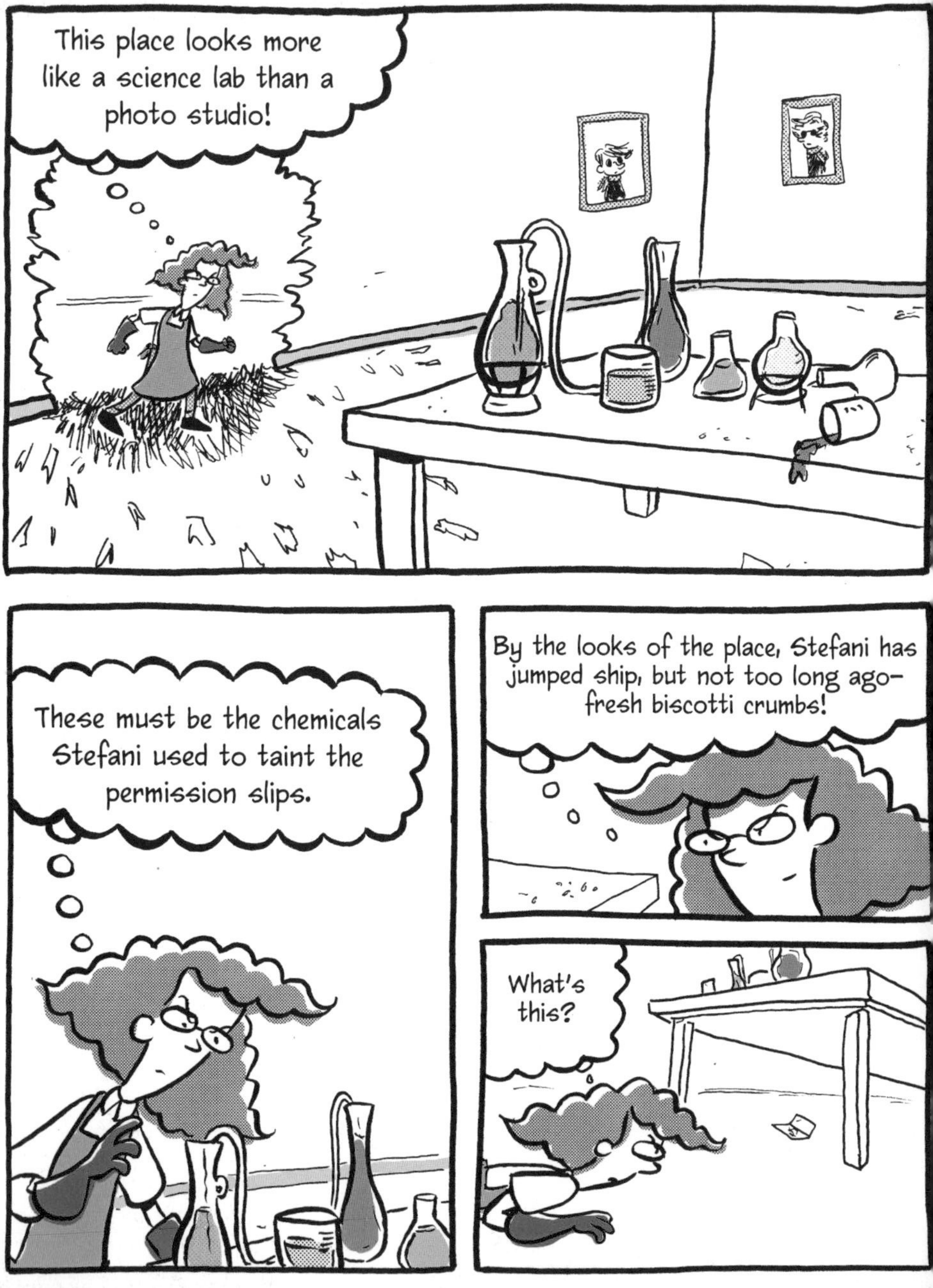
This place looks more like a science lab than a photo studio!
These must be the chemicals Stefani used to taint the permission slips.
By the looks of the place, Stefani has jumped ship, but not too long ago— fresh biscotti crumbs!
What's this?

Dearest Stefani,
It is all going as planned! Soon I will be in the city for Fashion Week. And then, with your help—PARIS! Together, we will rule the fashion industry! With my flair for design and your eye for photography, we will be unstoppable! I pity anyone who stands in our way!
Kiss, kiss,
Gerard
The soup thickens!

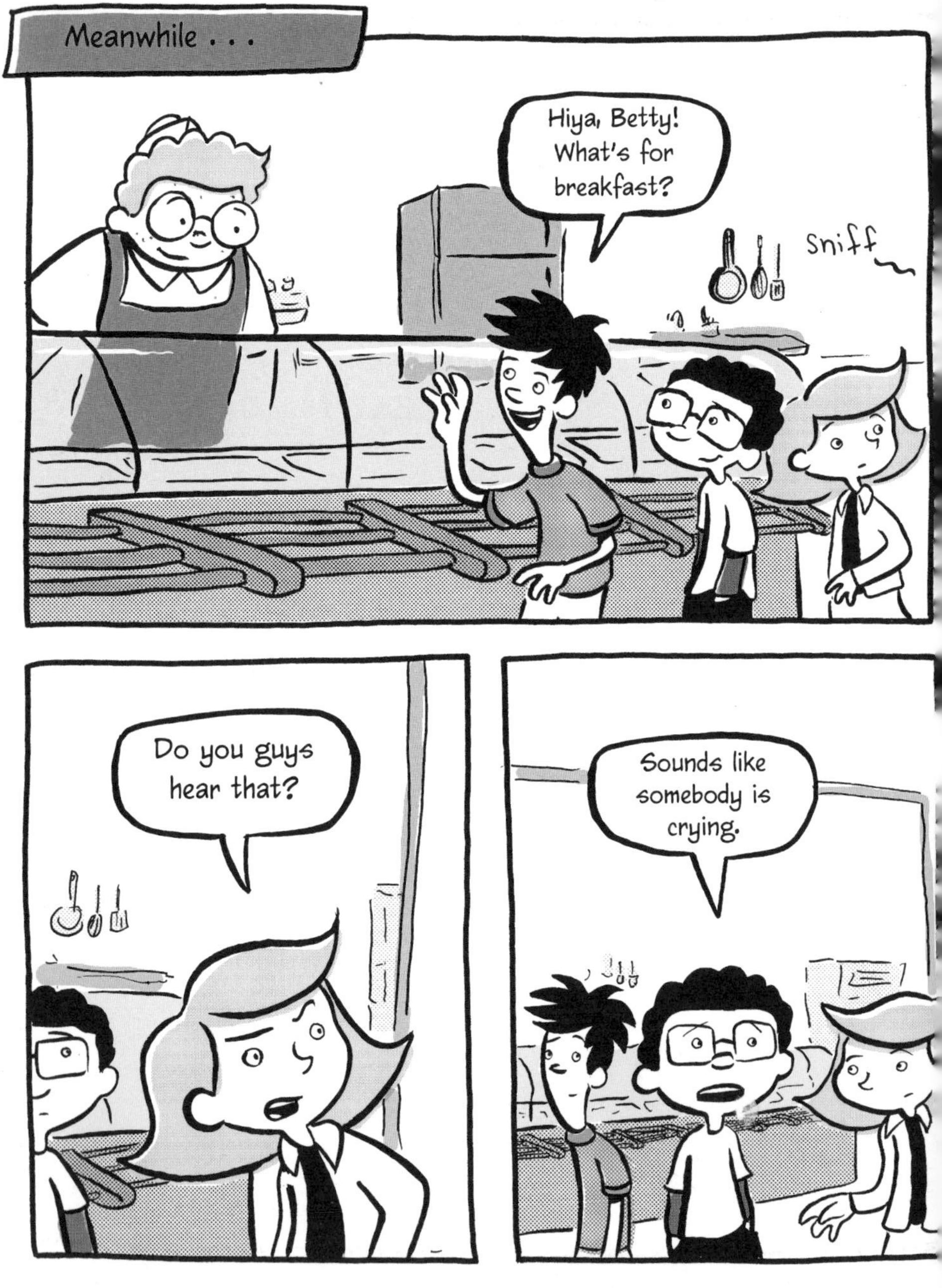
Meanwhile . . .
Hiya, Betty! What's for breakfast?
Sniff
Do you guys hear that?
Sounds like somebody is crying.

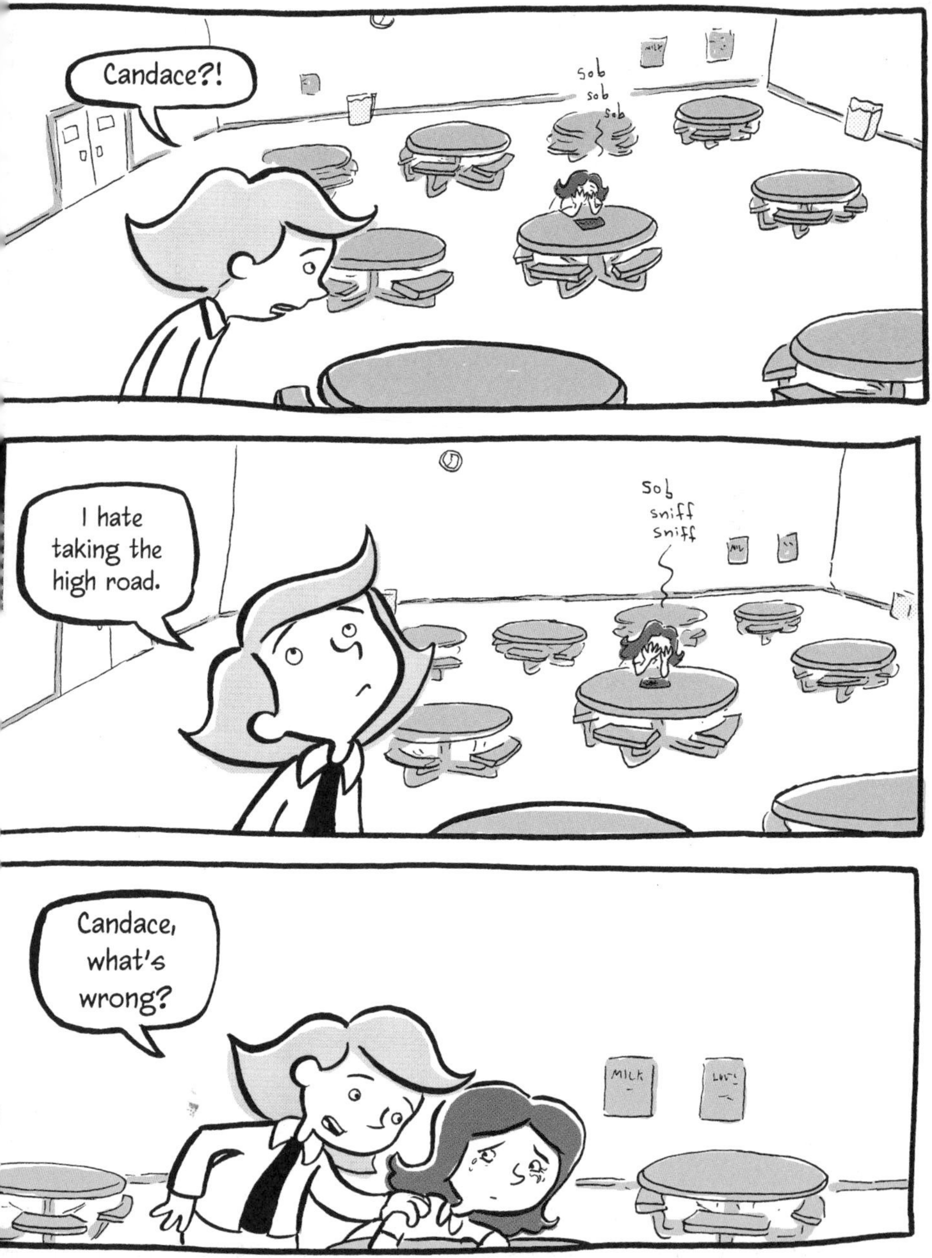
Candace?!
sob sob sob
I hate taking the high road.
sob sniff sniff
Candace, what's wrong?
MILK

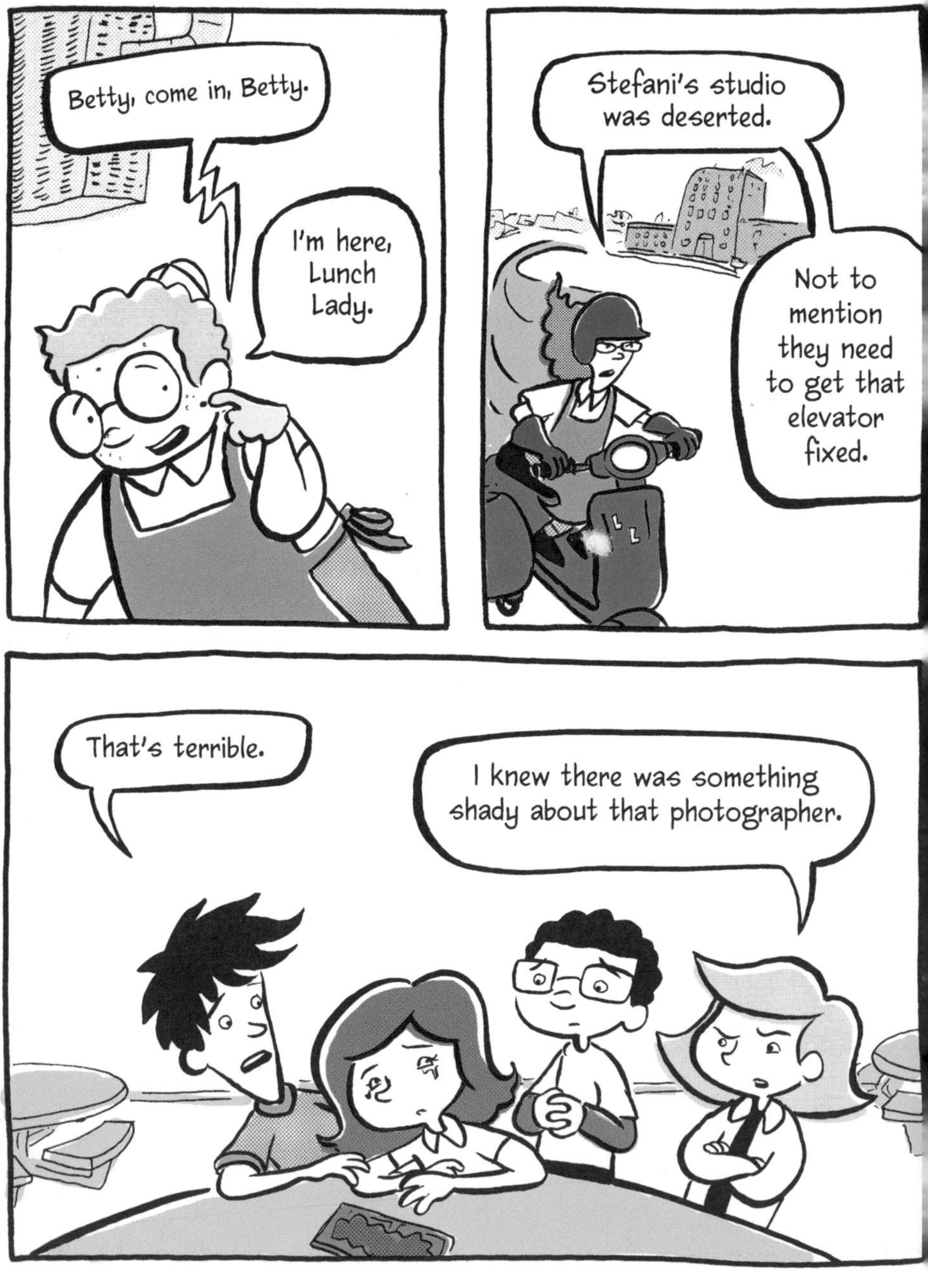
Betty, come in, Betty.
I'm here, Lunch Lady.
Stefani's studio was deserted.
Not to mention they need to get that elevator fixed.
That's terrible.
I knew there was something shady about that photographer.

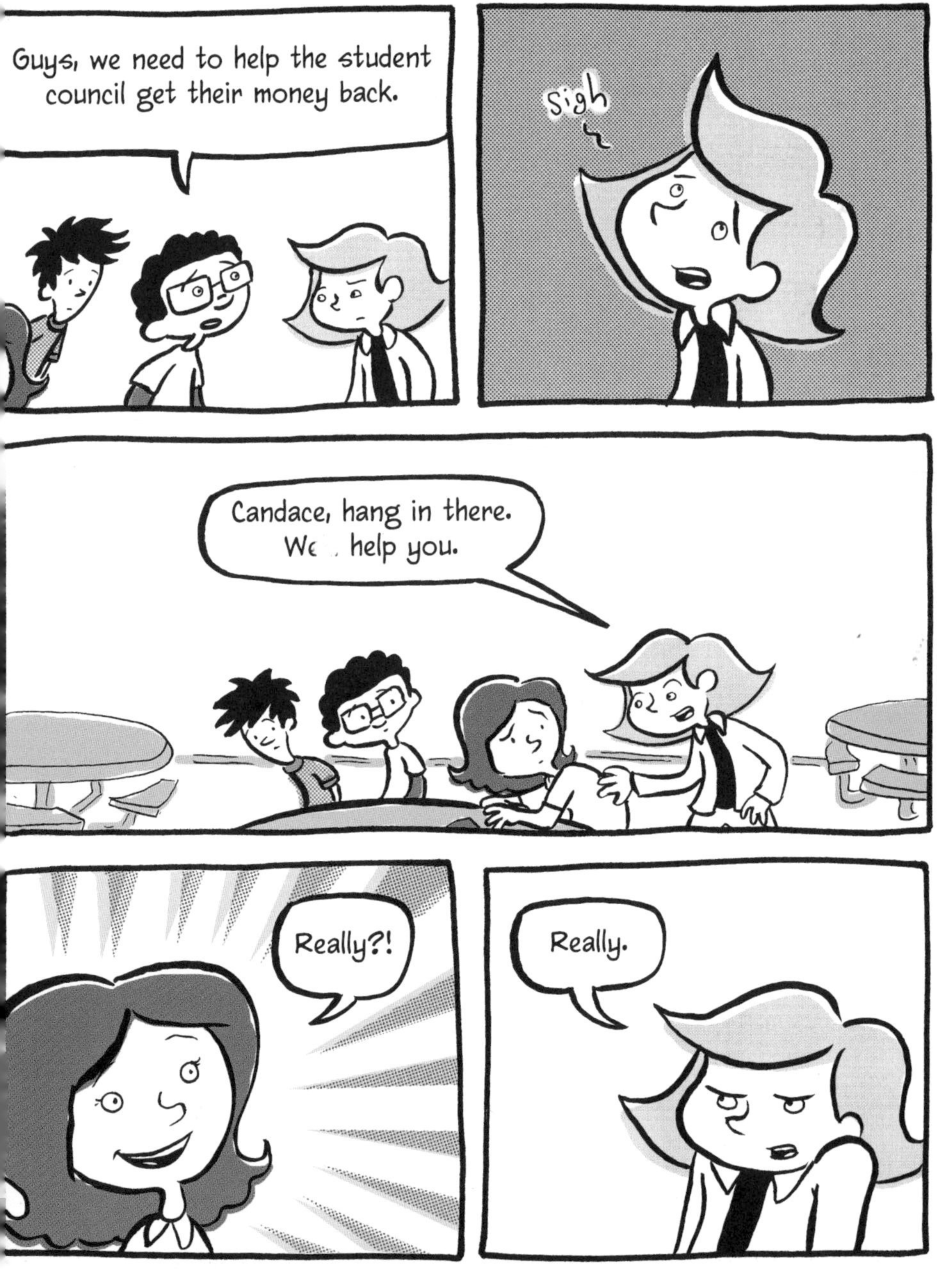
Guys, we need to help the student council get their money back.
Sigh
Candace, hang in there.
help you.
Really?!
Really.

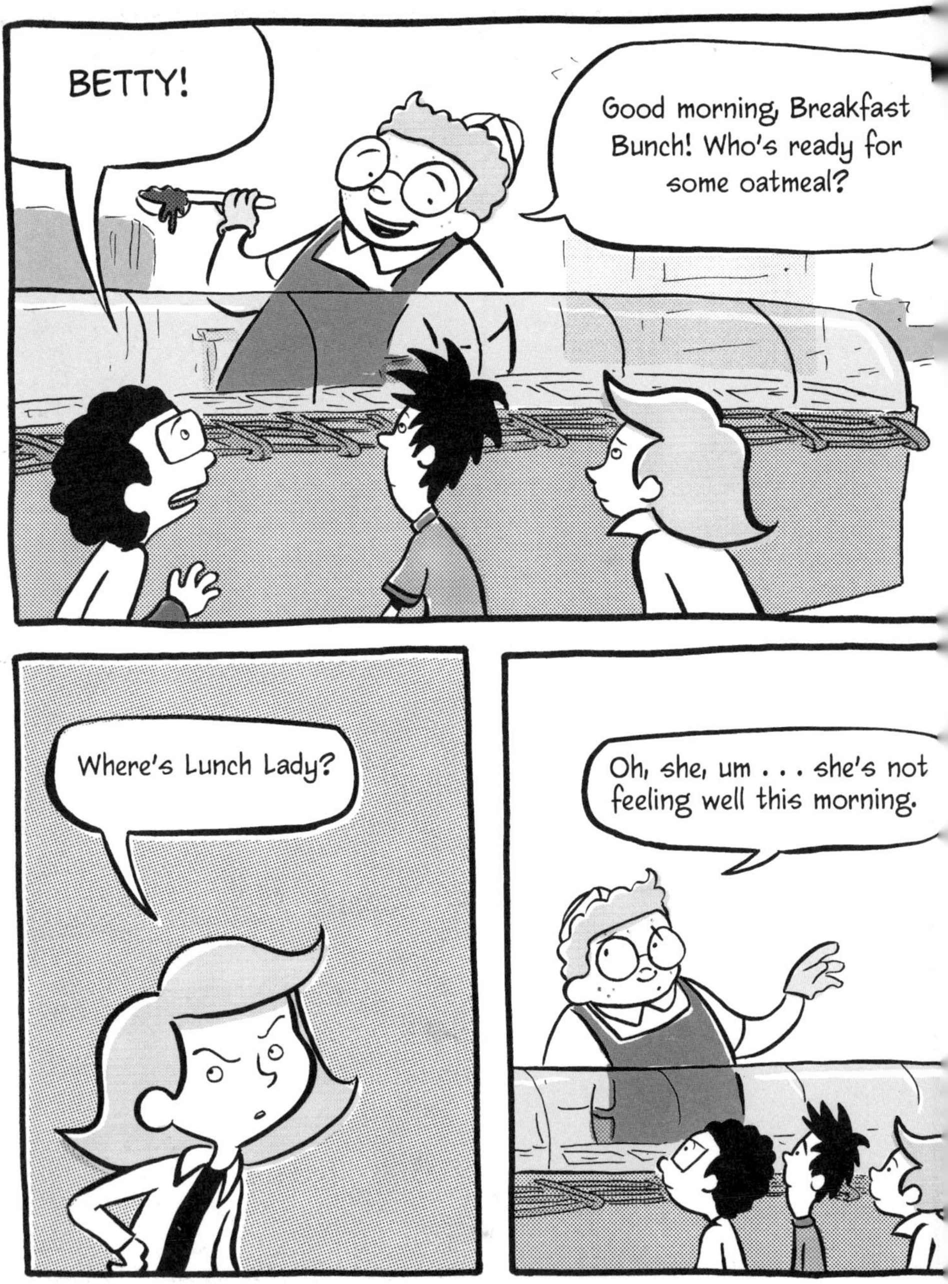
BETTY!
Good morning, Breakfast Bunch! Who's ready for some oatmeal?
Where's Lunch Lady?
Oh, she, um . . . she's not feeling well this morning.

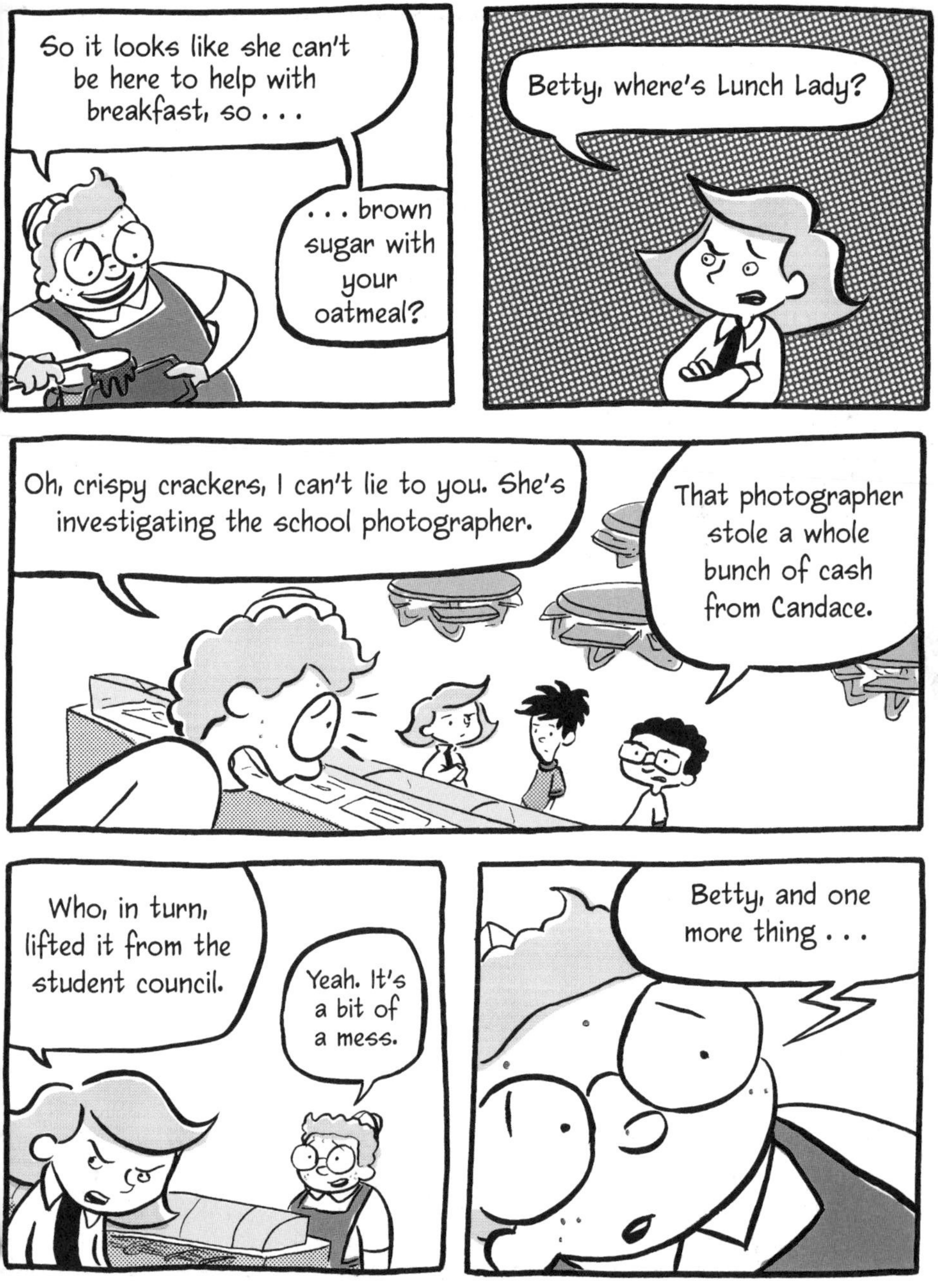
So it looks like she can't be here to help with breakfast, so . . .
. . . brown sugar with your oatmeal?
Betty, where's Lunch Lady?
Oh, crispy crackers, I can't lie to you. She's investigating the school photographer.
That photographer stole a whole bunch of cash from Candace.
Who, in turn, lifted it from the student council.
Yeah. It's a bit of a mess.
Betty, and one more thing . . .

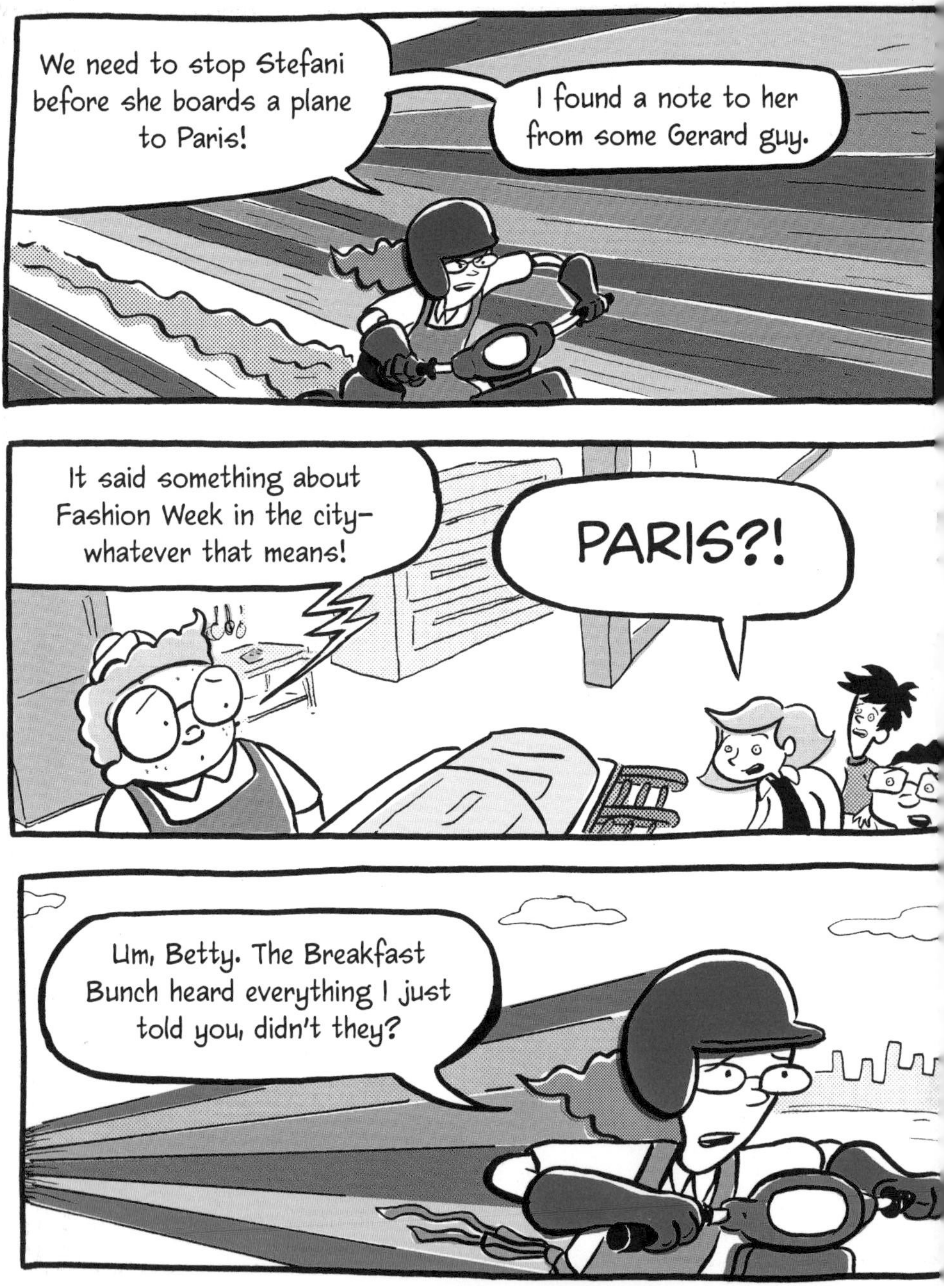
We need to stop Stefani before she boards a plane to Paris!
I found a note to her from some Gerard guy.
It said something about Fashion Week in the city-whatever that means!
PARIS?!
Um, Betty. The Breakfast Bunch heard everything I just told you, didn't they?

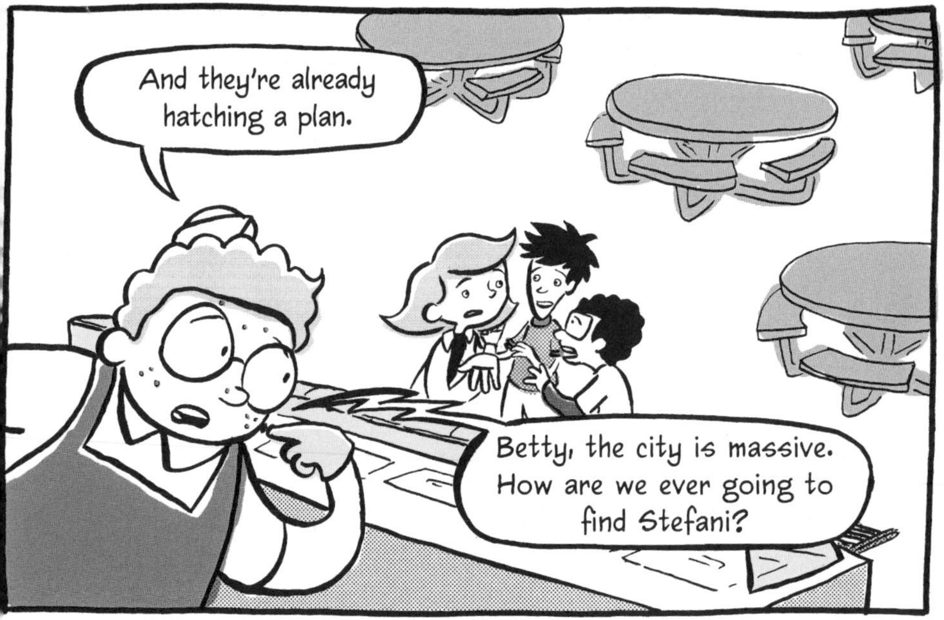
And they're already hatching a plan.
Betty, the city is massive. How are we ever going to find Stefani?

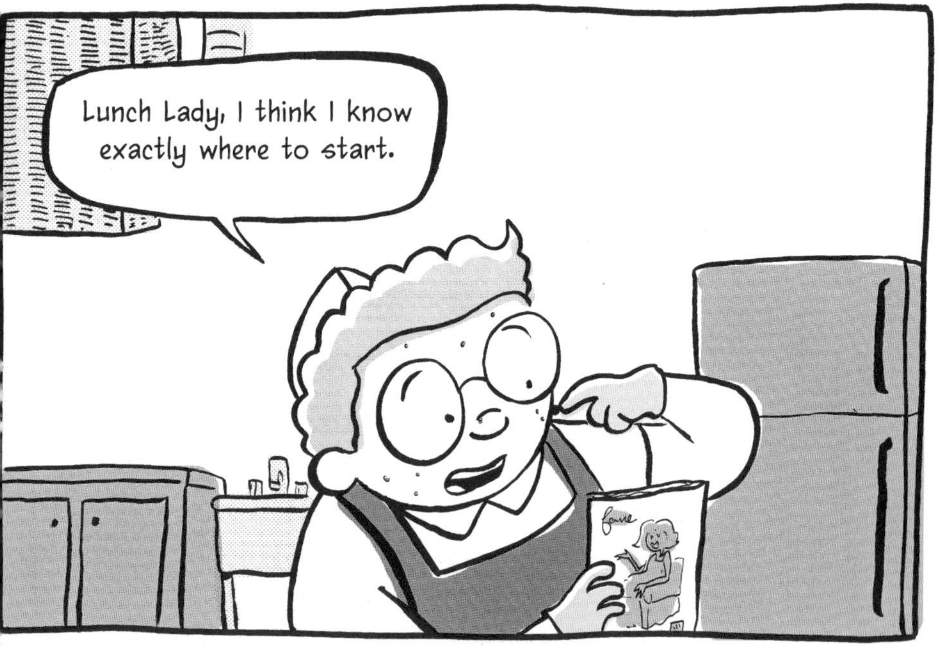
Lunch Lady, I think I know exactly where to start.

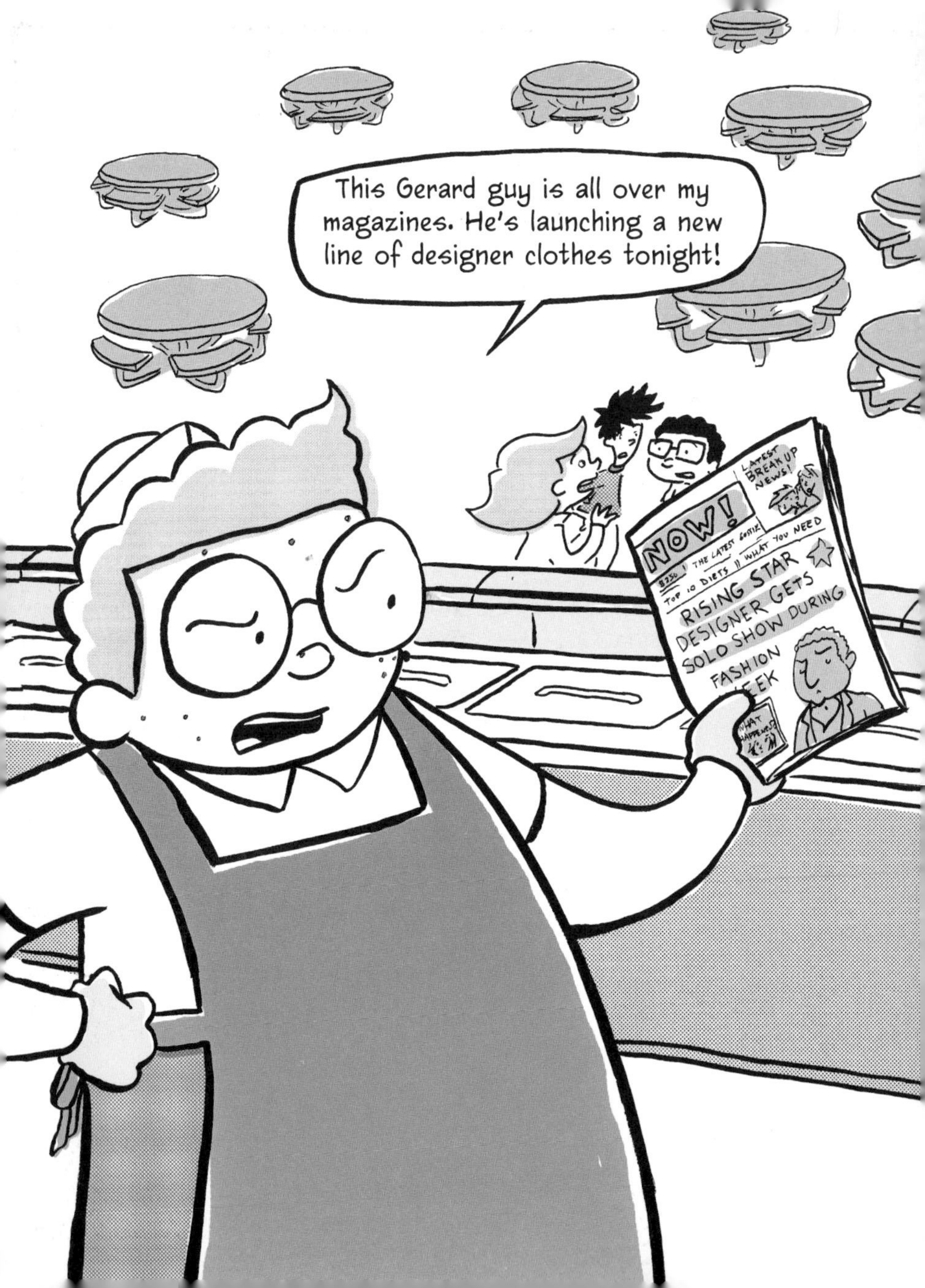
This Gerard guy is all over my magazines. He's launching a new line of designer clothes tonight!
NOW!
LATEST BREAK UP NEWS!
THE LATEST GOSSIP
WHAT YOU NEED
TOP 10 DIETS
RISING STAR DESIGNER GETS SOLO SHOW DURING FASHION

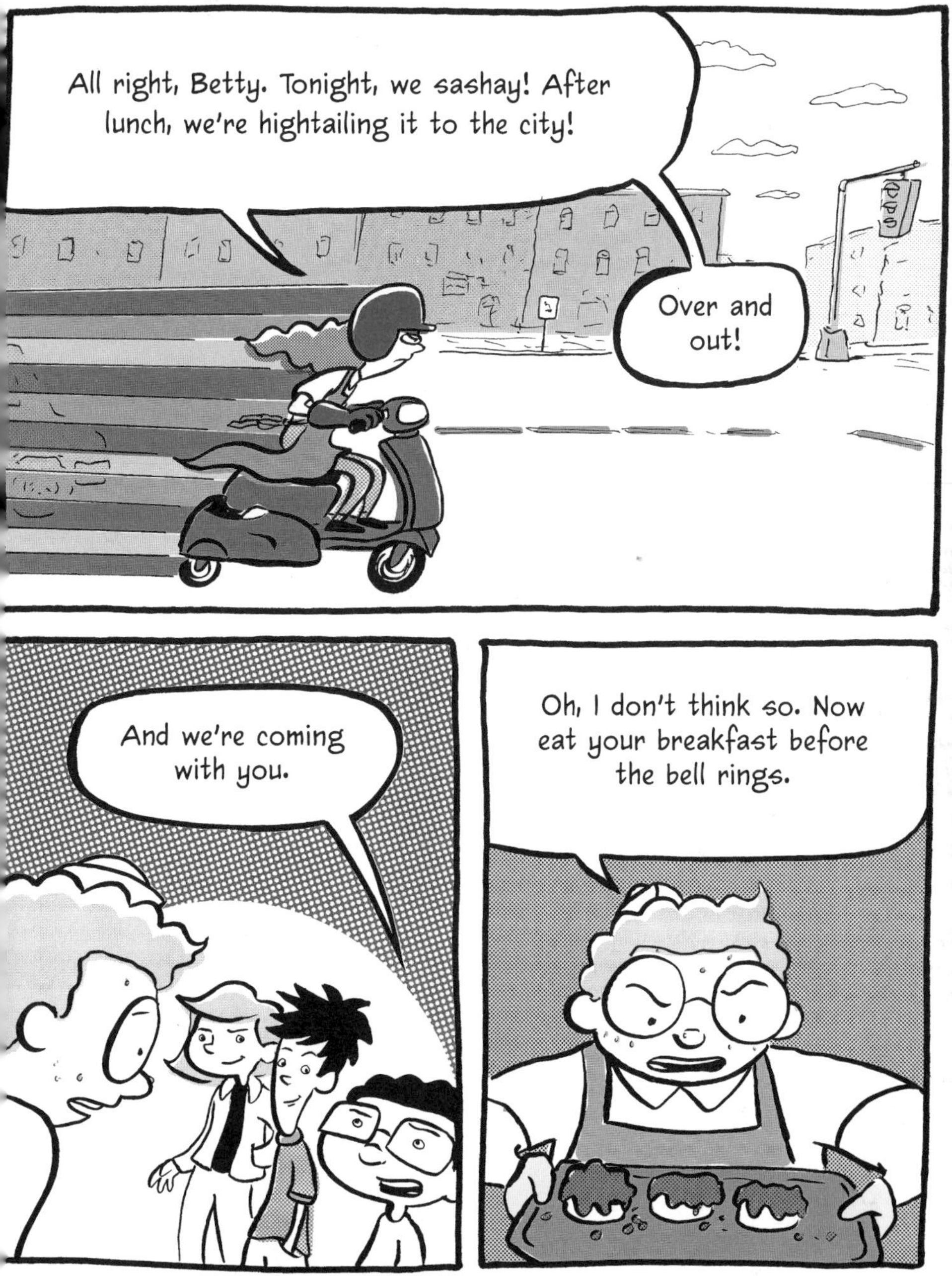
All right, Betty. Tonight, we sashay! After lunch, we're hightailing it to the city!
Over and out!
And we're coming with you.
Oh, I don't think so. Now eat your breakfast before the bell rings.

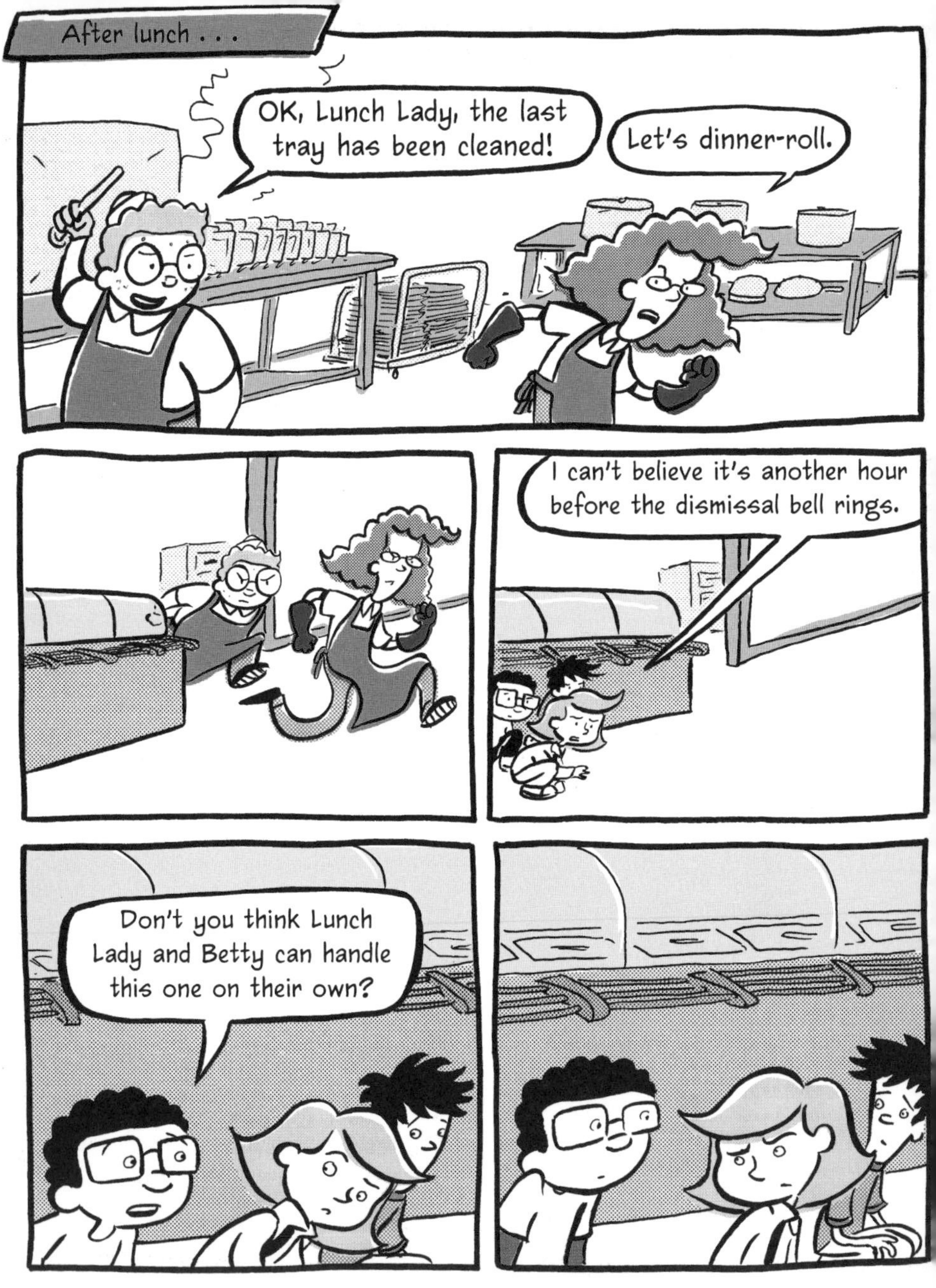
After lunch . . .
OK, Lunch Lady, the last tray has been cleaned!
Let's dinner-roll.
I can't believe it's another hour before the dismissal bell rings.
Don't you think Lunch Lady and Betty can handle this one on their own?

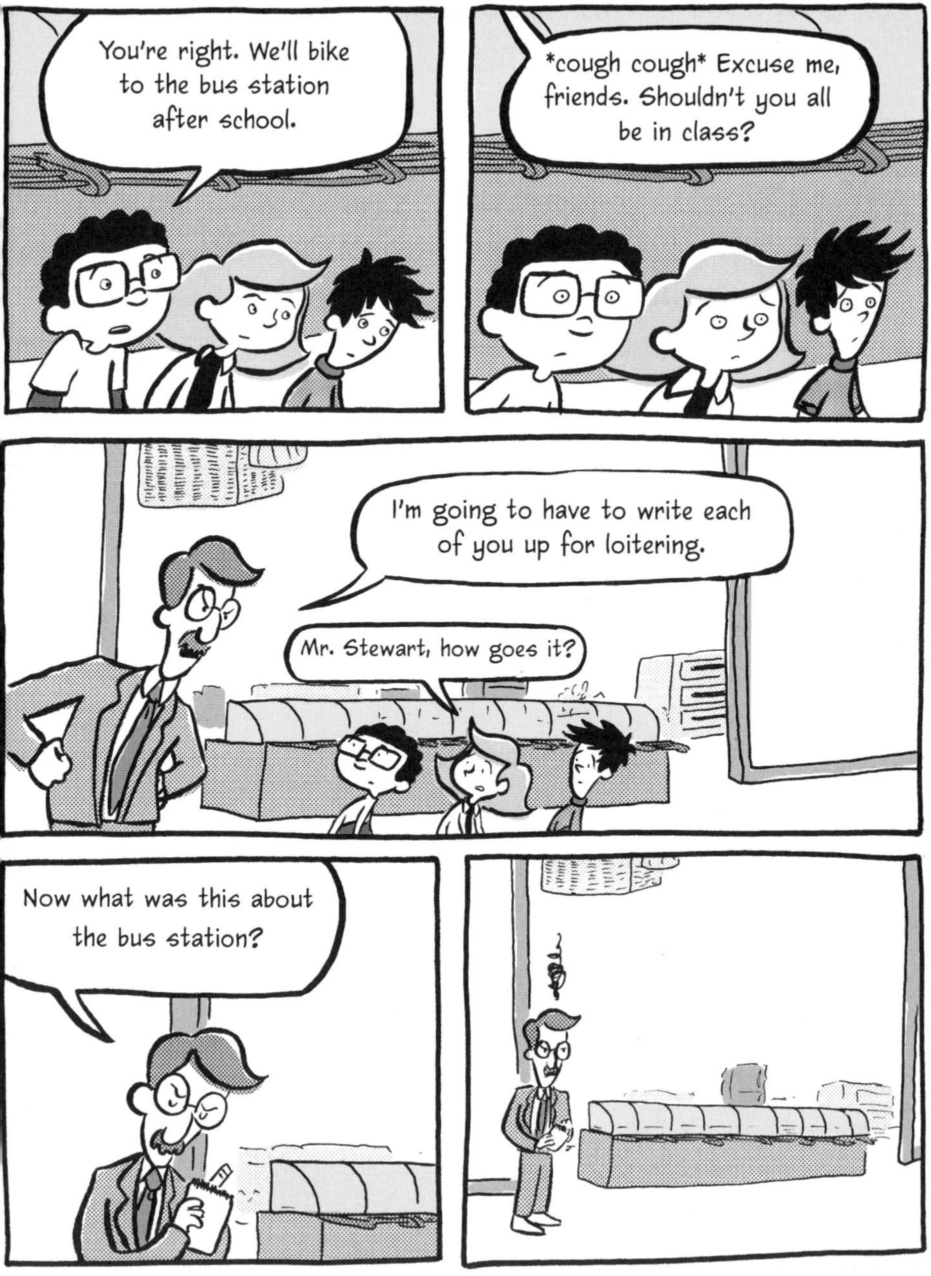
You're right. We'll bike to the bus station after school.
cough cough Excuse me, friends. Shouldn't you all be in class?
Mr. Stewart, how goes it?
I'm going to have to write each of you up for loitering.
Now what was this about the bus station?

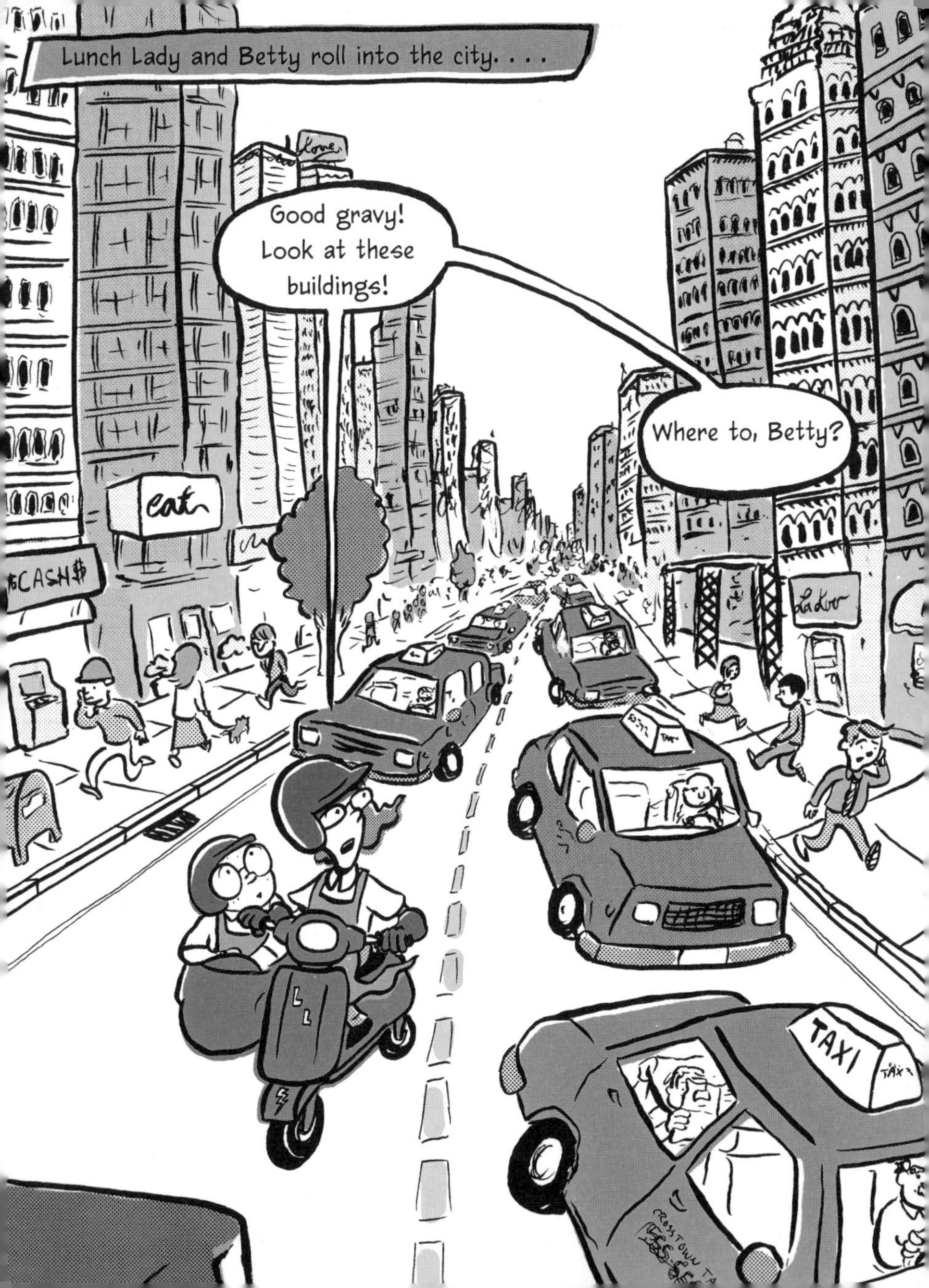

Lunch Lady and Betty roll into the city. . . .
Good gravy! Look at these buildings!
Where to, Betty?
eat
CASH$
TAXI

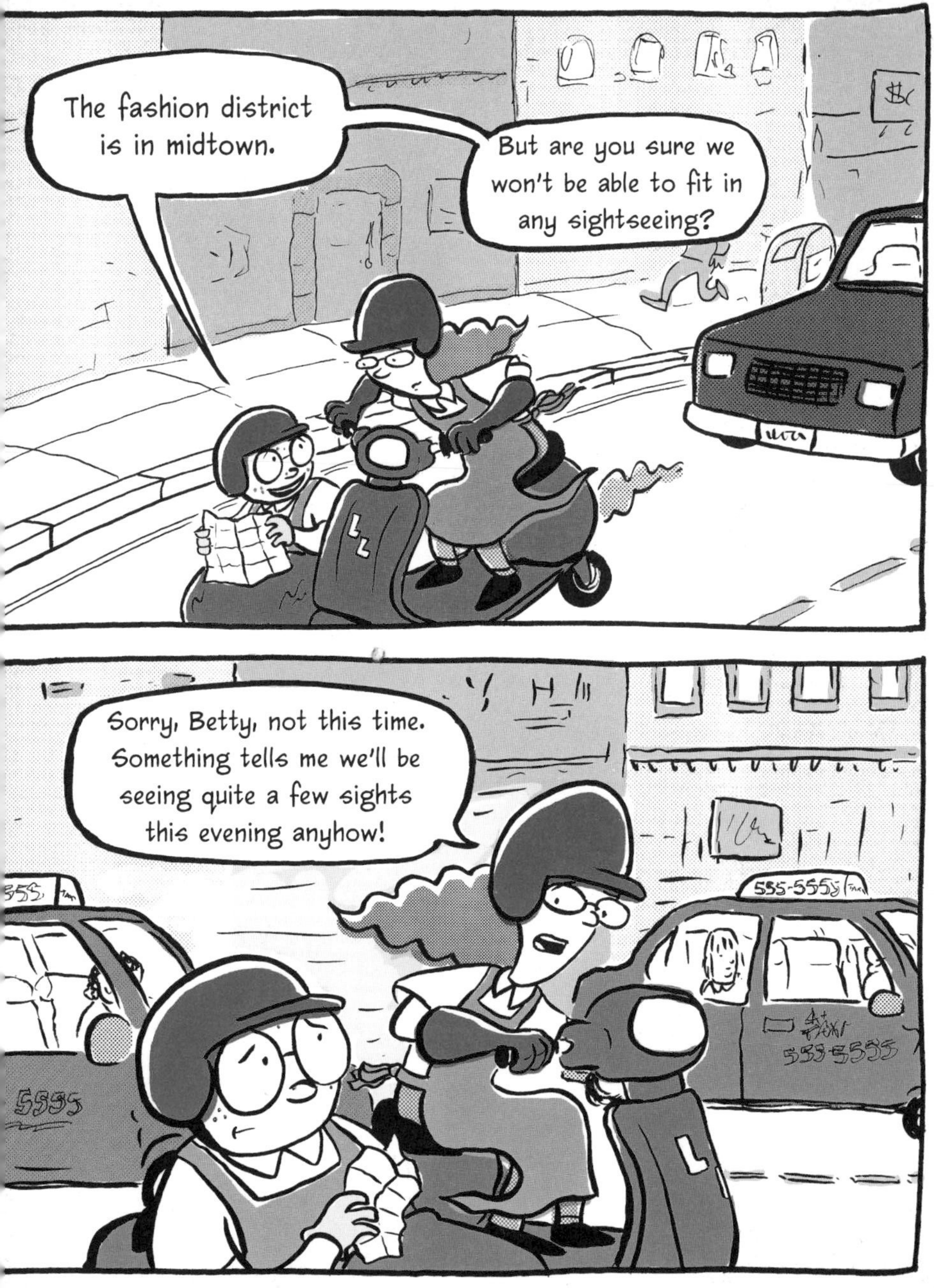
The fashion district is in midtown.
But are you sure we won't be able to fit in any sightseeing?
Sorry, Betty, not this time. Something tells me we'll be seeing quite a few sights this evening anyhow!
555-5555

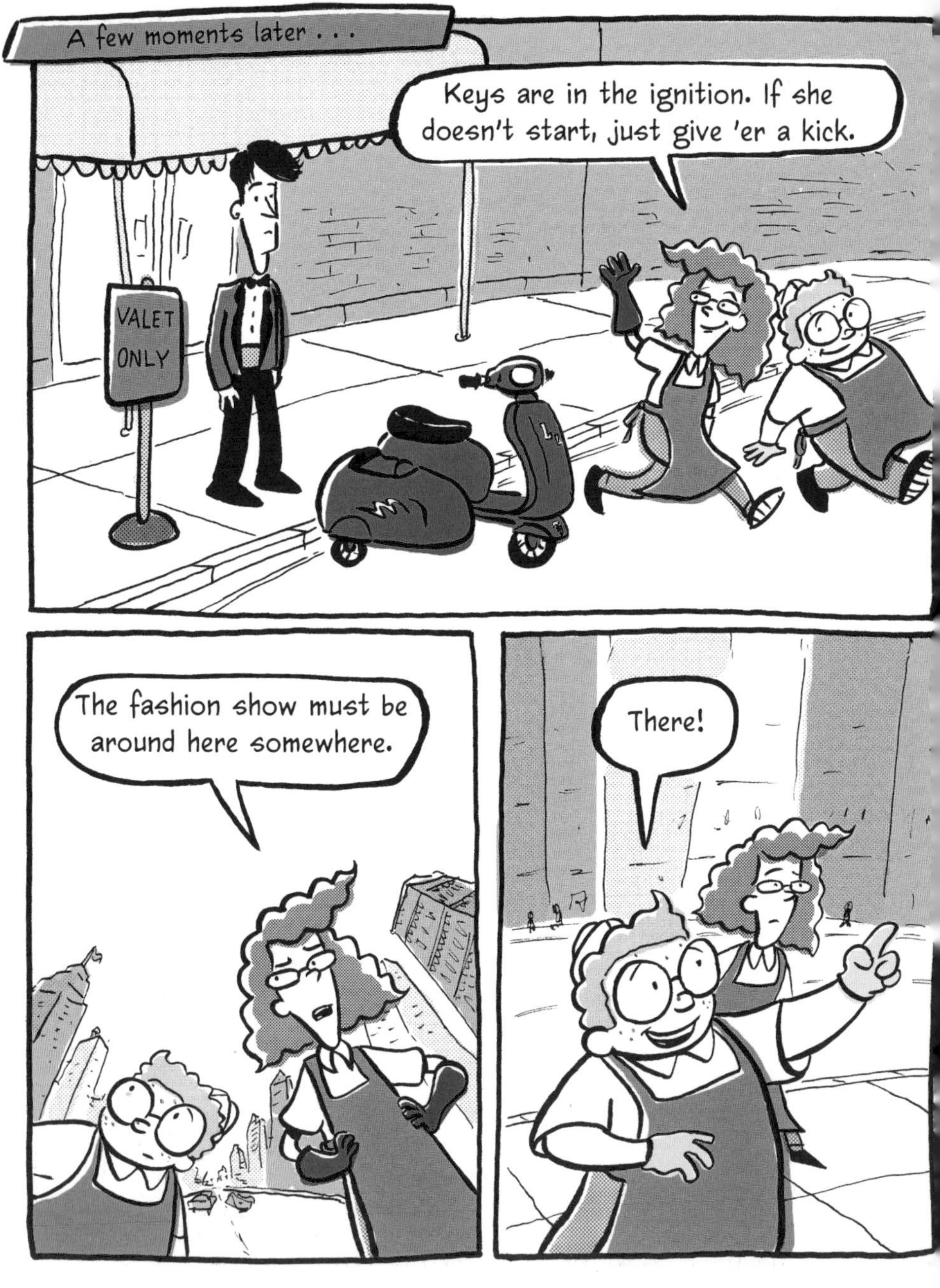
A few moments later . . .
Keys are in the ignition. If she doesn't start, just give 'er a kick.
VALET ONLY
The fashion show must be around here somewhere.
There!

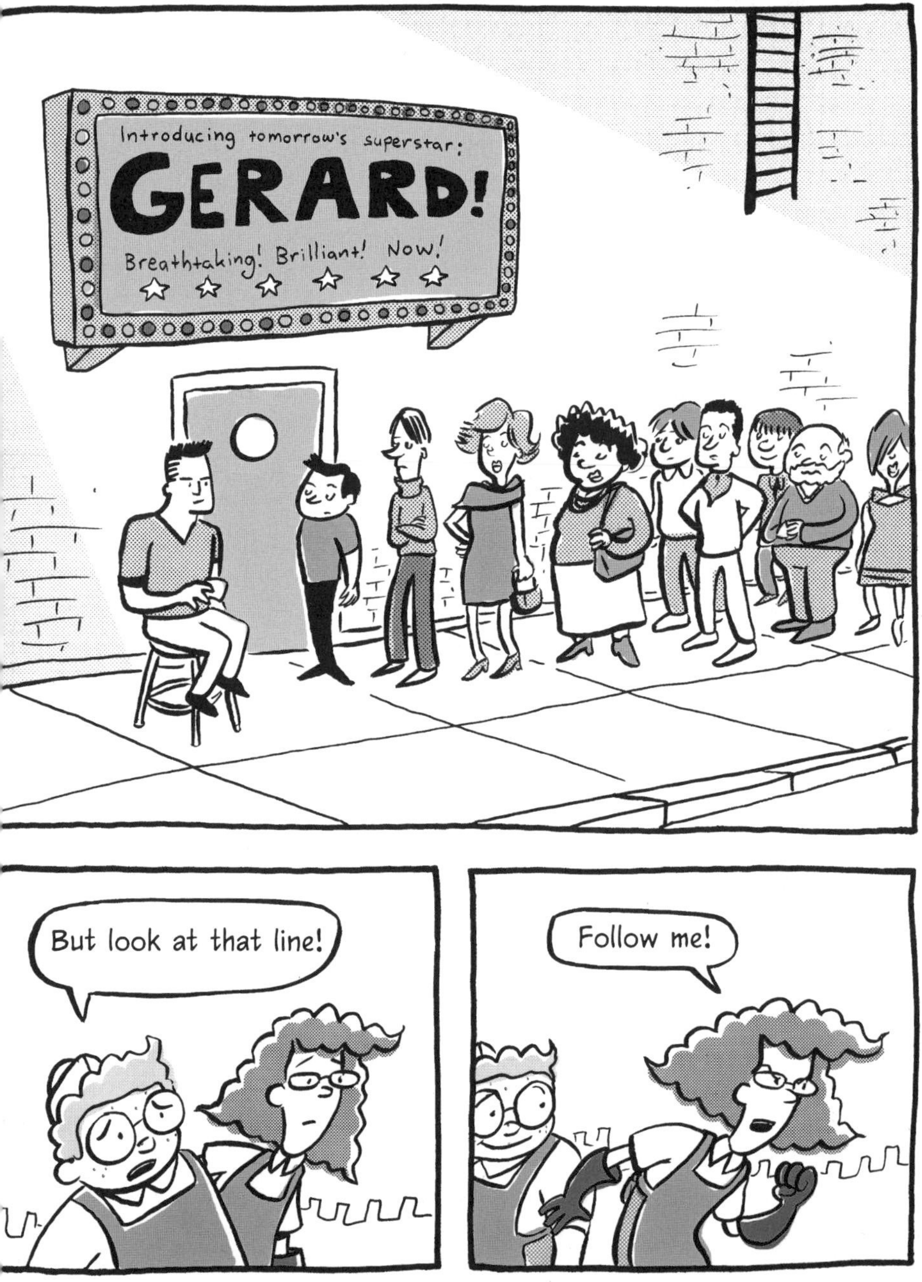
Introducing tomorrow's superstar:
GERARD!
Breathtaking! Brilliant! Now!
But look at that line!
Follow me!

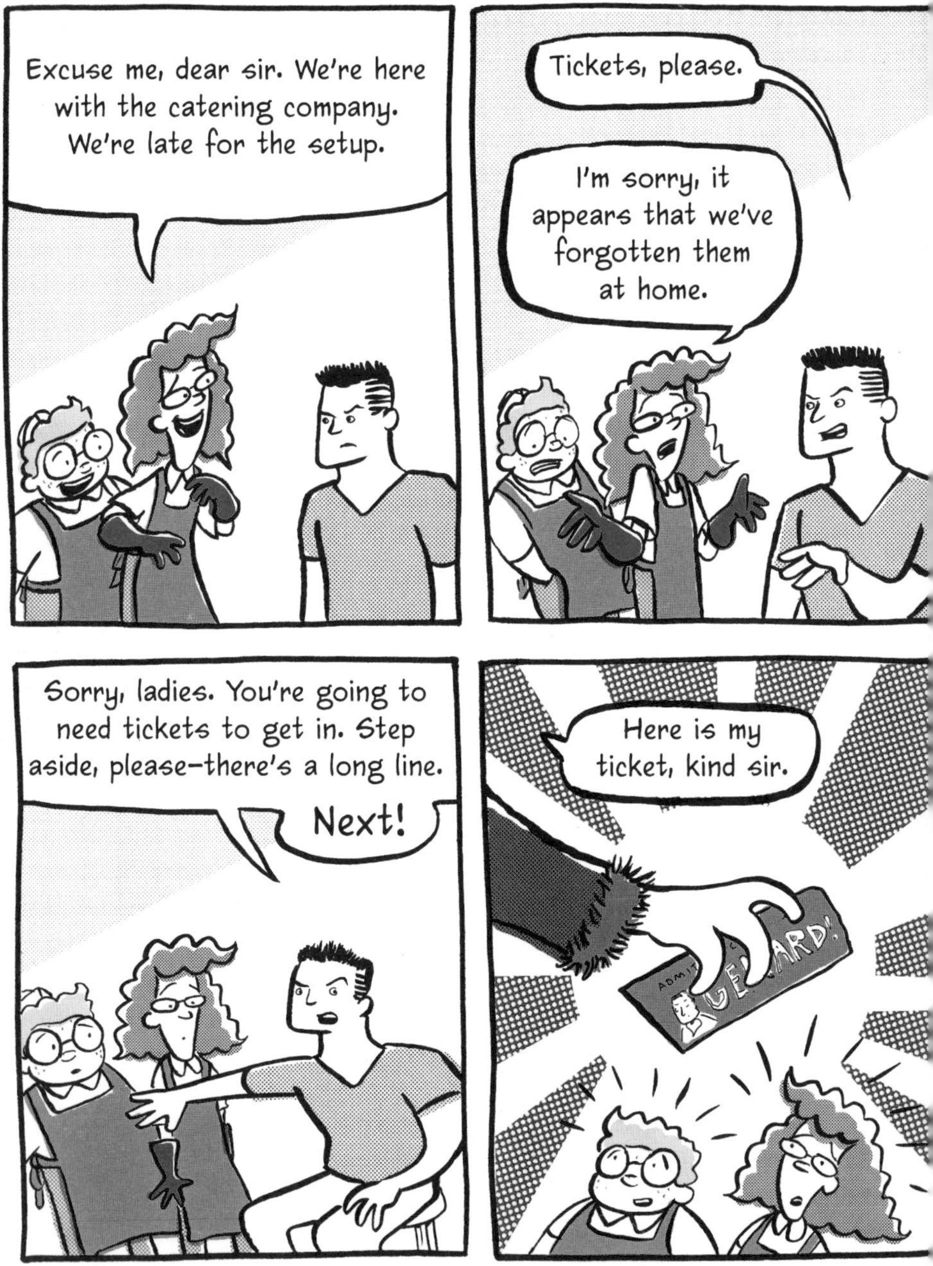
Excuse me, dear sir. We're here with the catering company. We're late for the setup.
Tickets, please.
I'm sorry, it appears that we've forgotten them at home.
Sorry, ladies. You're going to need tickets to get in. Step aside, please—there's a long line.
Next!
Here is my ticket, kind sir.

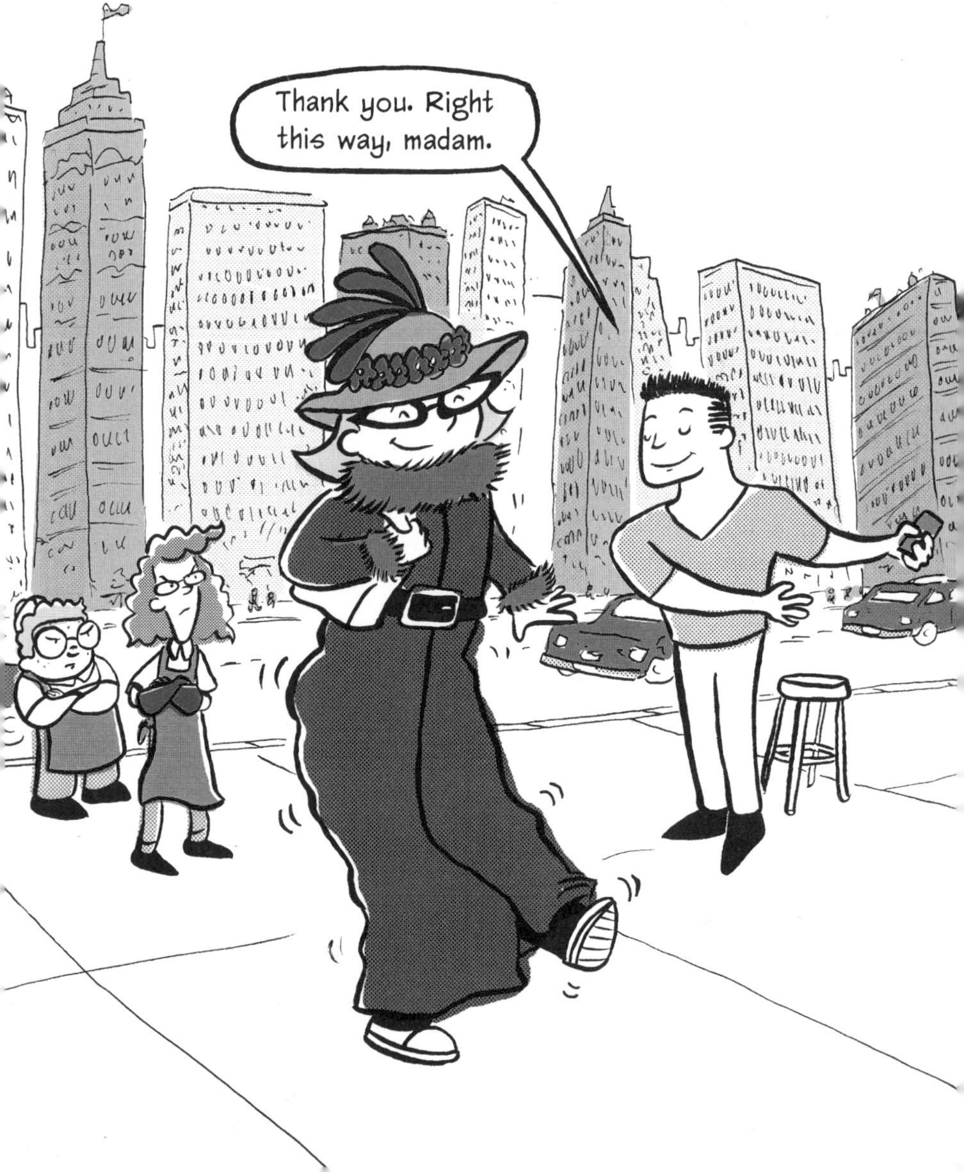
Thank you. Right this way, madam.

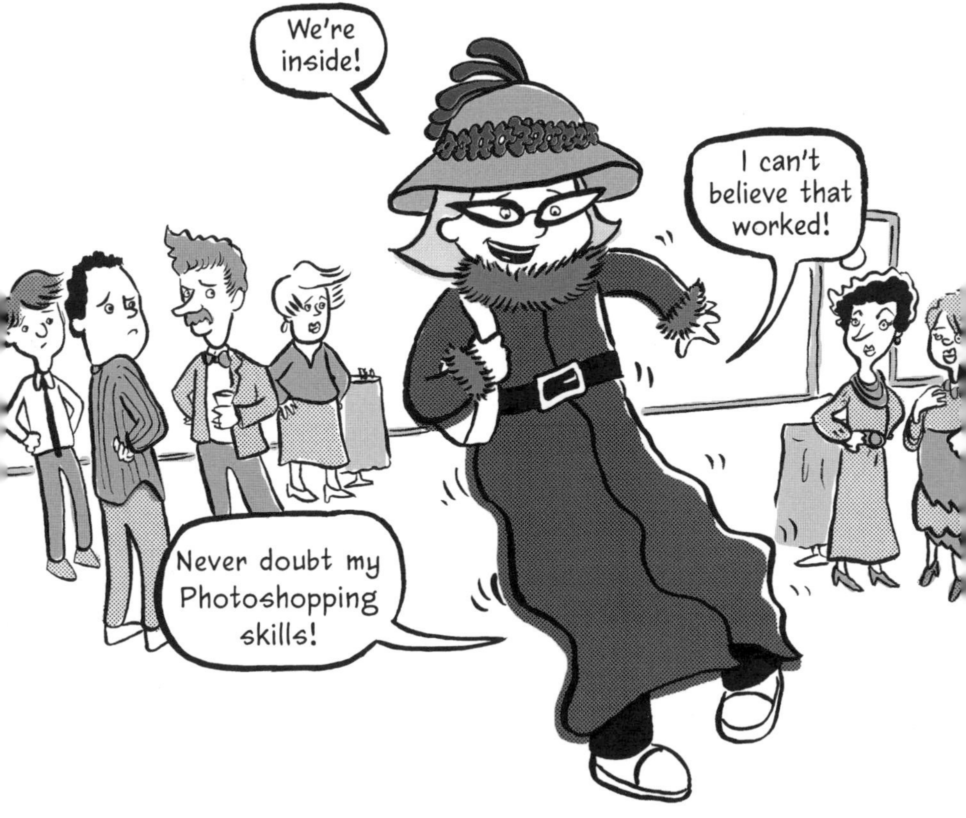
We're inside!
I can't believe that worked!
Never doubt my Photoshopping skills!

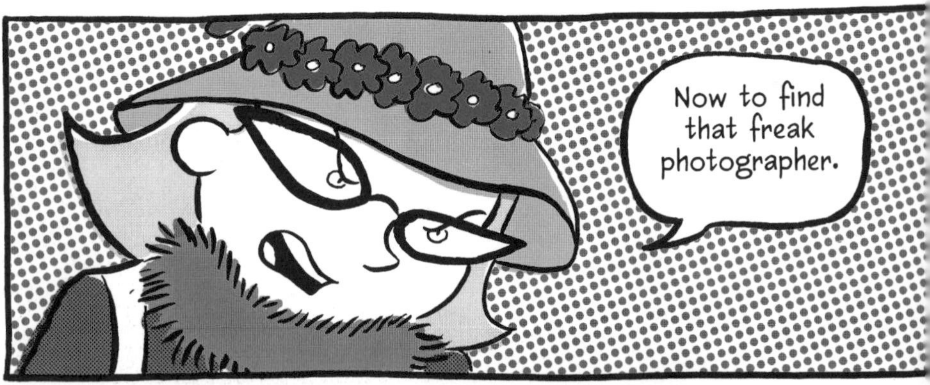
Now to find that freak photographer.

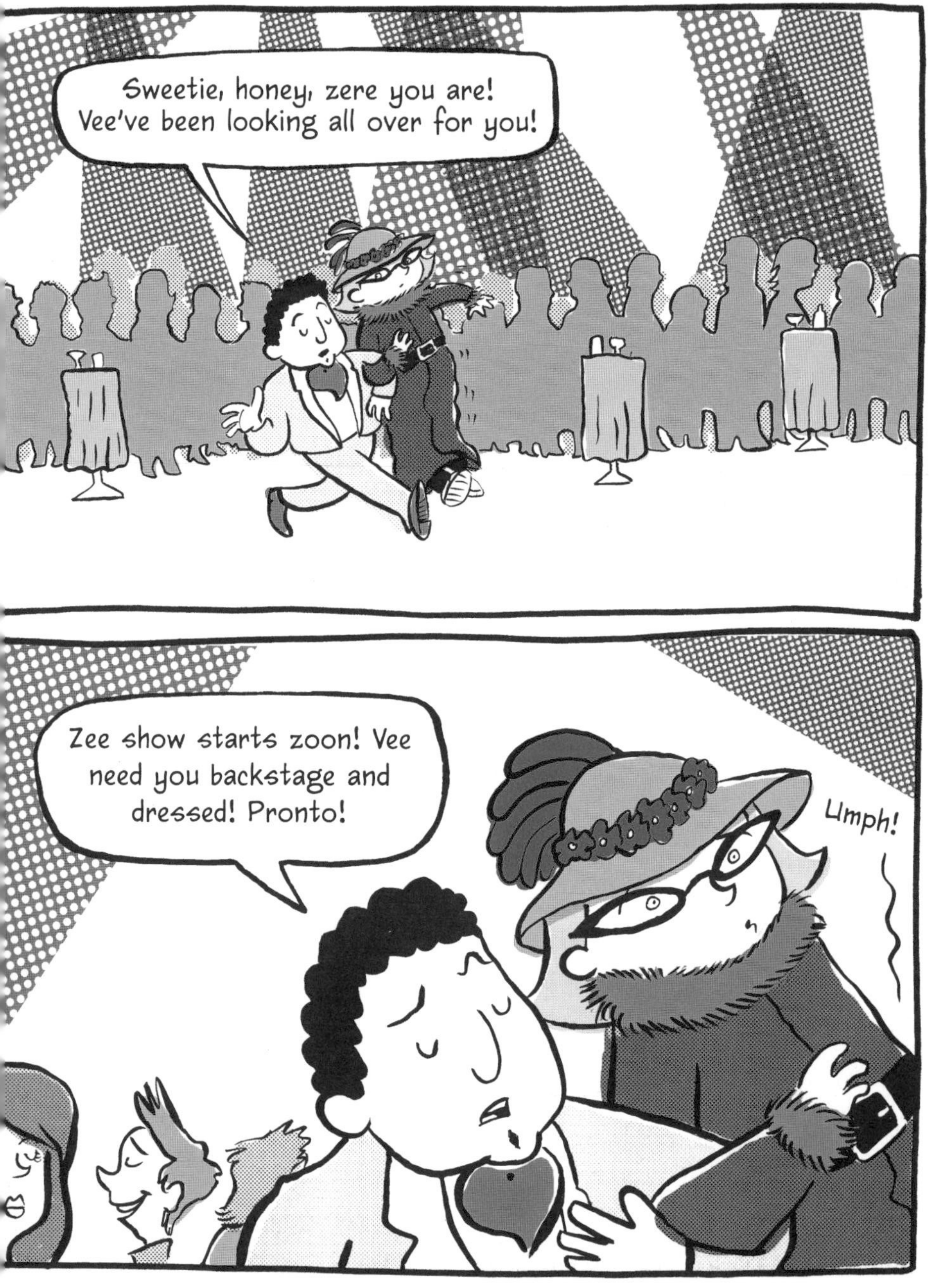
Sweetie, honey, zere you are! Vee've been looking all over for you!
Zee show starts zoon! Vee need you backstage and dressed! Pronto!
Umph!

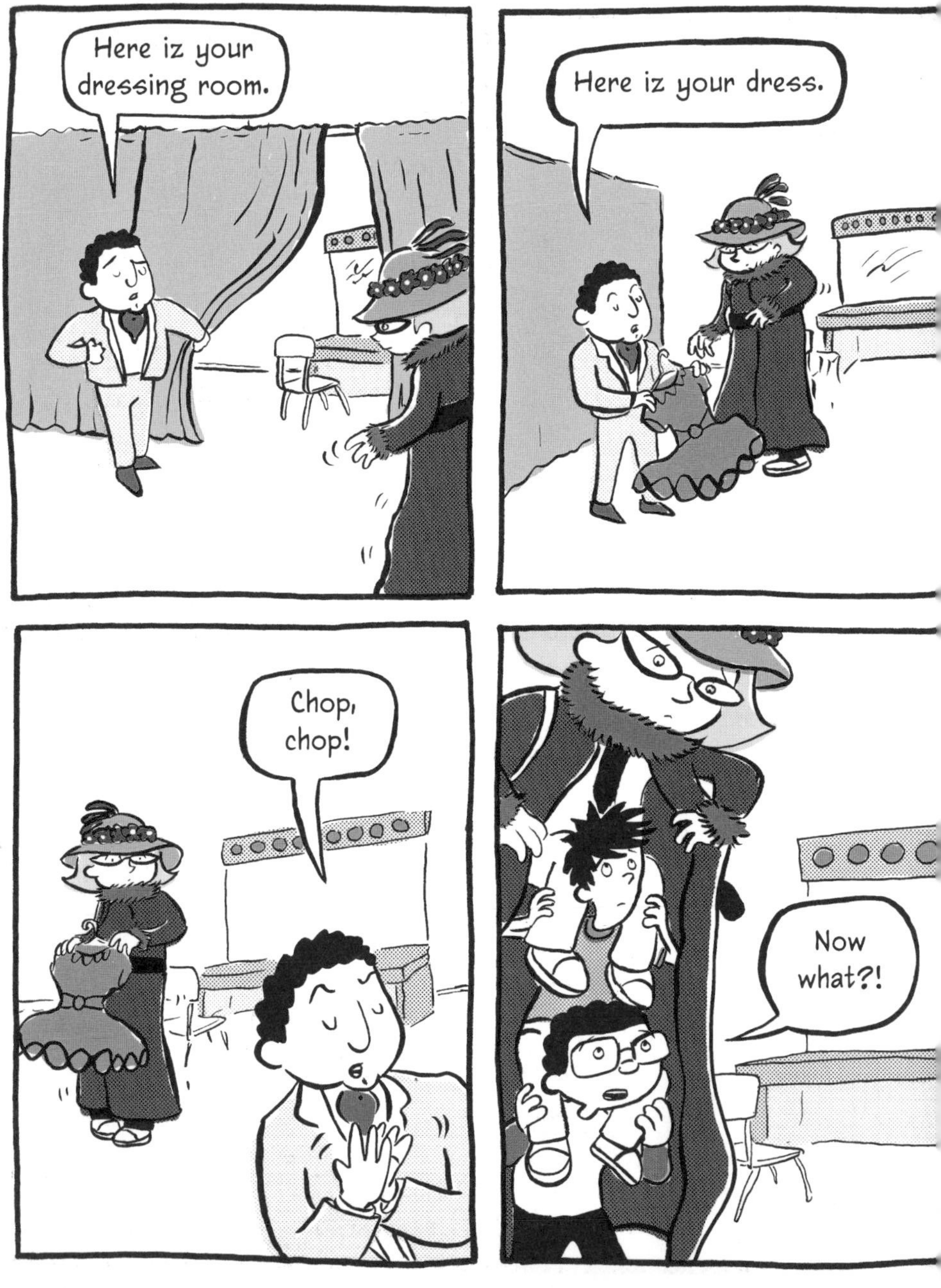
Here iz your dressing room.
Here iz your dress.
Chop, chop!
Now what?!

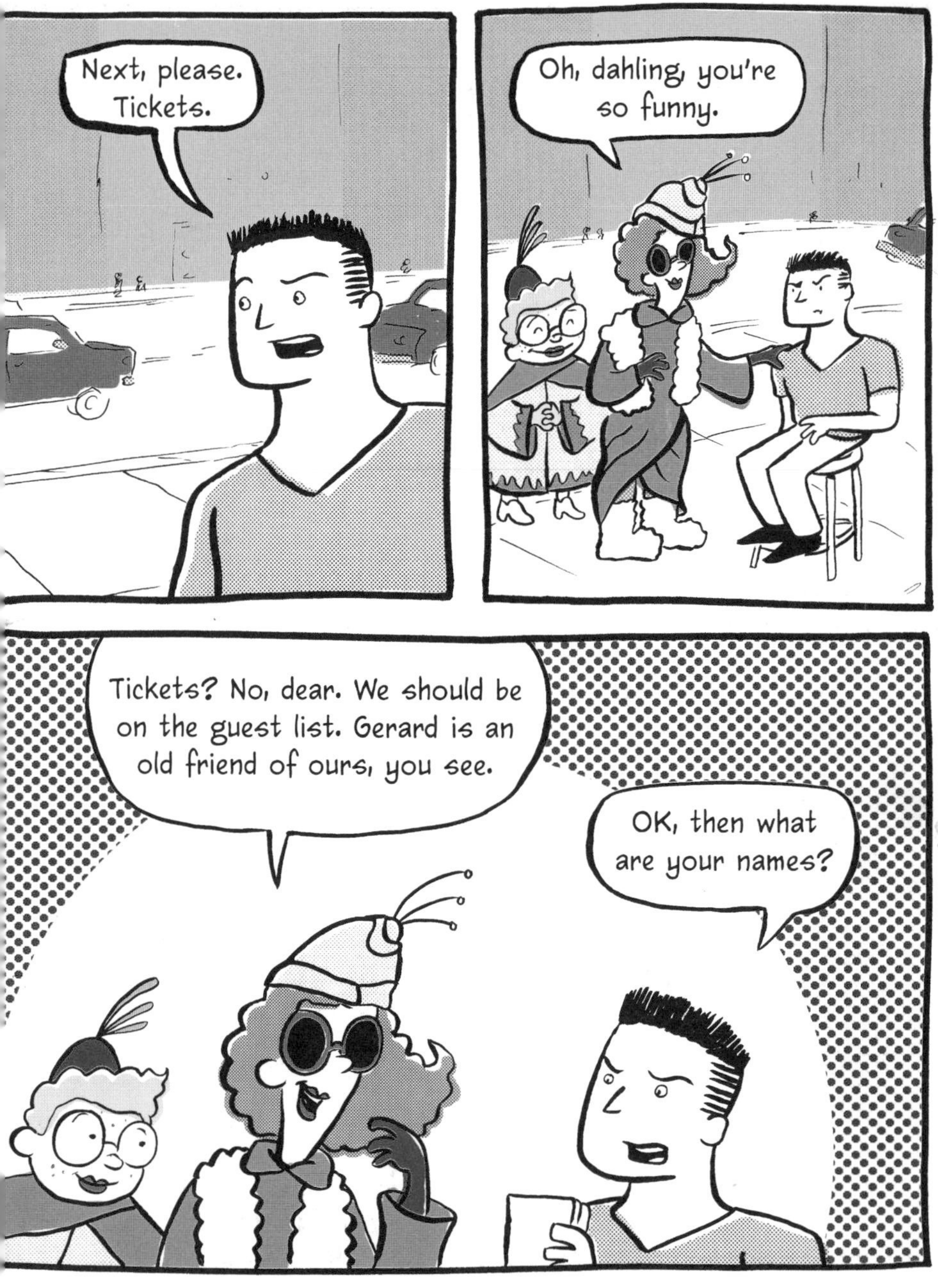
Next, please.
Tickets.
Oh, dahling, you're so funny.
Tickets? No, dear. We should be on the guest list. Gerard is an old friend of ours, you see.
OK, then what are your names?

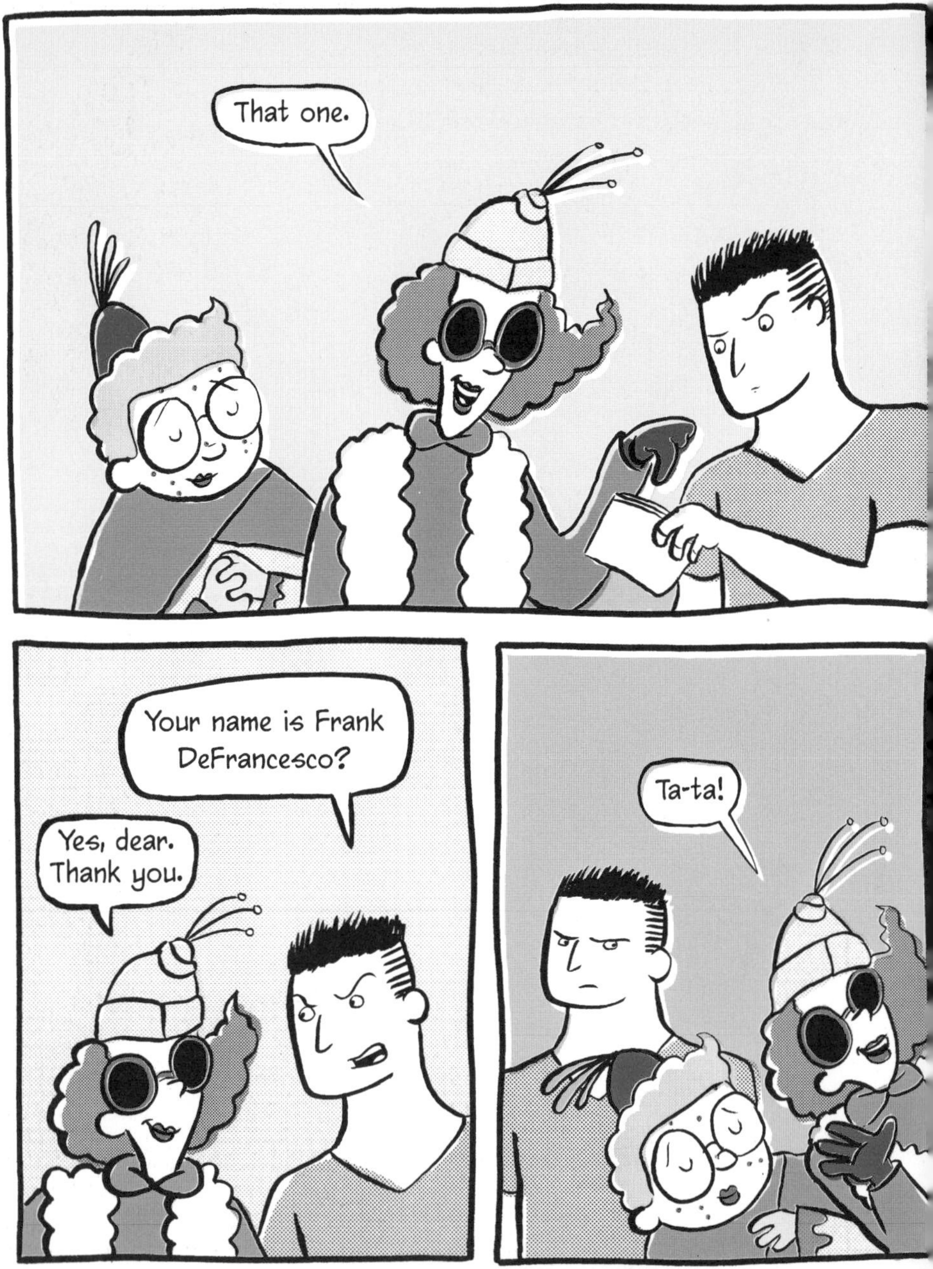
That one.
Your name is Frank DeFrancesco?
Yes, dear. Thank you.
Ta-ta!

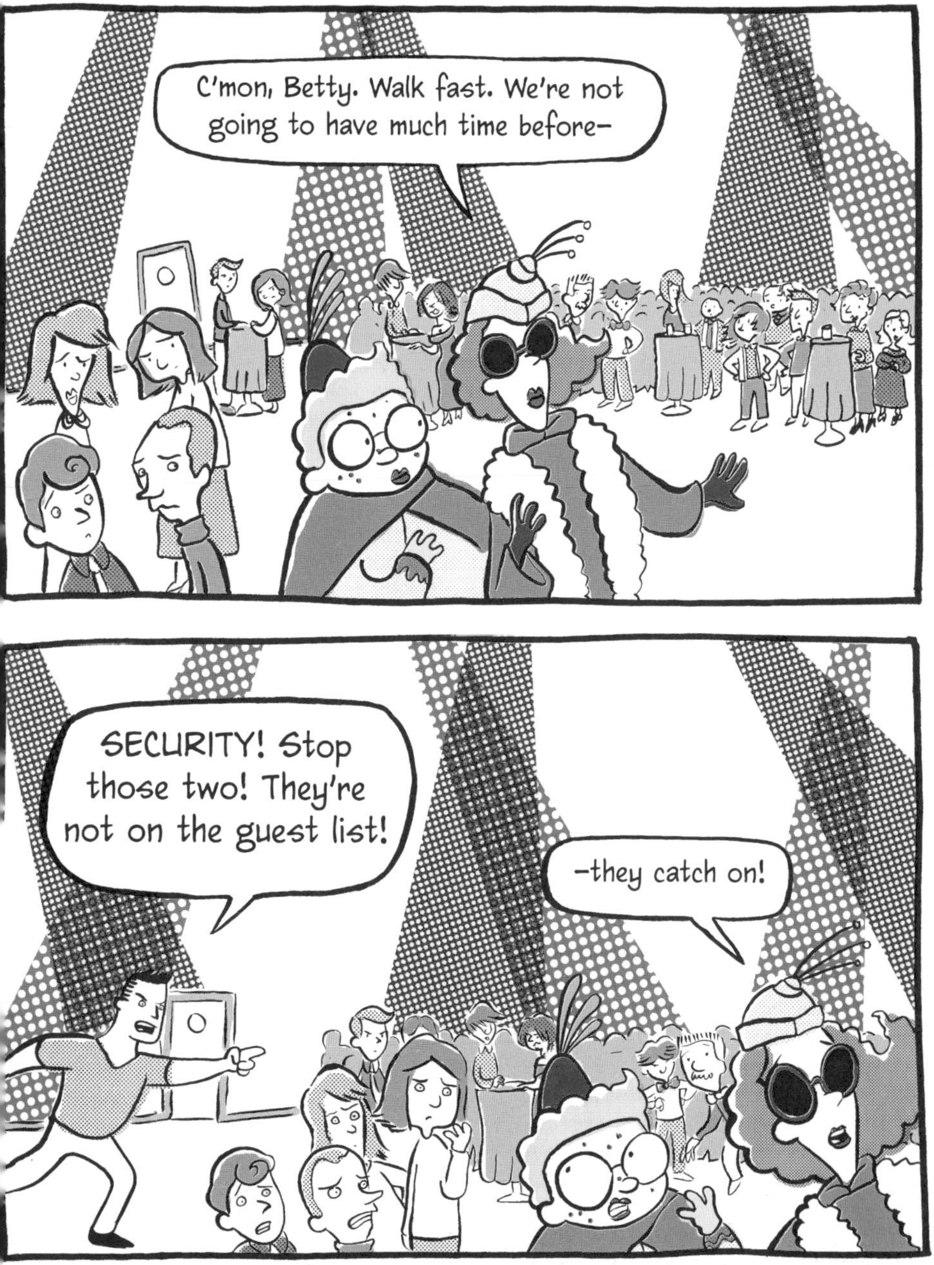
C'mon, Betty. Walk fast. We're not going to have much time before–
SECURITY! Stop those two! They're not on the guest list!
–they catch on!

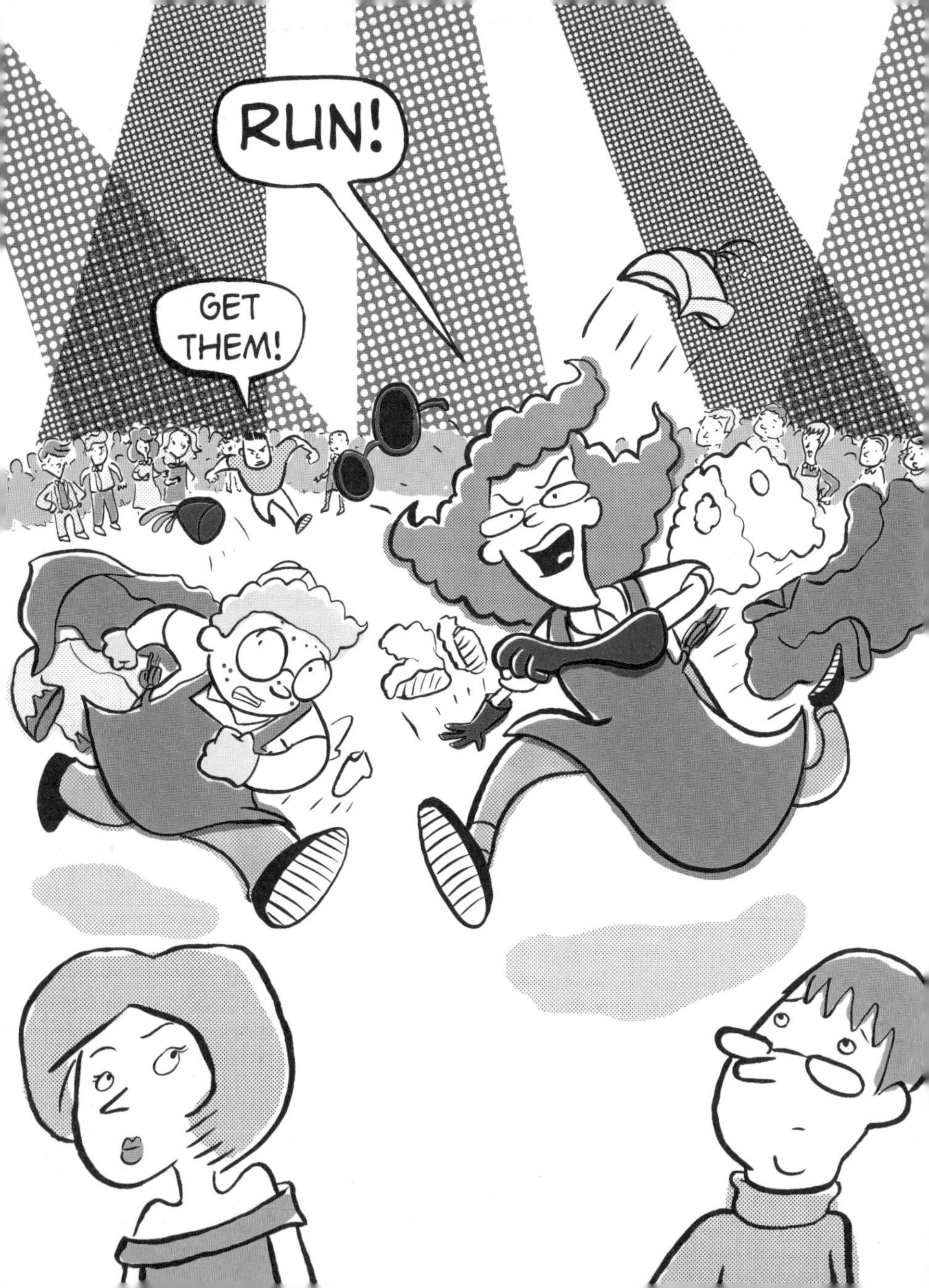
RUN!
GET THEM!

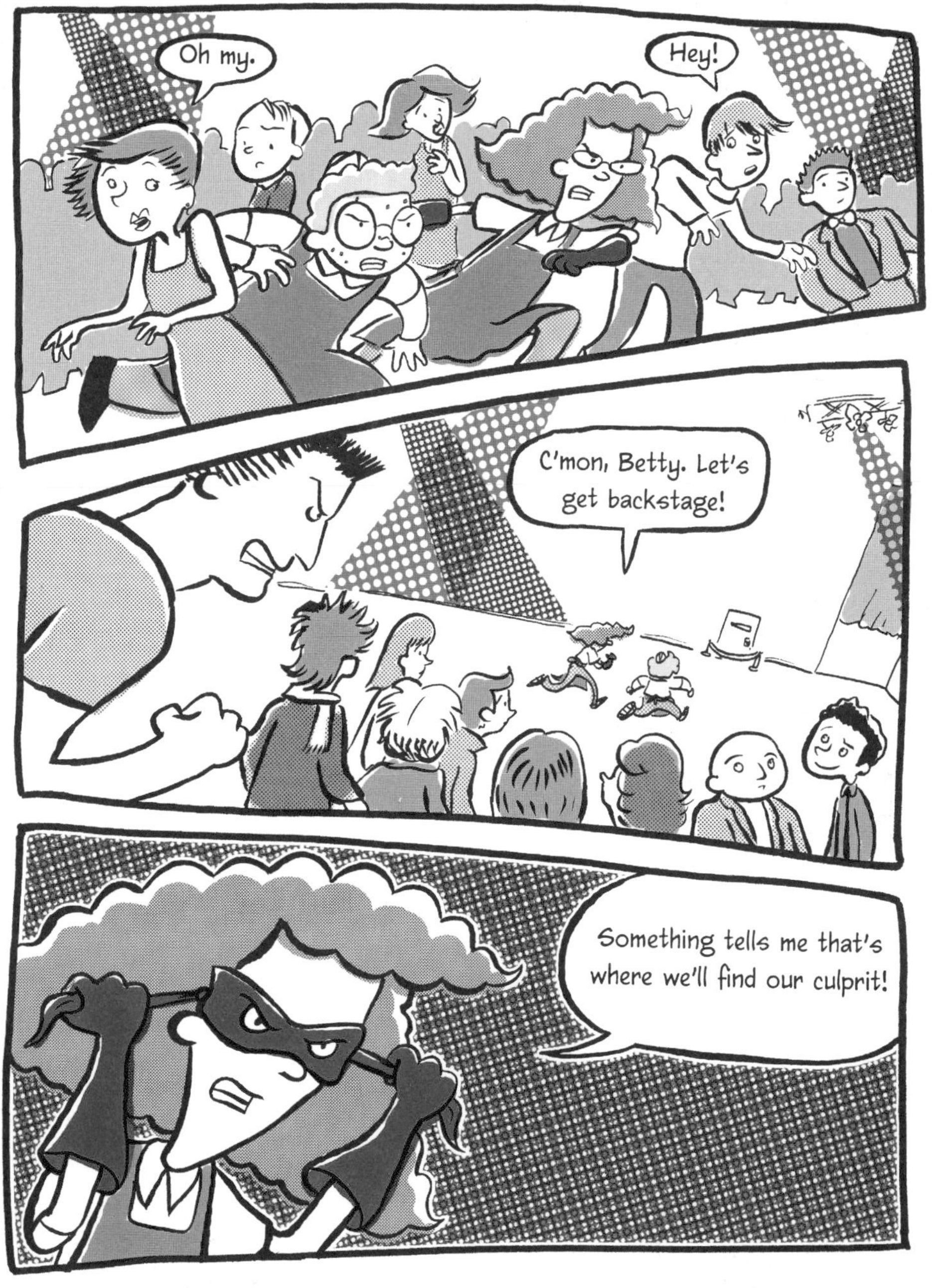
Oh my.
Hey!
C'mon, Betty. Let's get backstage!
Something tells me that's where we'll find our culprit!

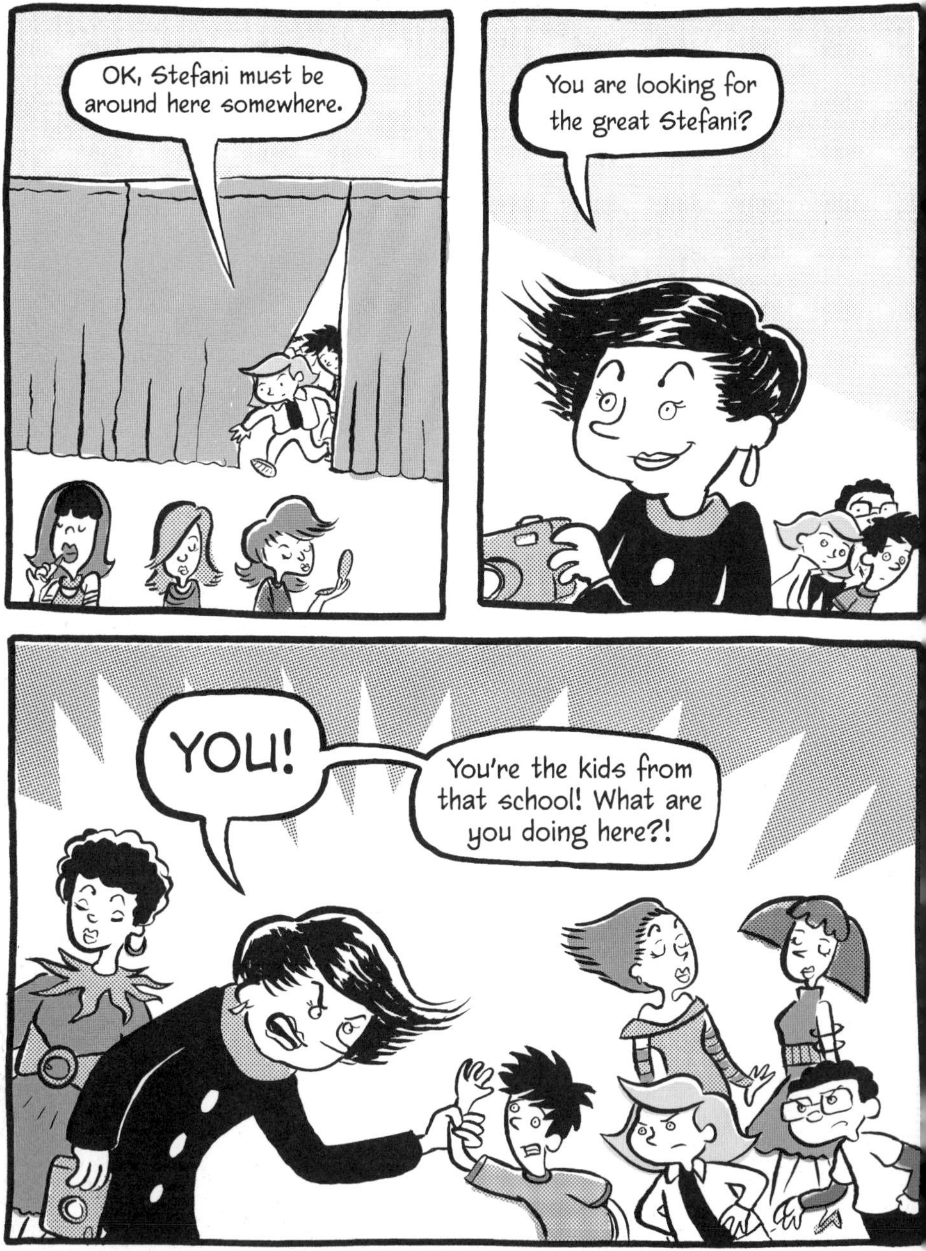
OK, Stefani must be around here somewhere.
You are looking for the great Stefani?
YOU!
You're the kids from that school! What are you doing here?!

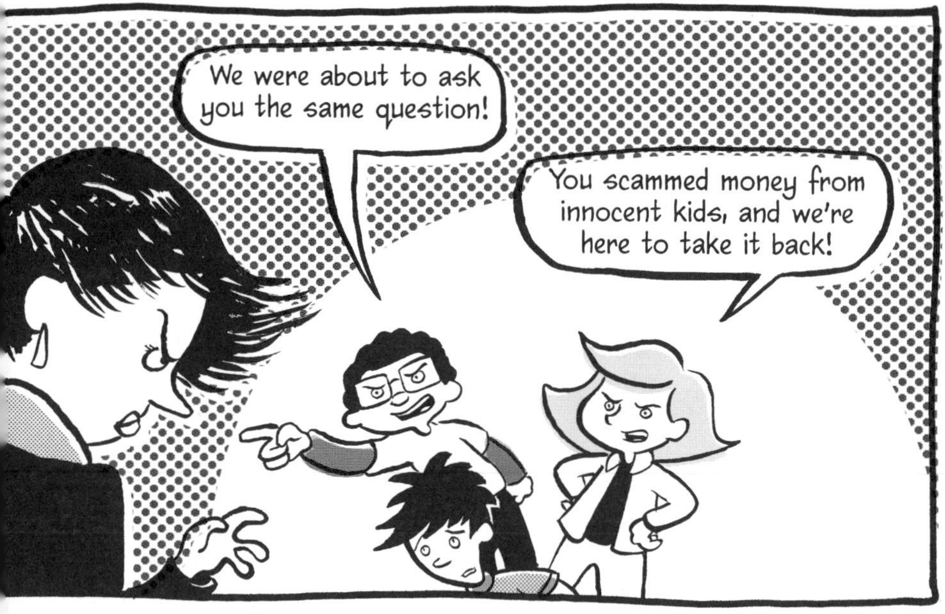
We were about to ask you the same question!
You scammed money from innocent kids, and we're here to take it back!

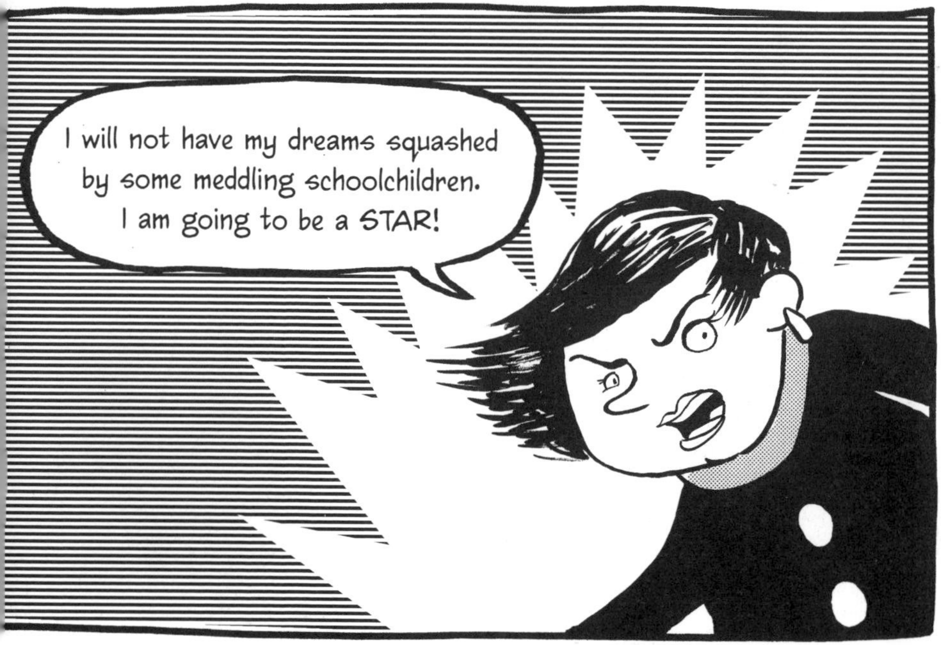
I will not have my dreams squashed by some meddling schoolchildren. I am going to be a STAR!

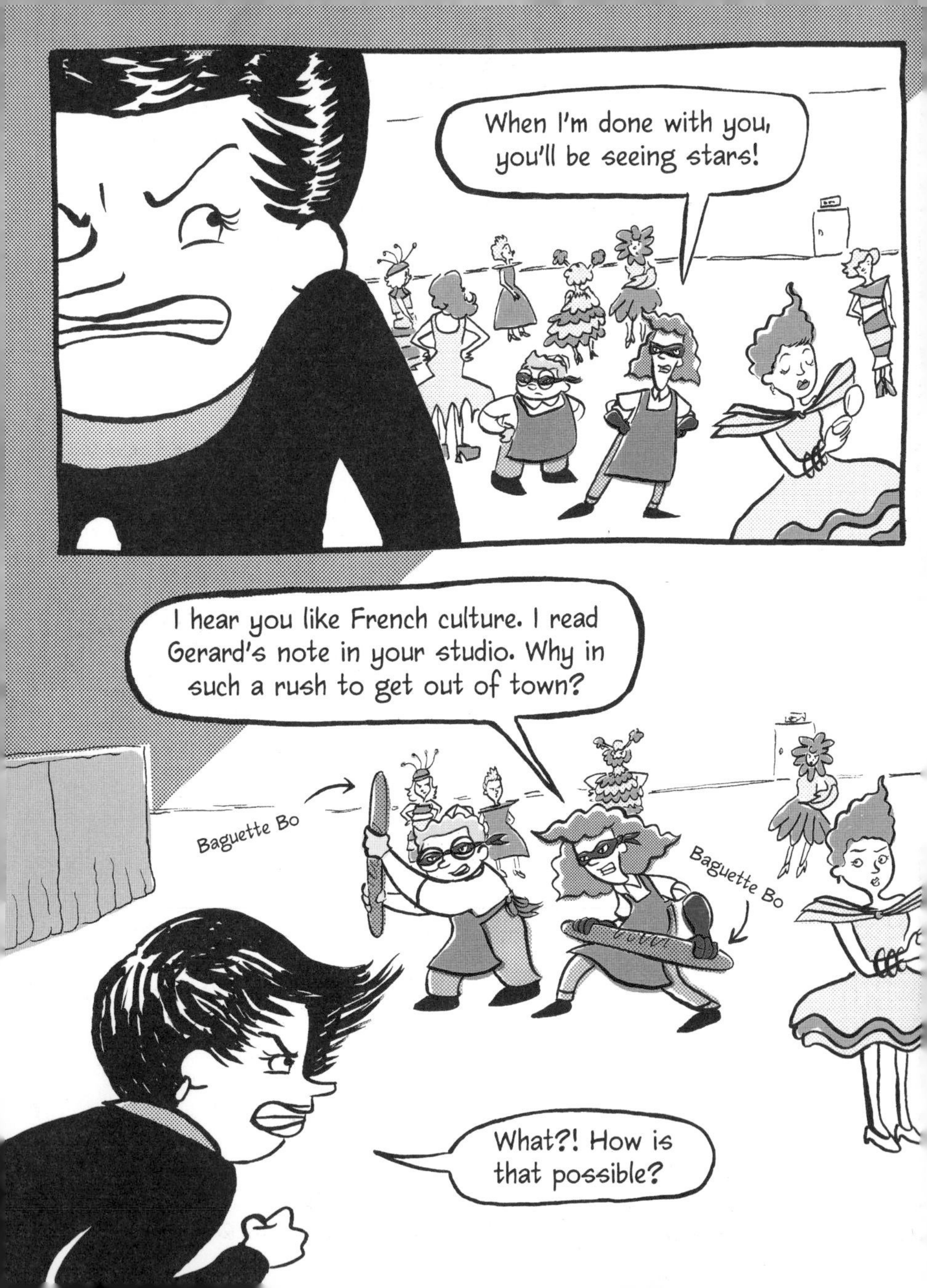
When I'm done with you, you'll be seeing stars!
I hear you like French culture. I read Gerard's note in your studio. Why in such a rush to get out of town?
Baguette Bo
Baguette Bo
What?! How is that possible?

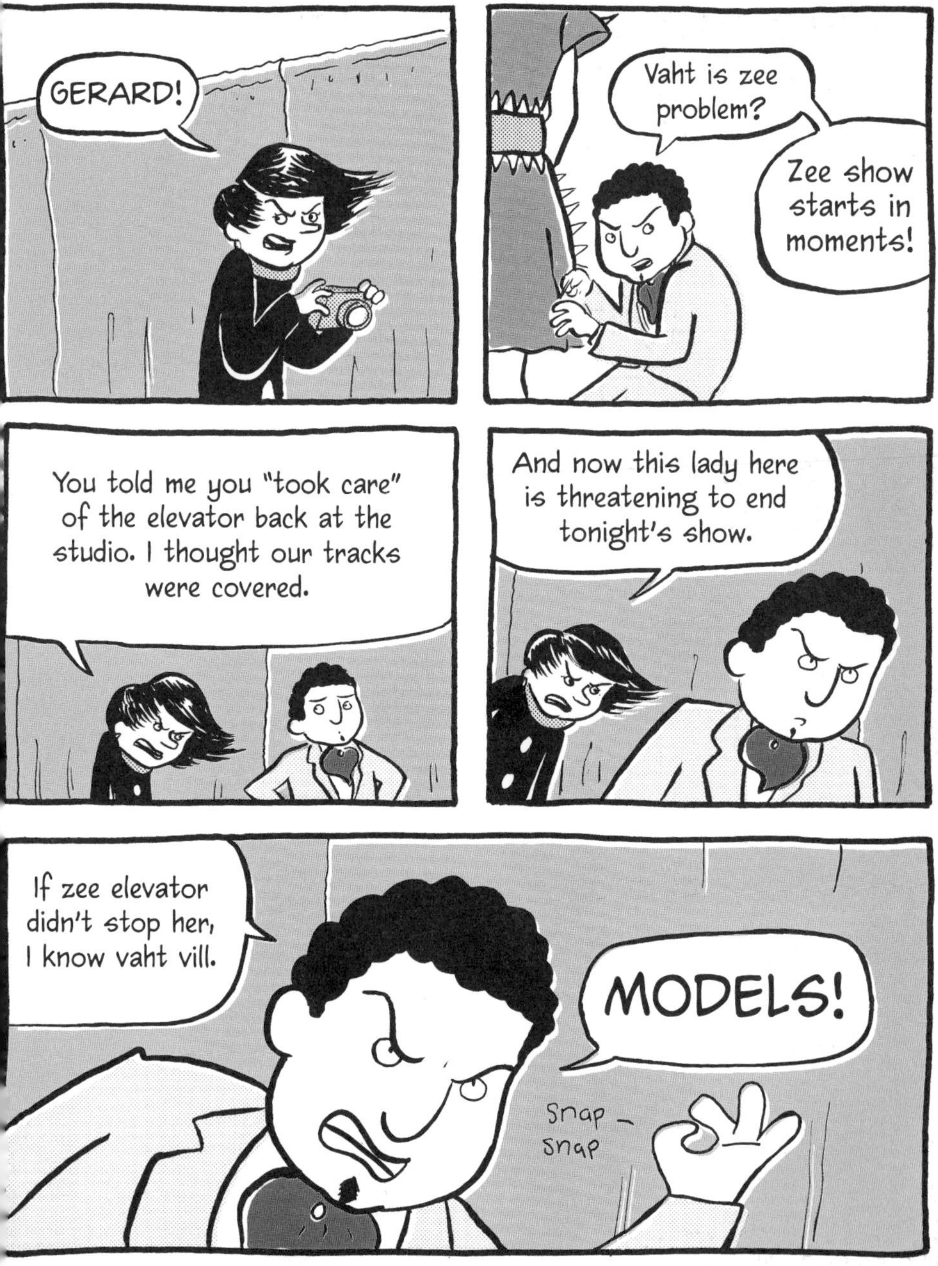
GERARD!
Vaht is zee problem?
Zee show starts in moments!
You told me you "took care" of the elevator back at the studio. I thought our tracks were covered.
And now this lady here is threatening to end tonight's show.
If zee elevator didn't stop her, I know vaht vill.
MODELS!
Snap - Snap

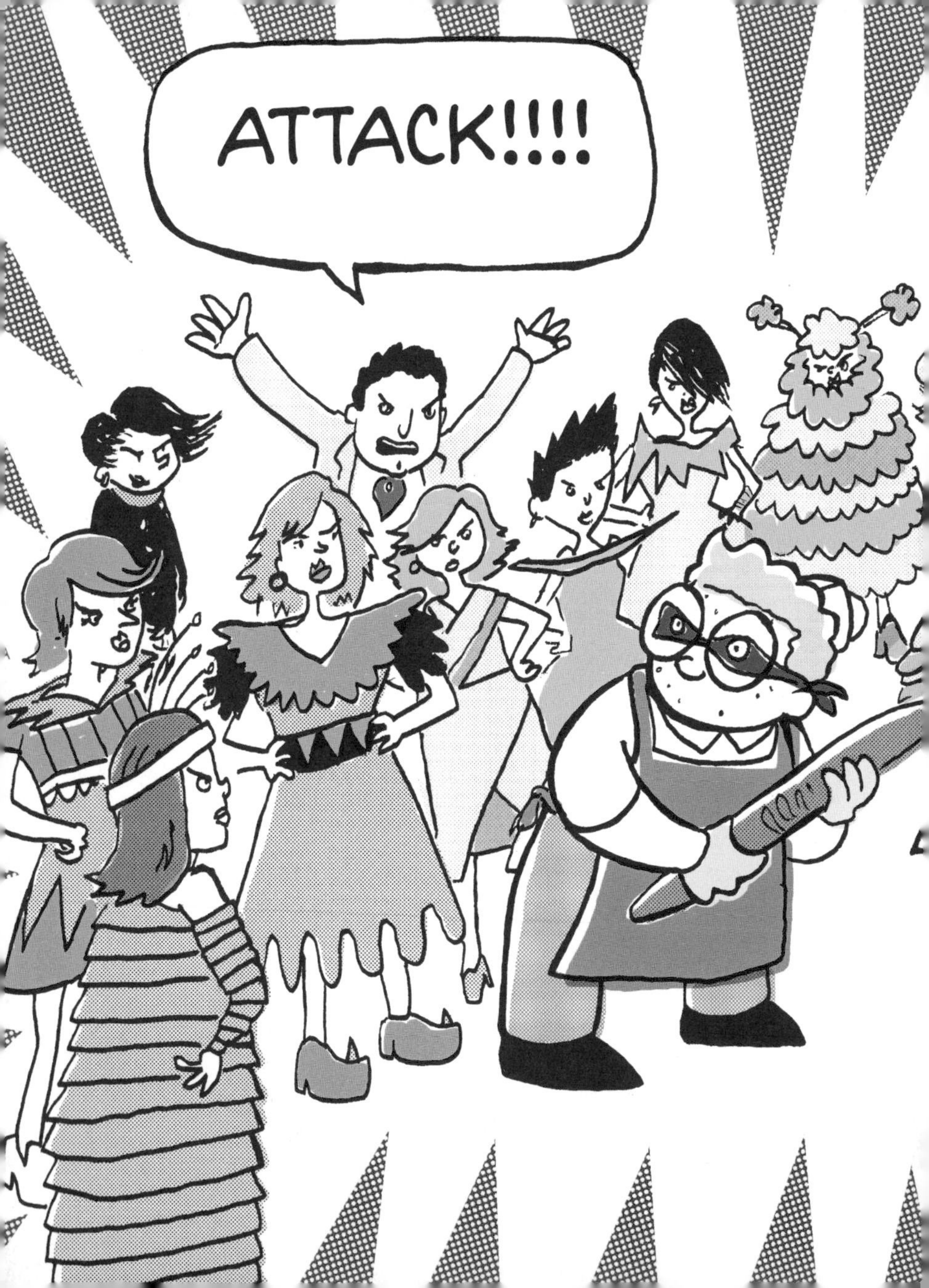
ATTACK!!!!

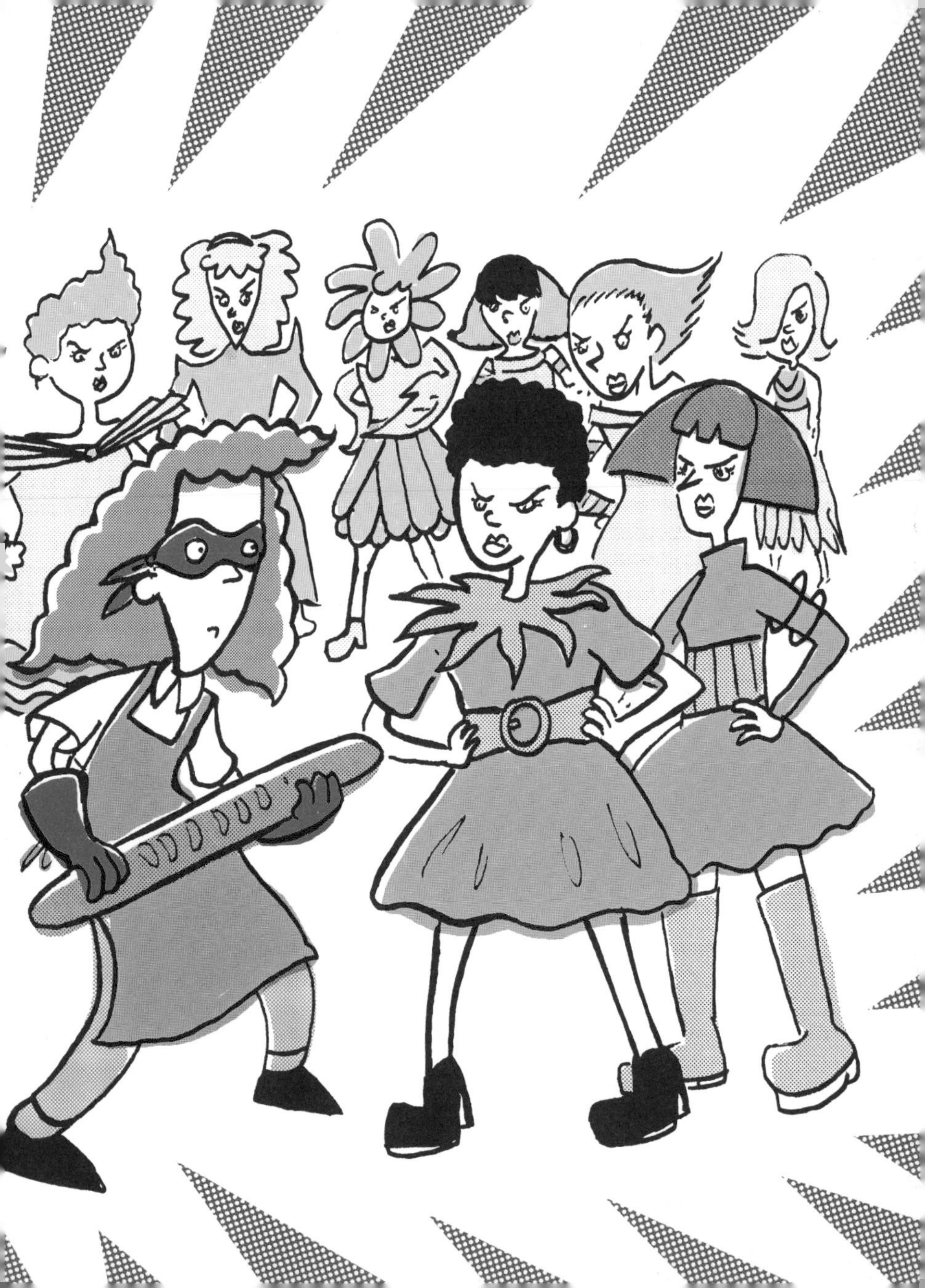

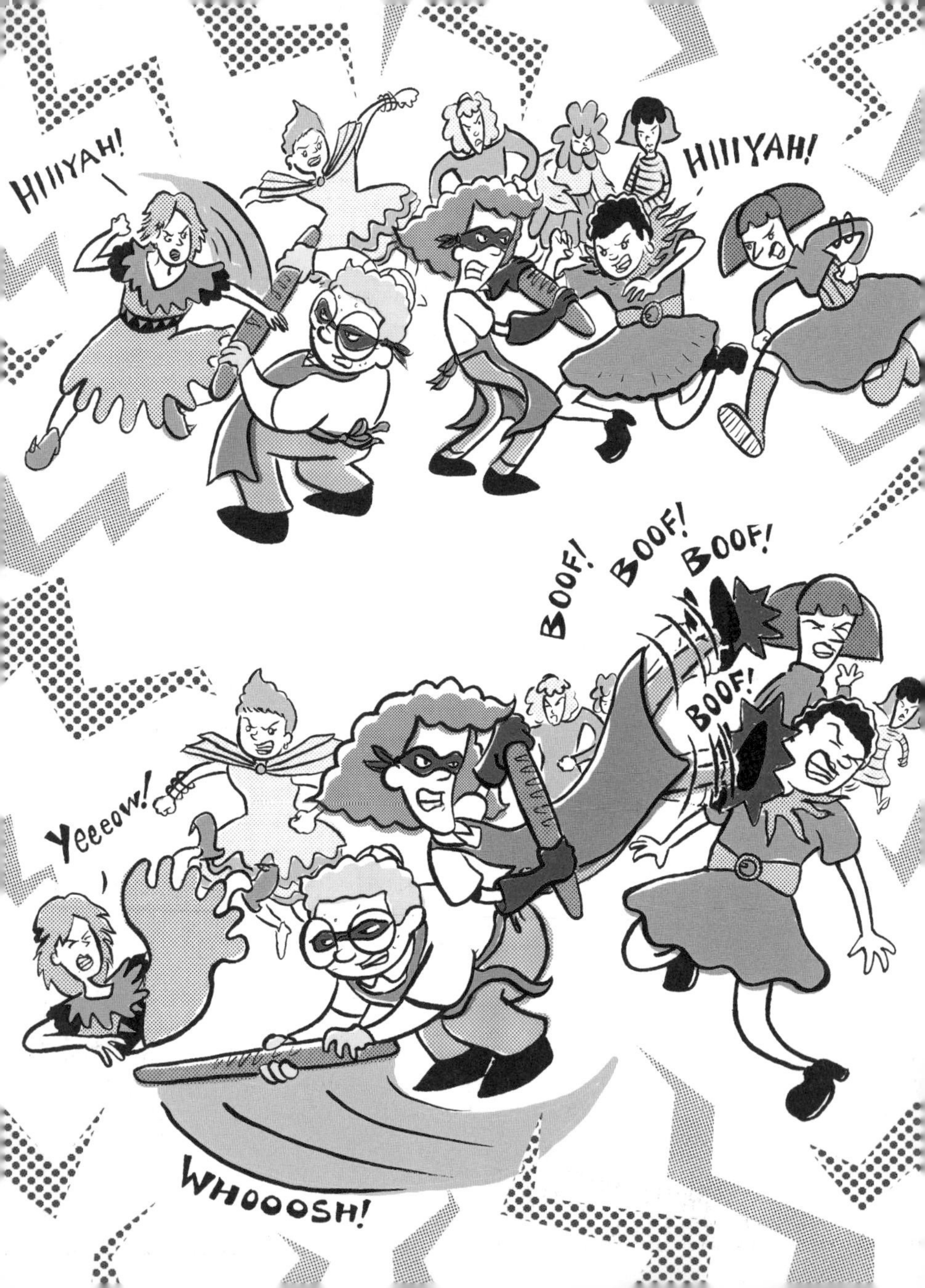
HIIIYAH!
HIIIYAH!
BOOF!
BOOF!
BOOF!
BOOF!
Yeeeow!
WHOOOOSH!

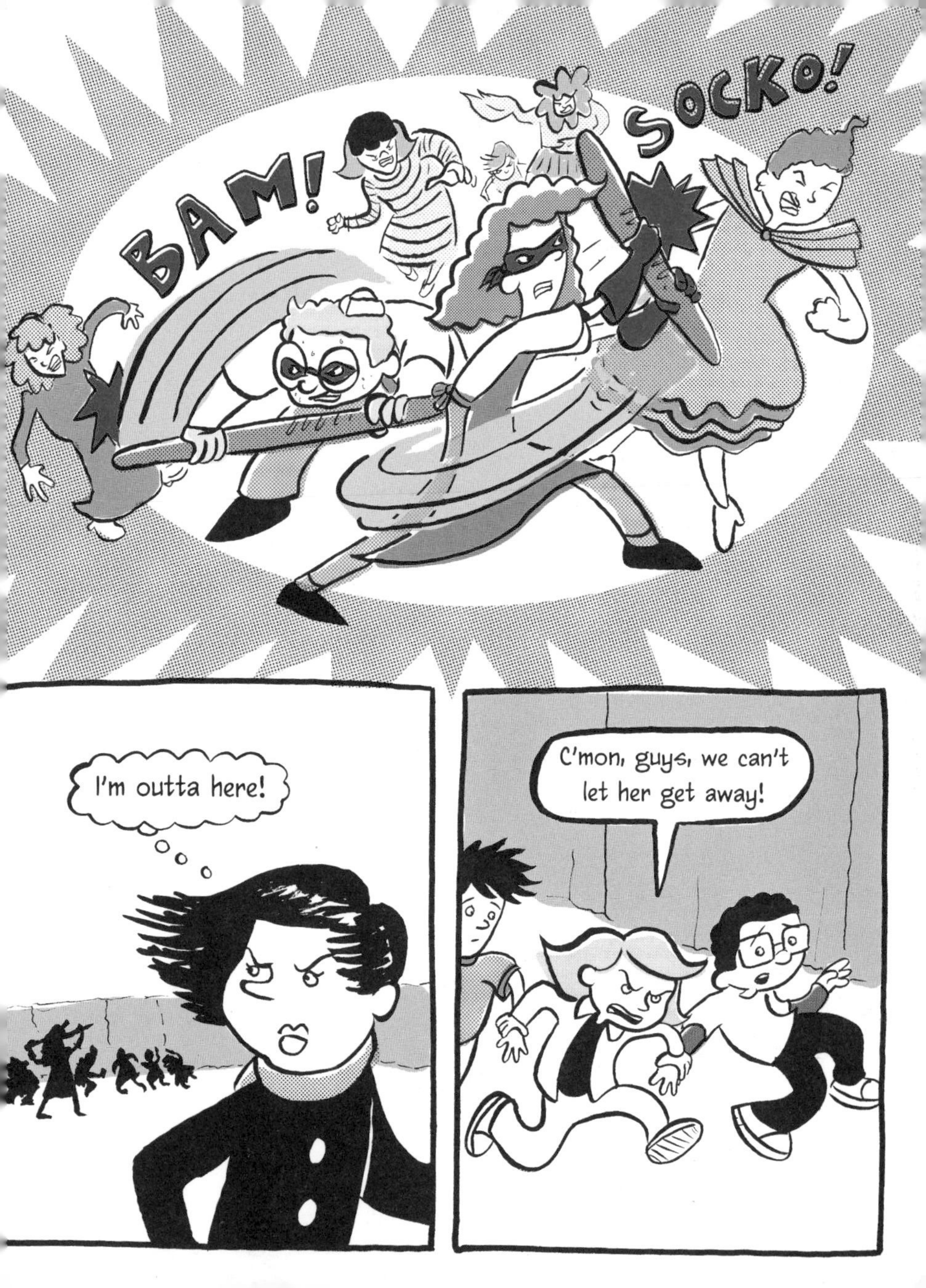
BAM!
SOCKO!
I'm outta here!
C'mon, guys, we can't let her get away!

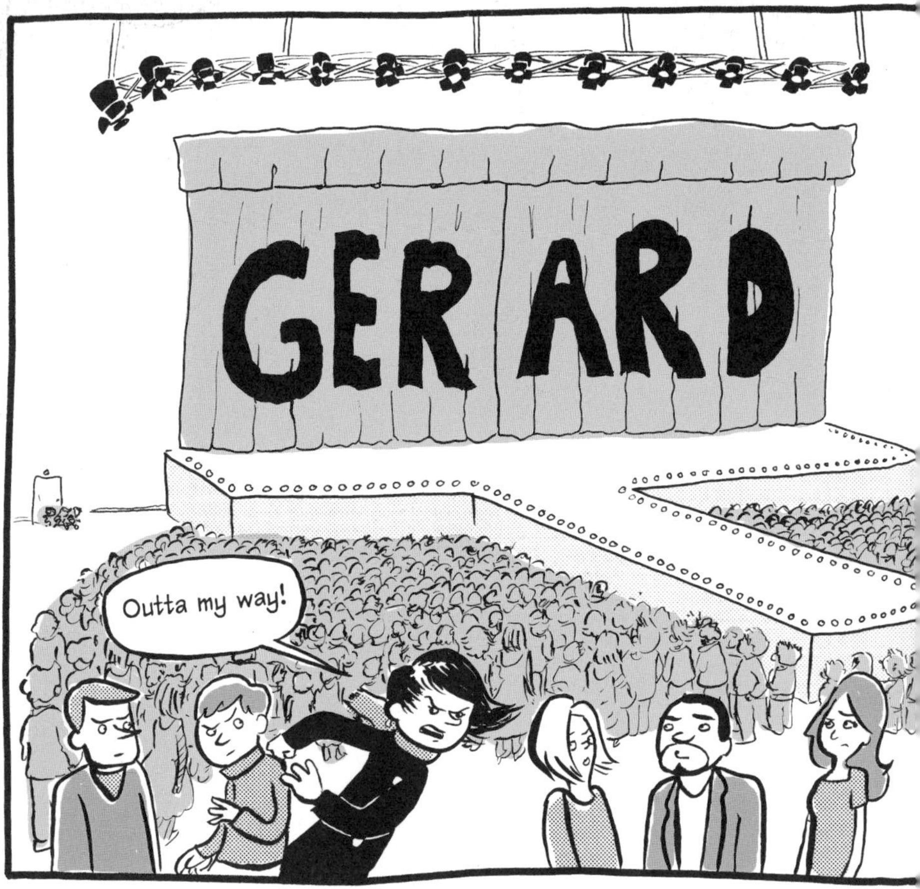
GERARD
Outta my way!
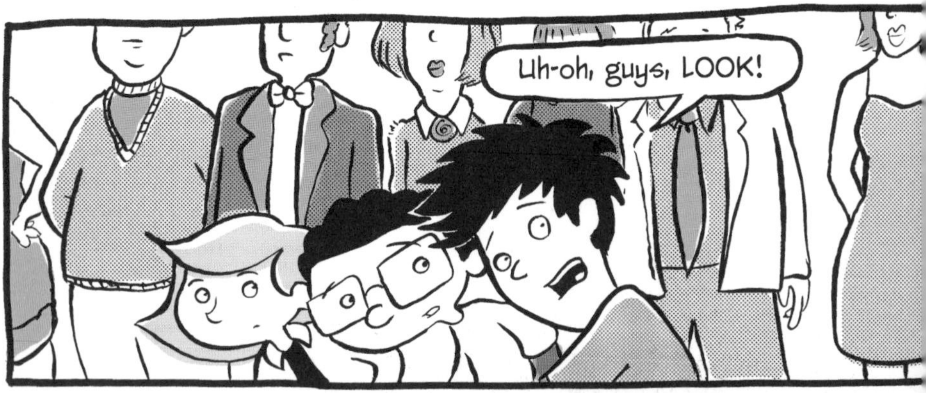
Uh-oh, guys, LOOK!

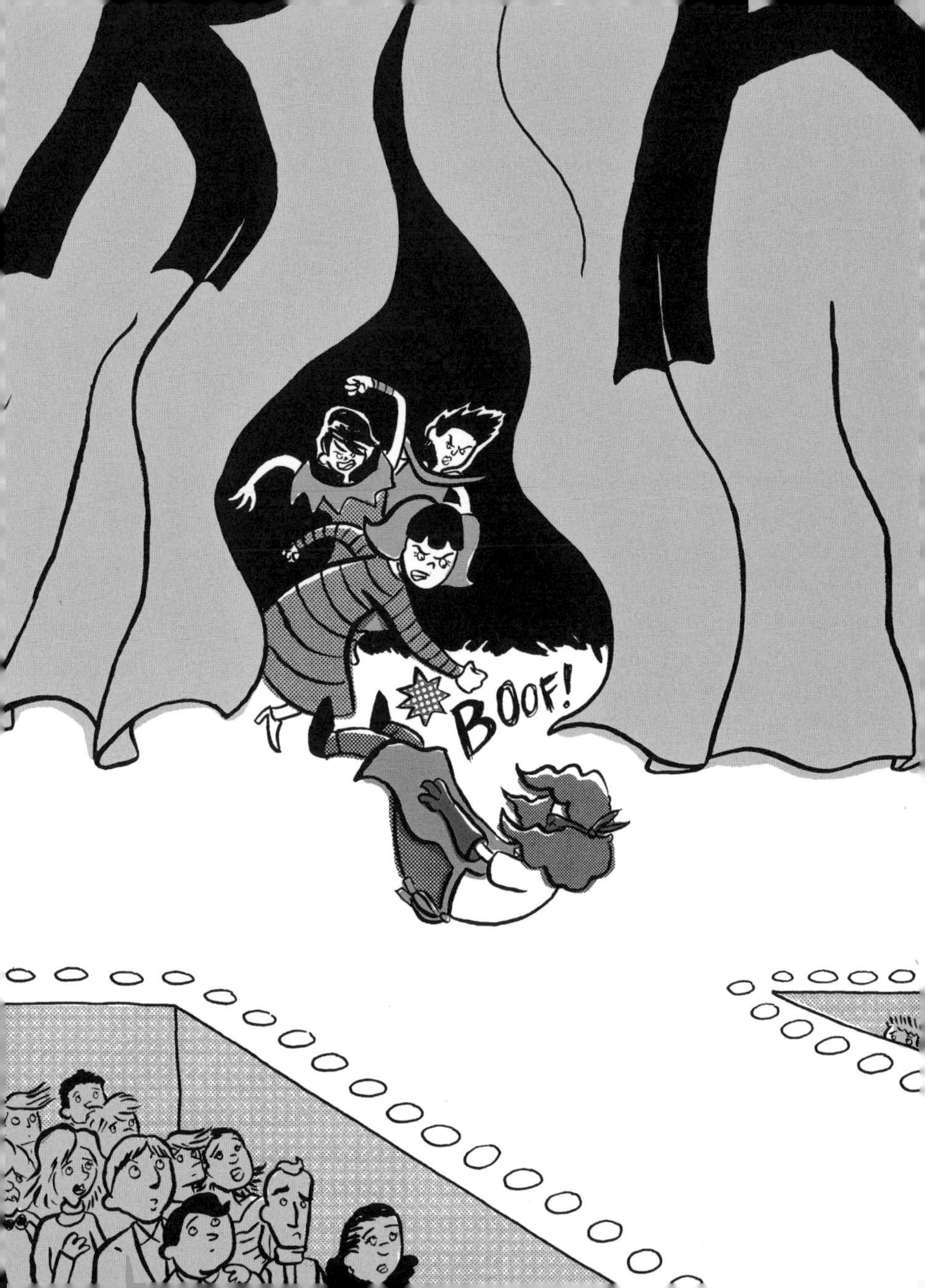
BOOF!

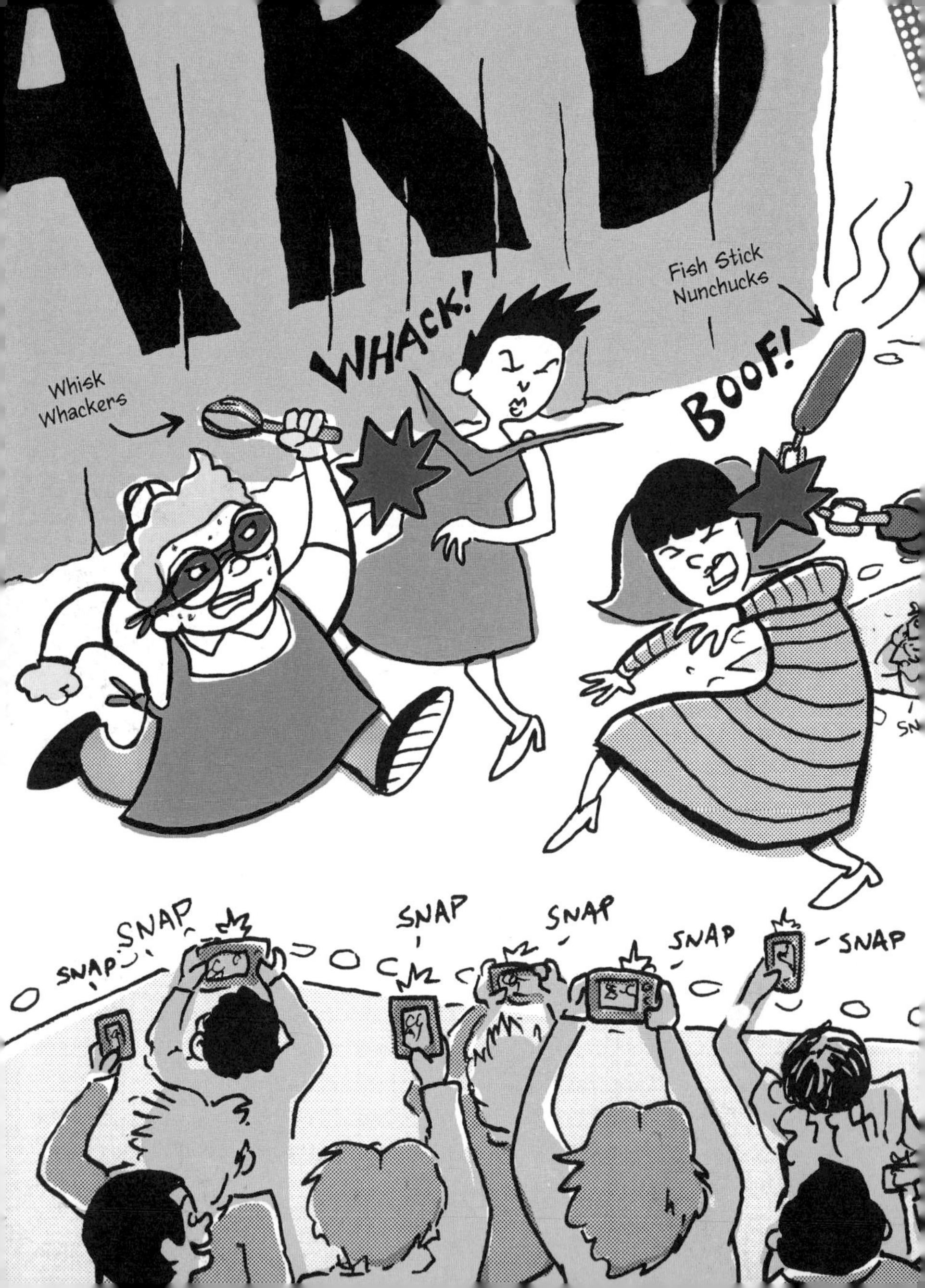
Fish Stick
Nunchucks
WHACK!
Whisk
Whackers
BOOF!
SNAP
SNAP
SNAP
SNAP
SNAP
SNAP
SNAP

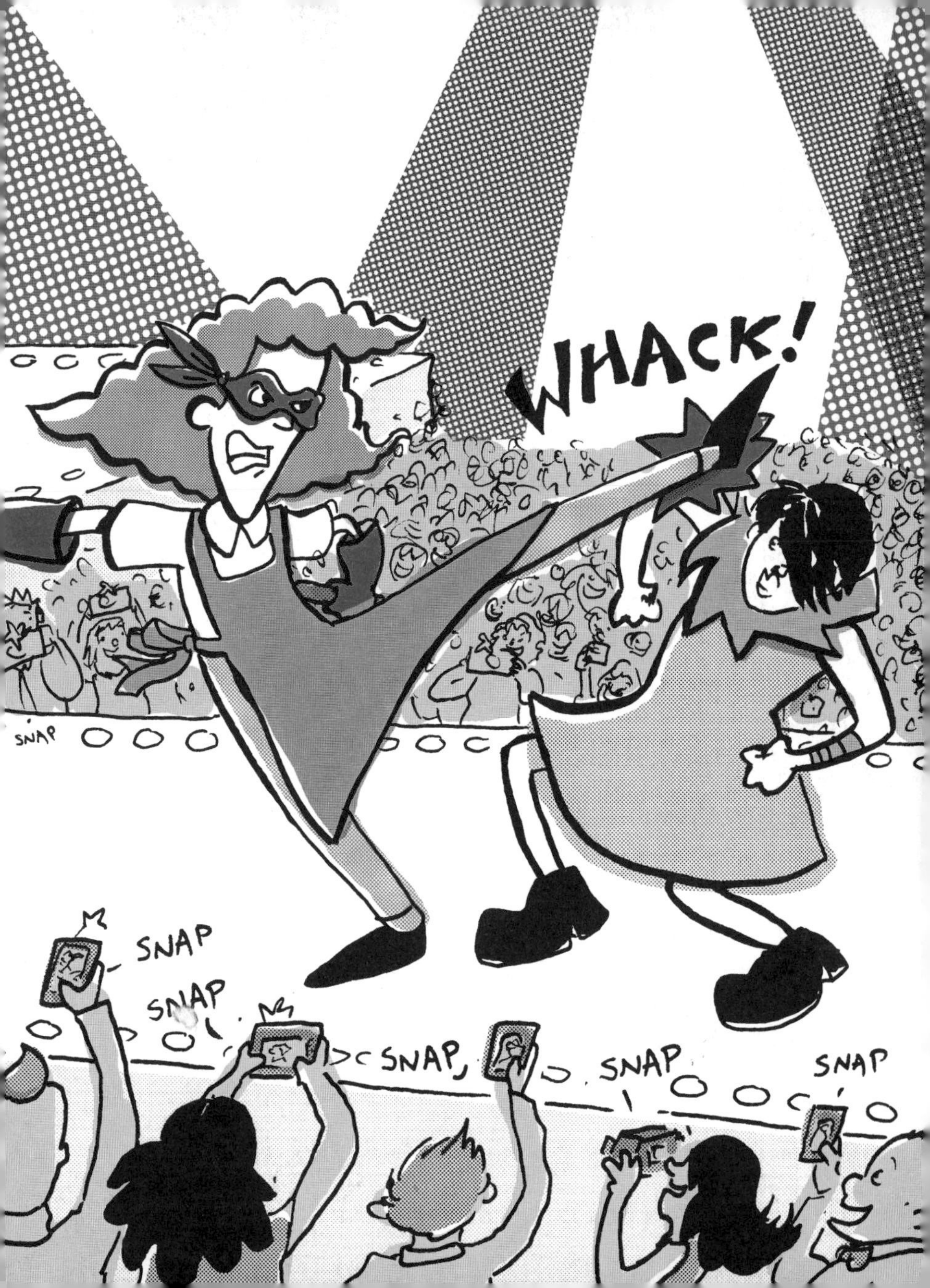
WHACK!
SNAP
SNAP
SNAP
SNAP,
SNAP
SNAP

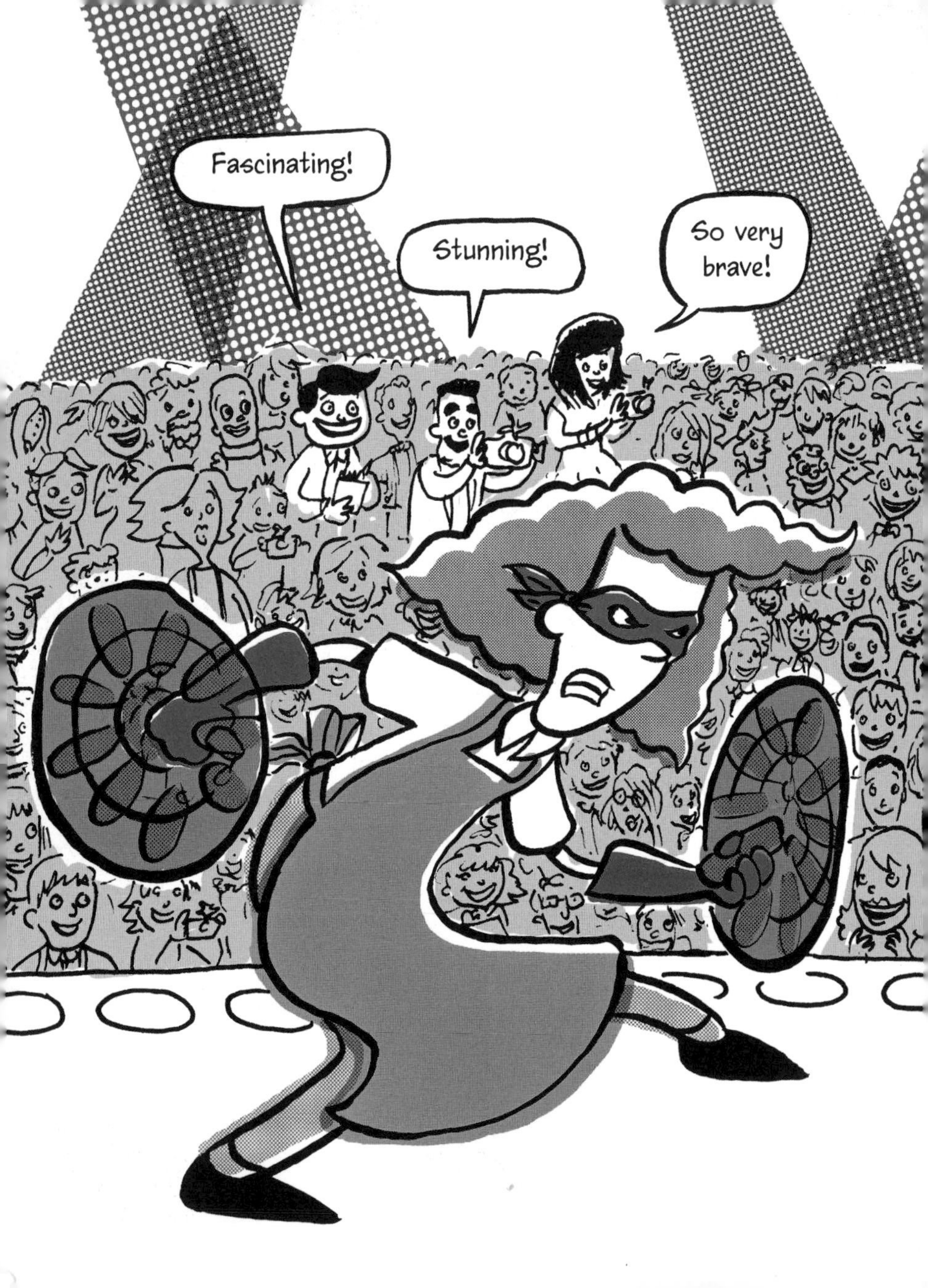
Fascinating!
Stunning!
So very brave!

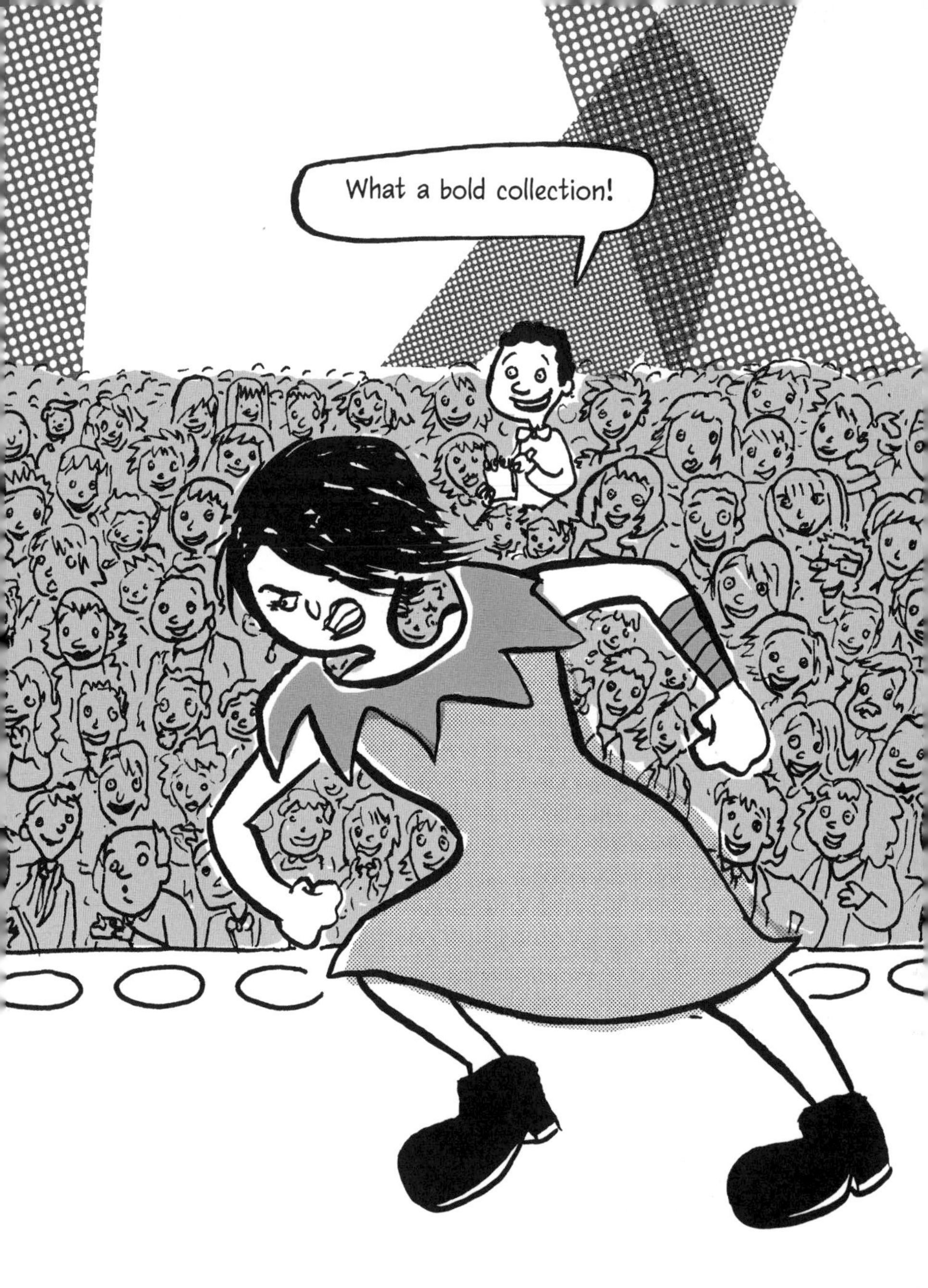
What a bold collection!

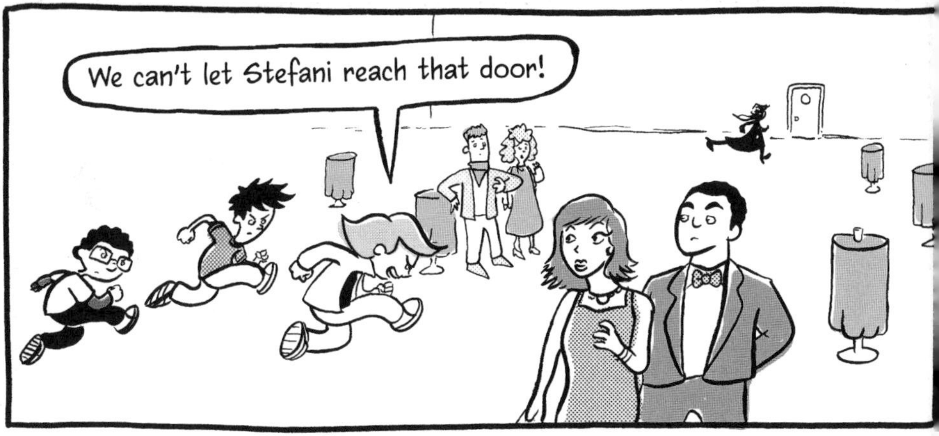
We can't let Stefani reach that door!

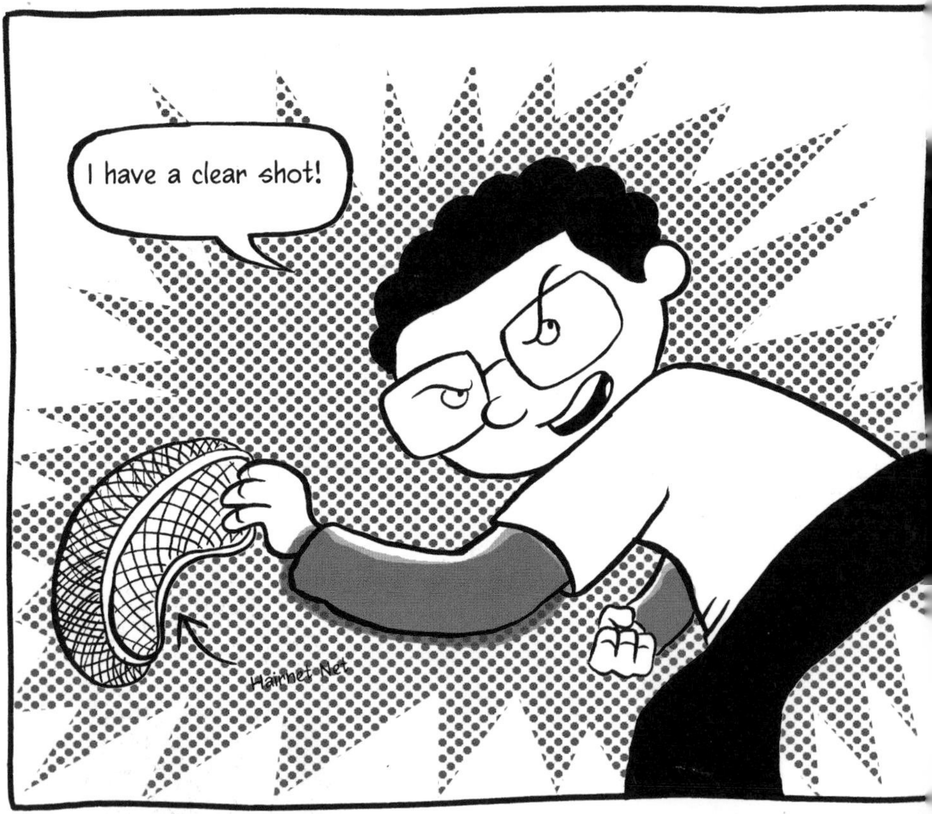
I have a clear shot!
Hairnet Net

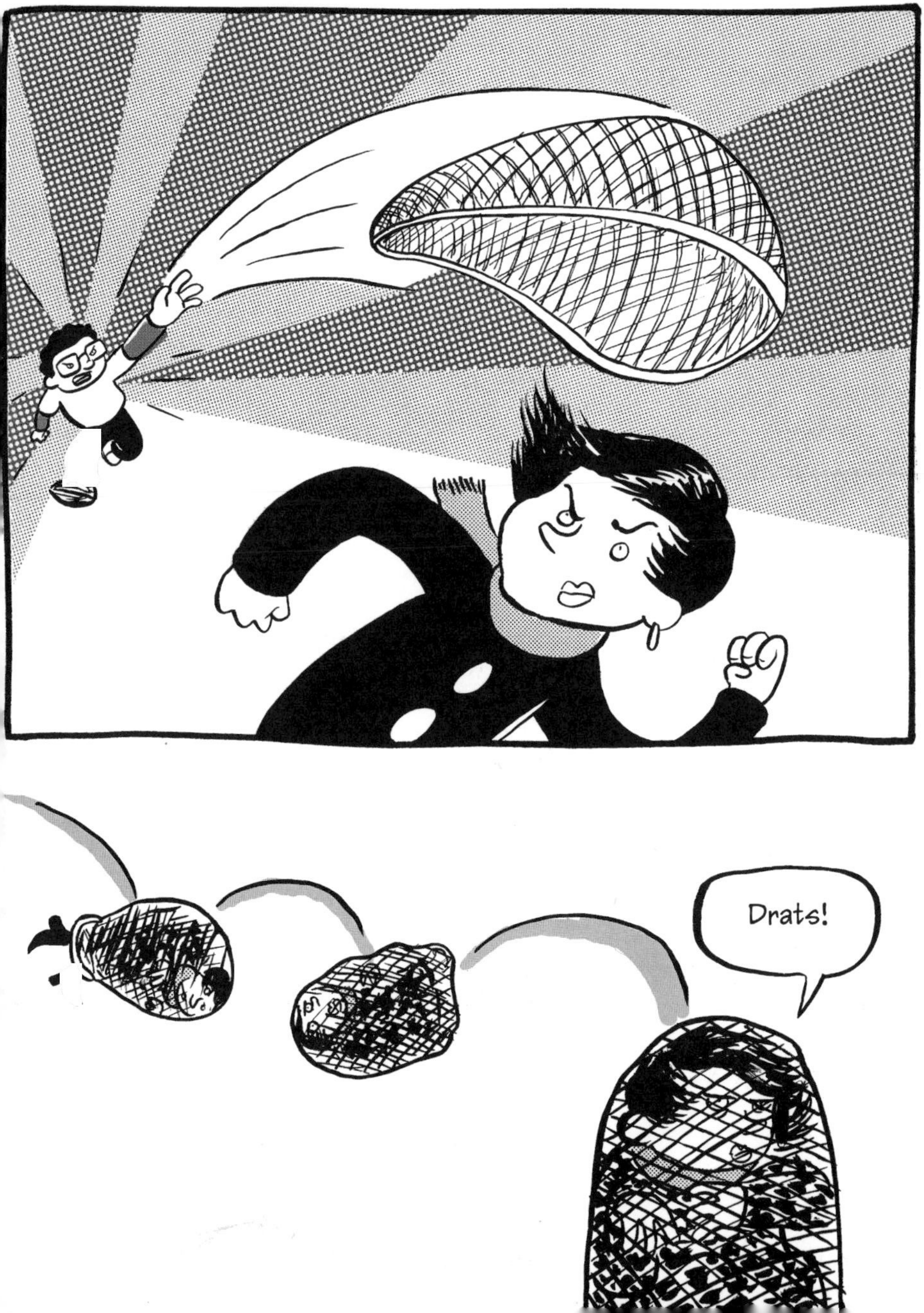
Drats!

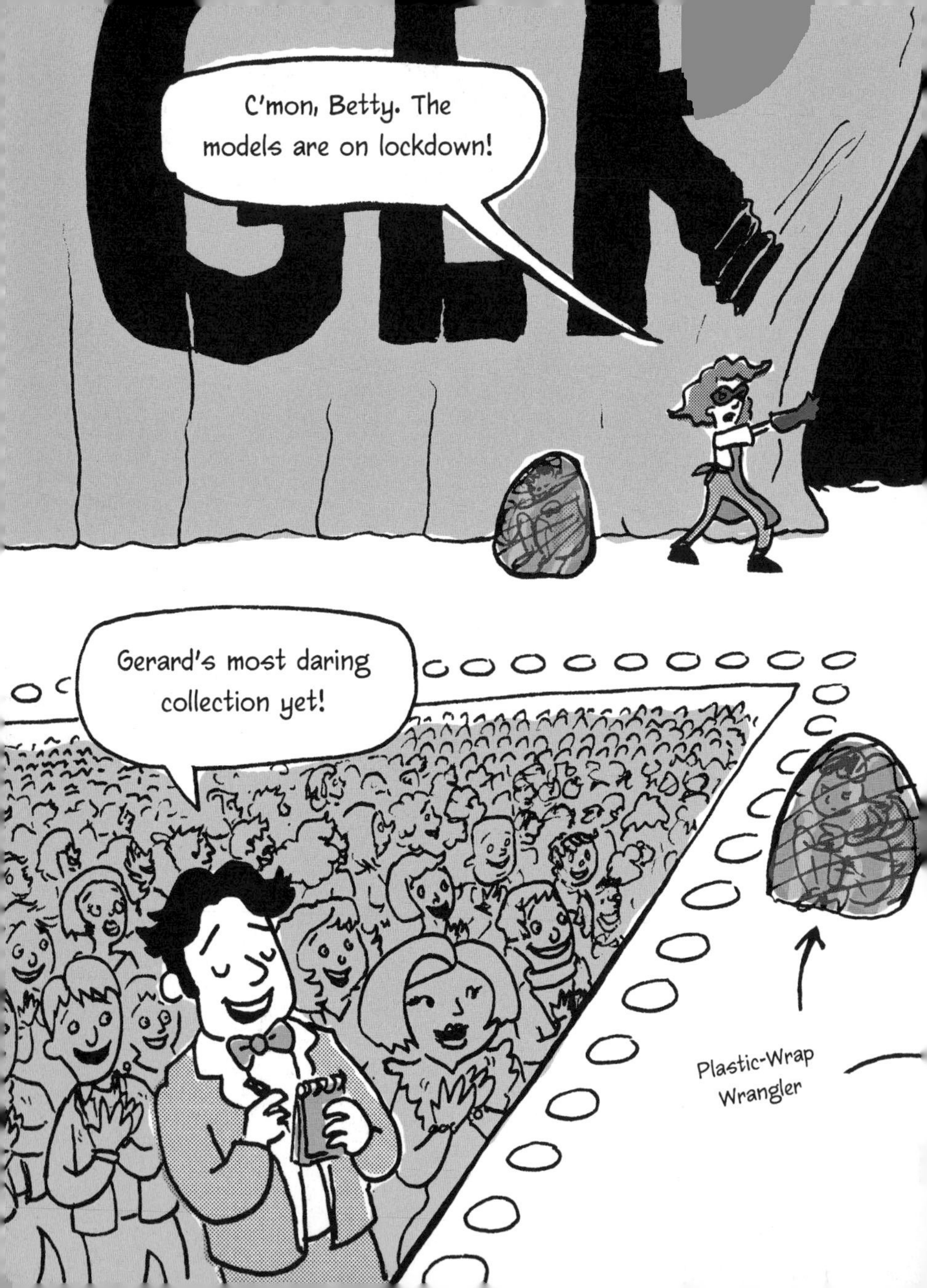
C'mon, Betty. The models are on lockdown!
Gerard's most daring collection yet!
Plastic-Wrap Wrangler

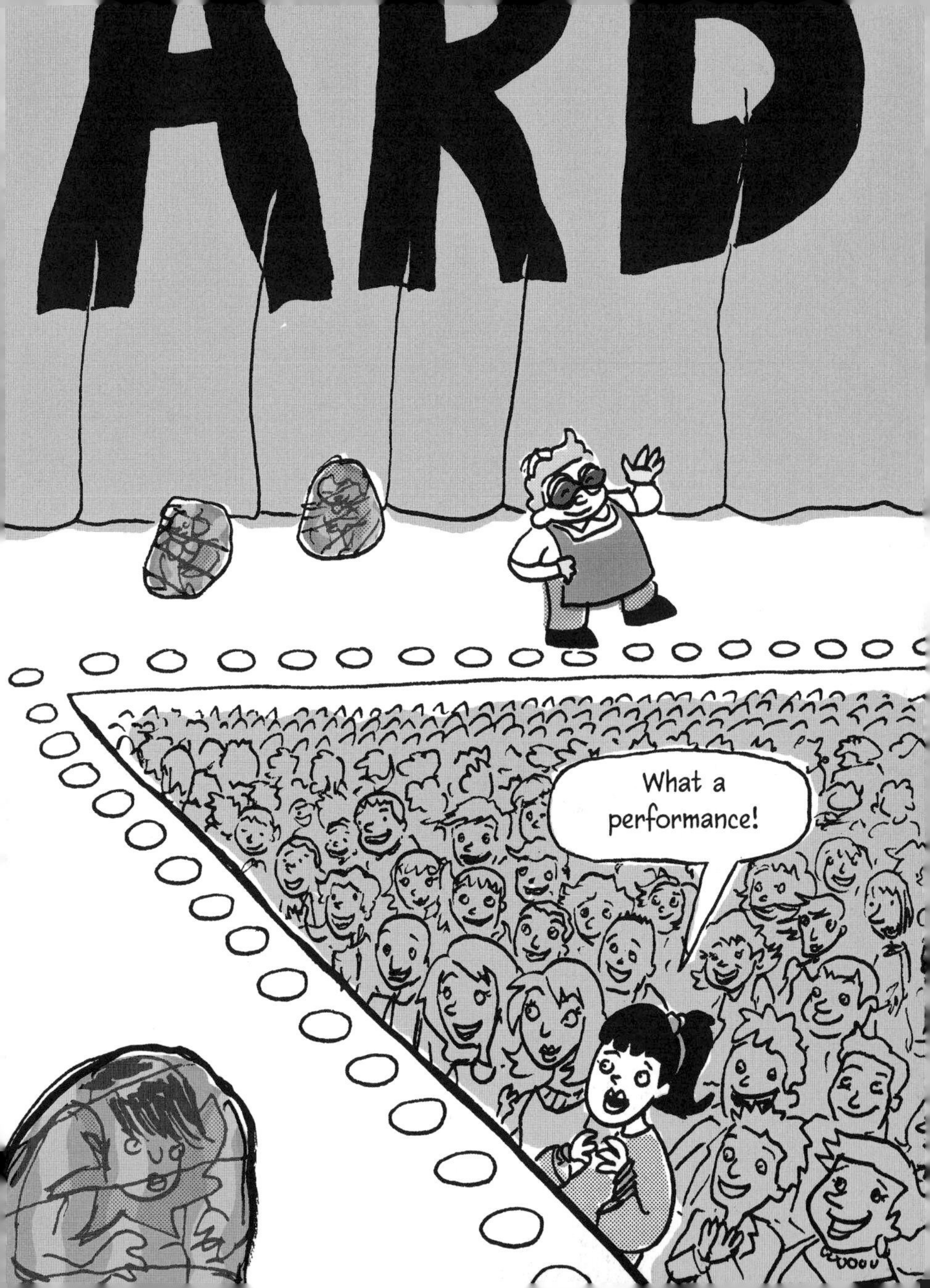
ARD
What a performance!

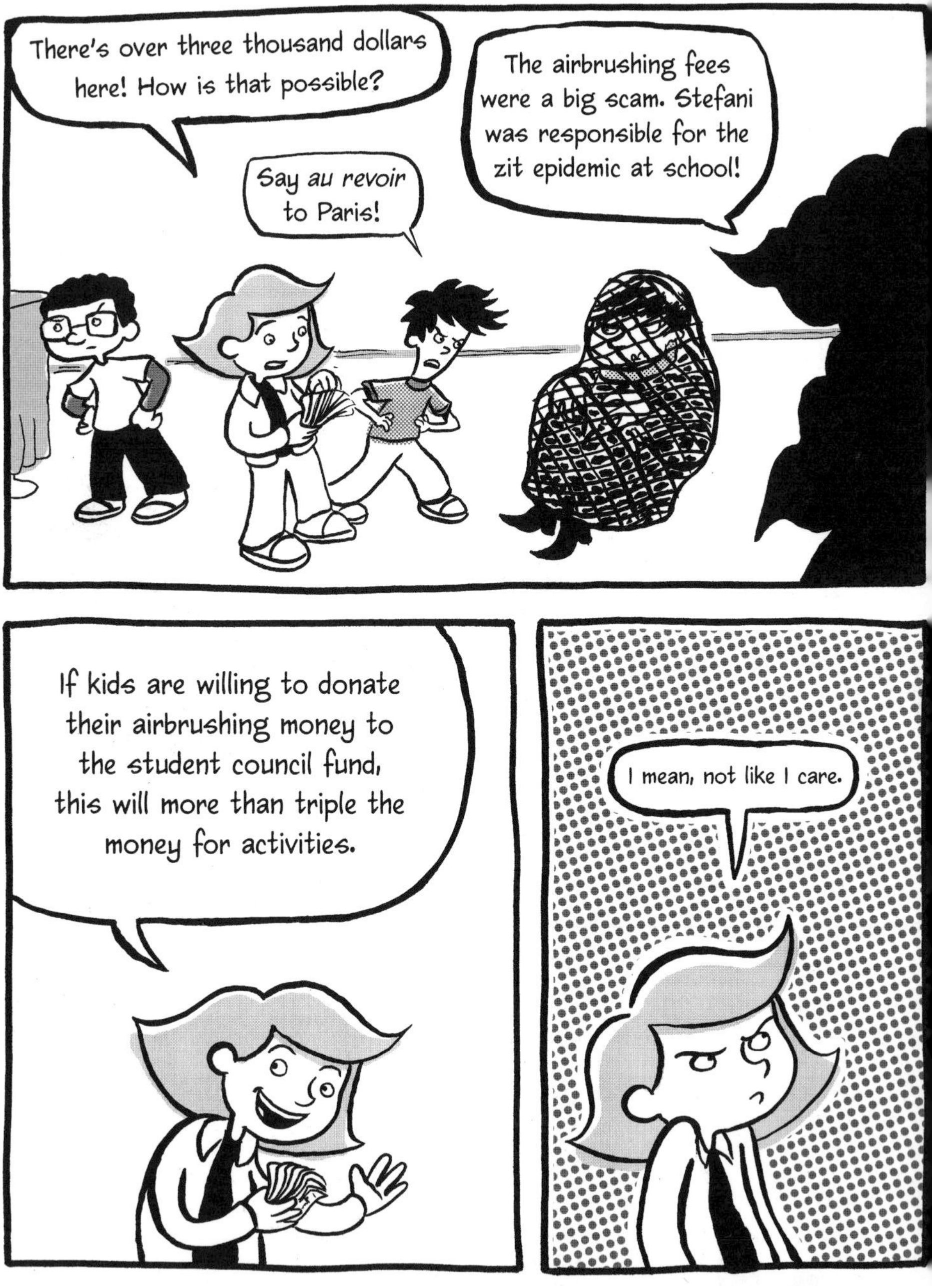
There's over three thousand dollars here! How is that possible?
Say *au revoir* to Paris!
The airbrushing fees were a big scam. Stefani was responsible for the zit epidemic at school!
If kids are willing to donate their airbrushing money to the student council fund, this will more than triple the money for activities.
I mean, not like I care.

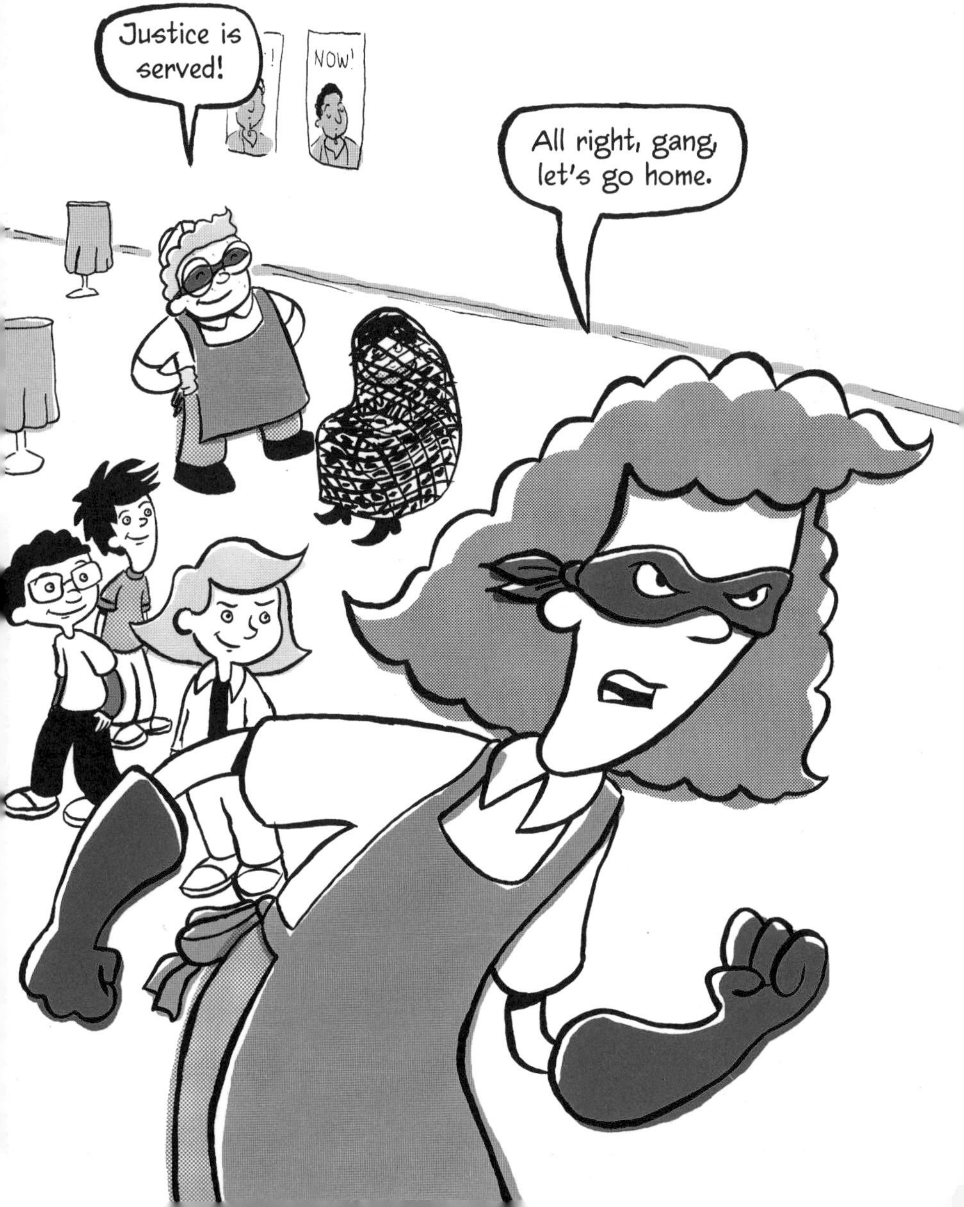
Justice is served!
NOW!
All right, gang, let's go home.

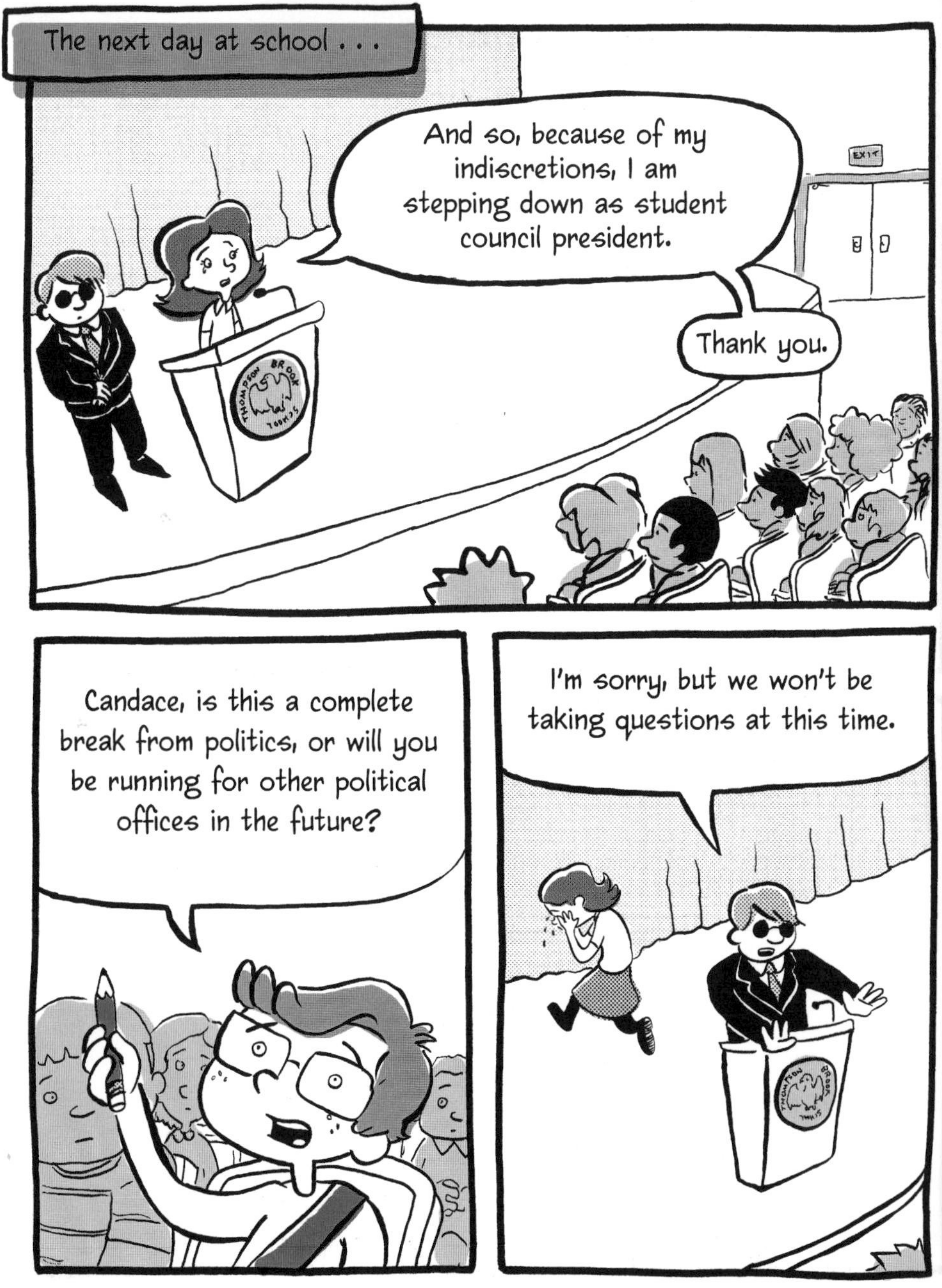
The next day at school . . .
And so, because of my indiscretions, I am stepping down as student council president.
Thank you.
THOMPSON BROOK SCHOOL
Candace, is this a complete break from politics, or will you be running for other political offices in the future?
I'm sorry, but we won't be taking questions at this time.

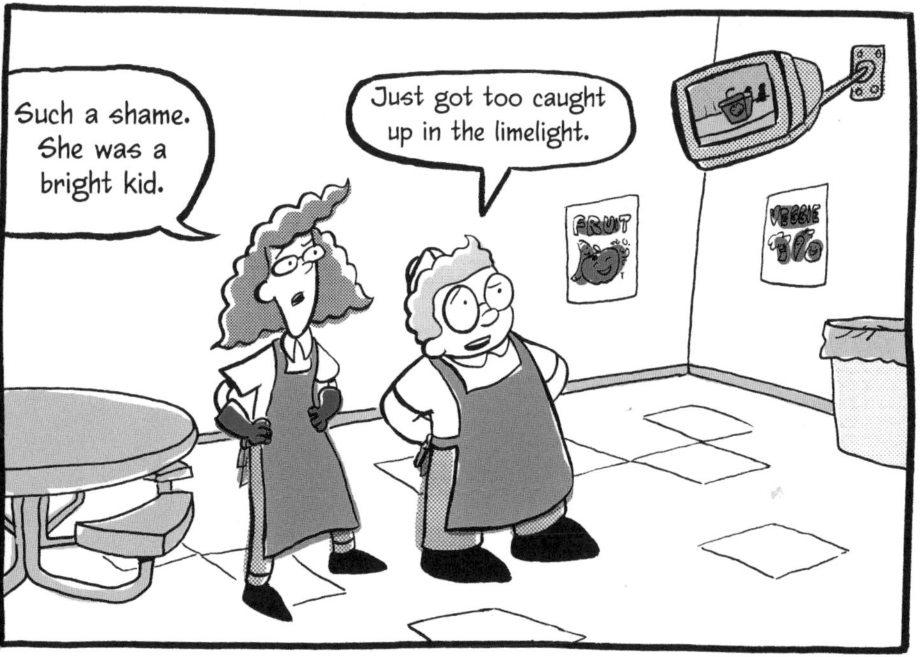
Such a shame. She was a bright kid.
Just got too caught up in the limelight.
FRUIT
VEGGIE

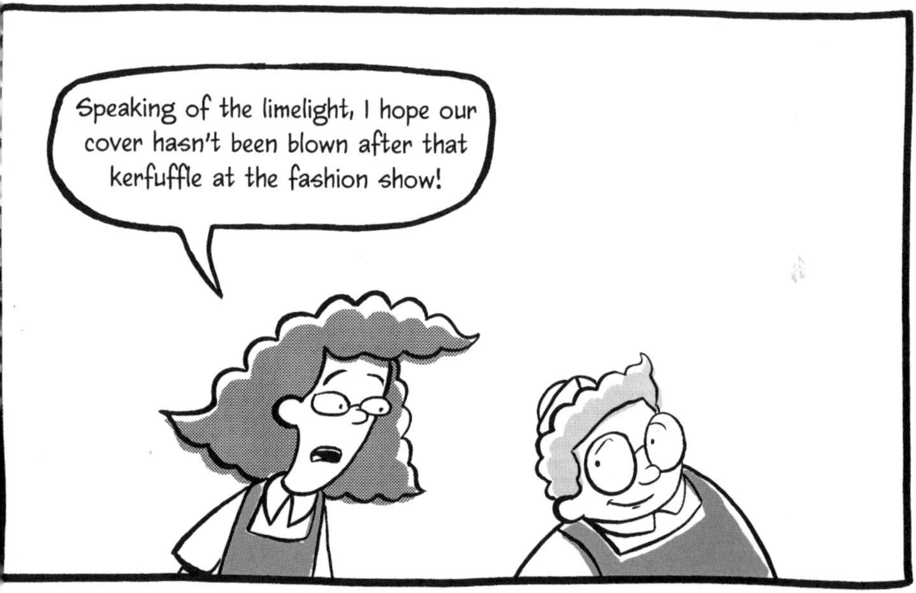
Speaking of the limelight, I hope our cover hasn't been blown after that kerfuffle at the fashion show!

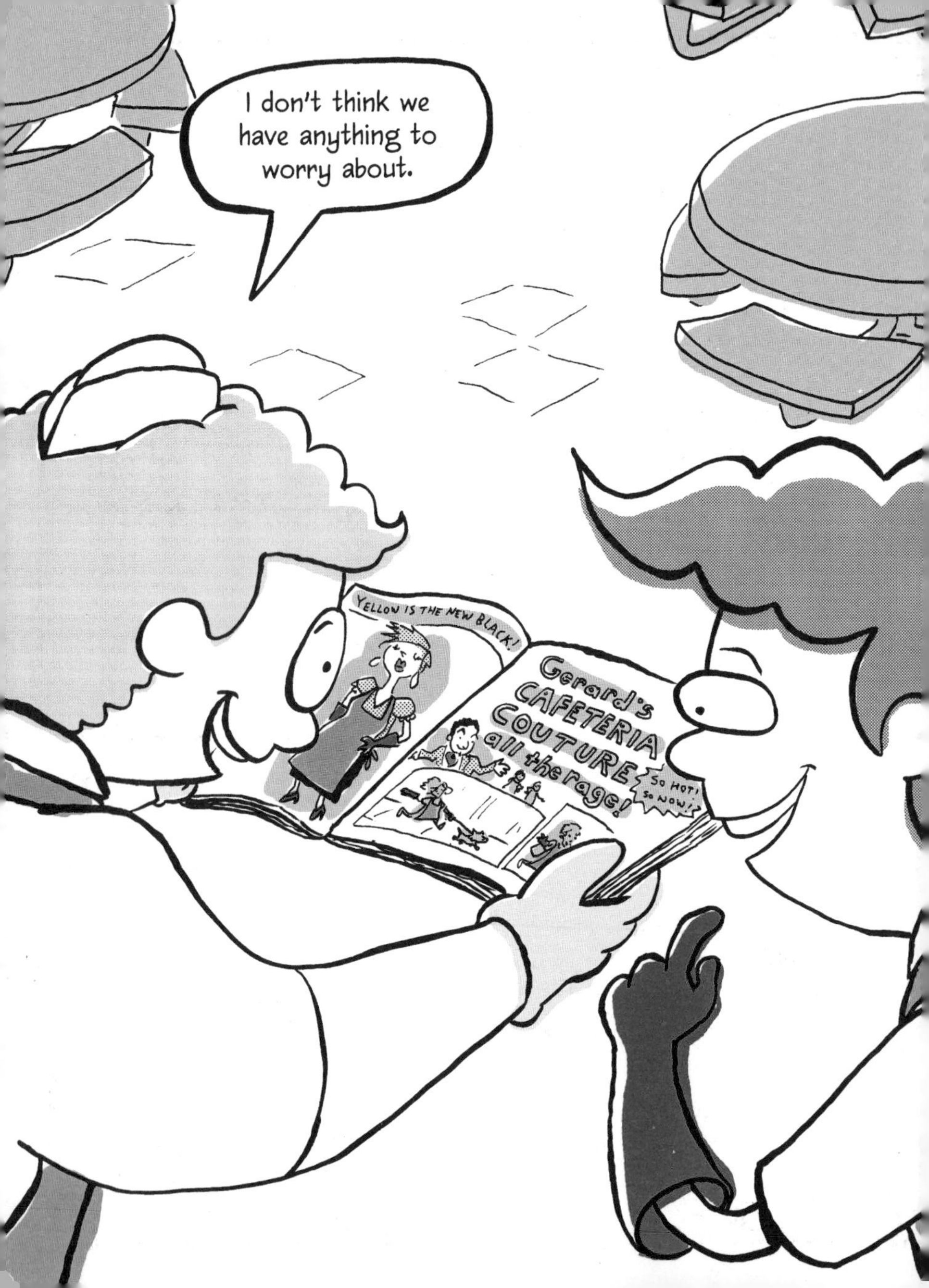
I don't think we have anything to worry about.
YELLOW IS THE NEW BLACK!
Gerard's CAFETERIA COUTURE all the rage!
SO HOT! SO NOW!

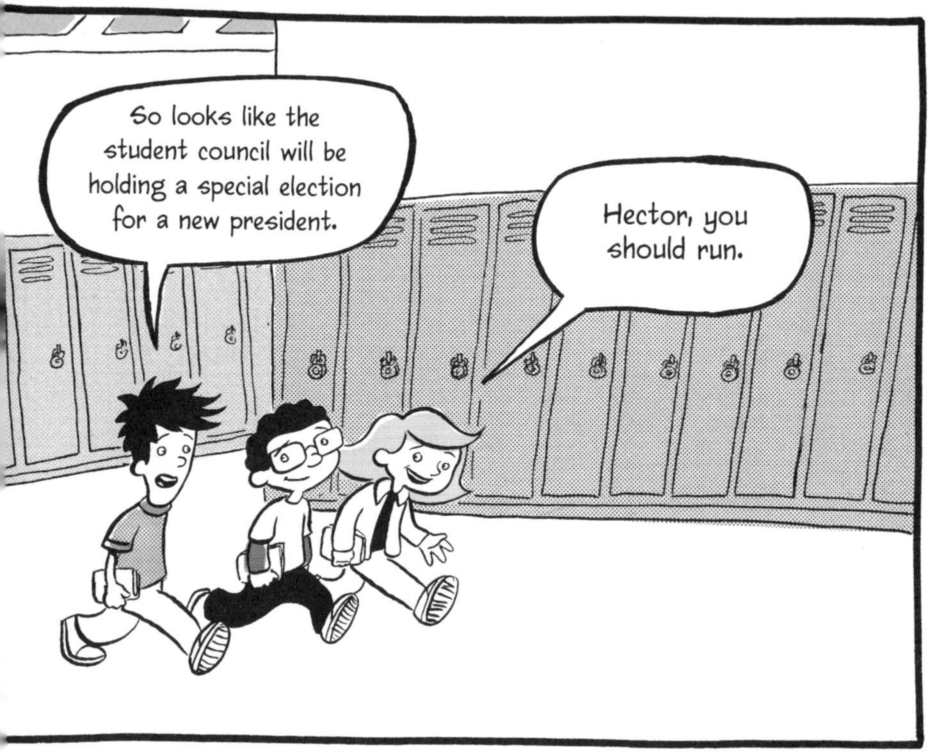
So looks like the student council will be holding a special election for a new president.
Hector, you should run.

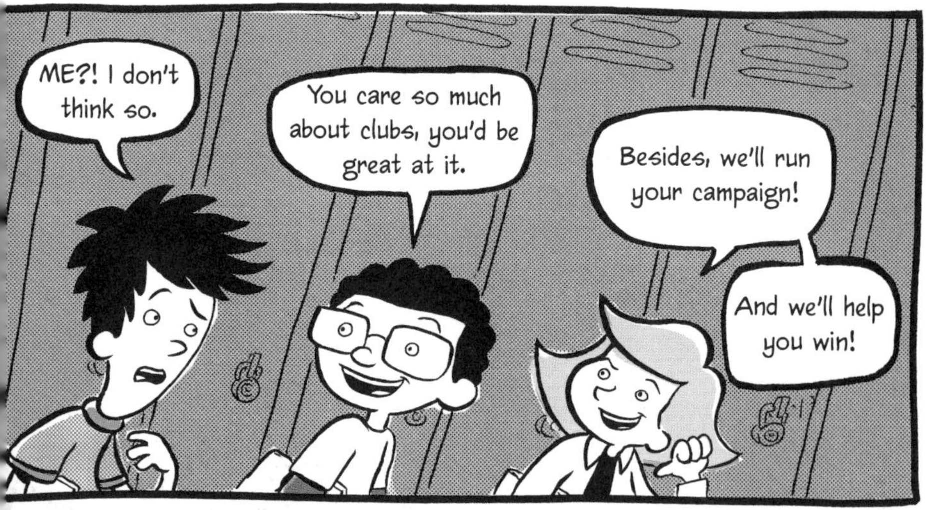
ME?! I don't think so.
You care so much about clubs, you'd be great at it.
Besides, we'll run your campaign!
And we'll help you win!

FOR JEANNIE AND BETTY
and all of their years of dedication and service to Gates Lane School

The author would like to acknowledge the color work in this book by Joey Weiser and Michele Chidester.

THIS IS A BORZOI BOOK PUBLISHED BY ALFRED A. KNOPF

This is a work of fiction. Names, characters, places, and incidents either are the product of the author's imagination or are used fictitiously. Any resemblance to actual persons, living or dead, events, or locales is entirely coincidental.

Visit us on the Web! randomhouse.com/kids

Educators and librarians, for a variety of teaching tools, visit us at RHTeachersLibrarians.com

Library of Congress Cataloging-in-Publication Data
Krosoczka, Jarrett.
Lunch lady and the picture day peril / Jarrett J. Krosoczka. — 1st ed.
p. cm. — (Lunch lady ; [8])
Summary: When eccentric photographer Stefani DePino comes to Thompson Brook to take school pictures in the midst of an acne epidemic, Lunch Lady, Betty, and the Breakfast Bunch learn that Stefani is using them to break into the world of high fashion.
ISBN 978-0-375-87035-4 (trade pbk.) — ISBN 978-0-375-97035-1 (lib. bdg.)
1. Graphic novels. [1. Graphic novels. 2. School lunchrooms, cafeterias, etc.—Fiction. 3. Schools—Fiction. 4. Photographers—Fiction. 5. Fashion—Fiction. 6. Mystery and detective stories.] I. Title.
PZ7.7.K76Lup 2012
741.5'973—dc23
2011047994

The text of this book is set in Hedge Backwards.
The illustrations were created using ink on paper and digital coloring.

MANUFACTURED IN MALAYSIA
September 2012
10 9 8 7 6 5 4

First Edition